KILLERS IN MASCARA

HUW COLLINGBOURNE

This edition: 2020
Copyright © 2011 by Huw Collingbourne
ISBN: 978-1-913132-00-2
Revision: 1.4b
Published by: Dark Neon

http://www.darkneon.com/

Table Of Contents

Preface

During the 1980s I became involved in a number of extraordinary events in and around the music and club scene of London. At the time I was fresh from university and, having no great ambitions in life other than to enjoy myself, I embarked upon a career of freelance journalism. I wrote for numerous magazines such as "Flexipop!", "My Guy", "Jackie" and "Great Hits". During that period I interviewed and, in some cases, became friends with musicians who have, in later years, been grouped together under the title: *The New Romantics*.

At the time (that is, at the start of 1980), the phrase "New Romantic" either had not yet been coined or, if it had, it had not gained common currency. For that reason you will notice that it never once occurs in the text of this book. Except in this preface, that is.

The version of the book you are holding is based on a manuscript which I typed up, on my venerable Imperial 66 typewriter, shortly after the events which it describes. I had always planned to publish it as a book. However, bearing in mind my close personal involvement with some of the principal persons in the story and the tragic character of the events, I came to the conclusion that it would be better to save the manuscript for publication at a later date.

More than thirty years have now passed. Some of the people in this story are no longer alive, others no longer care. I felt the time was right, finally, to publish my account. I have tried to make as few changes to my original manuscript at possible though I have rewritten some sections to add (for example) brief explanations to help the reader understand certain details of the music and club scene which, at the time, would have been common knowledge.

At the time, the tabloid press dubbed the case, "Killers In Mascara". While I always thought the name was overly sensational, it is nonetheless, the name by which these events continue to be known to this day. This book is not intended as a substitute for the well-documented accounts which have appeared elsewhere. It is, rather, a personal perspective on the bizarre and terrible events in which I was a participant and which began on New Year's Eve, 1979.

Principal Characters

Spivz Nightclub
Theodora – joint manager and figurehead of the club
Zipgun Dandy – joint manager, Theodora's partner
Brigitte – glamorous young man, shares duties at the door
Bad Tommy – not so glamorous young man, shares duties at door
The Ape – the bouncer
Velma – officially, Theodora's 'girlfriend'
Lady Vlad – club DJ

Chuttle Studios
Clifton Chuttle – studio owner, band manager, record producer
Janis – Chuttle's personal assistant

The Sexteens
Pete de Gré – singer
Lala Los Alamos – synthesiser player
Adam Xeon – synthesiser player/song-writer
Squirrel – drum-machine player

Mascara Addiction
Dave Buzzard – lead singer/guitarist
Dusty Evsky – keyboard player
Joe Jonson – bass guitarist
Anvil Evans – Drummer

Great Hits Magazine
Sanford Bouche-Torrington – publisher/editor
Gladys – secretary
Ingrid – art editor
Kev – freelance photographer

Others
Tyrone – freelance physicist/computer programmer
Scruffy – dog

Spivz Floor Plans

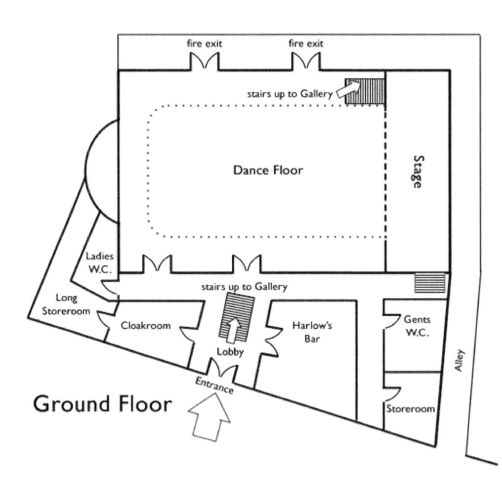

fire exit fire exit

stairs up to Gallery

Dance Floor

Stage

Ladies W.C.

Long Storeroom

Cloakroom

stairs up to Gallery

Harlow's Bar

Gents W.C.

Lobby

Entrance

Alley

Ground Floor

Storeroom

8

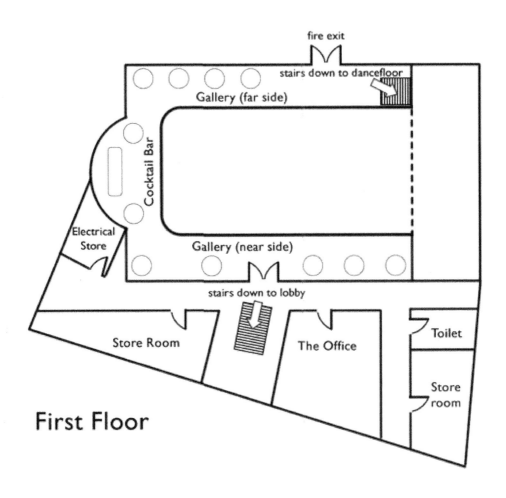

fire exit

stairs down to dancefloor

Gallery (far side)

Cocktail Bar

Electrical
Store

Gallery (near side)

stairs down to lobby

Store Room

The Office

Toilet

Store
room

First Floor

The London Broadsheet

Saturday, December 8, 1979

Invasion Of The Dandies

by Helen Royce (staff writer)

Move over Sex Pistols! Punk is out. The Dandies are in!

They wear frills and flounces, makeup and mascara – and that's just the men! It's the latest youth craze to hit London and it's the most shocking yet.

They call themselves The Futurists or The New Dandies and they have names to match. There is Princess Julia and Zipgun Dandy, Lala Los Alamos, Marilyn and Brigitte. Those last two, by the way, are men but if you saw them in the street you'd probably never guess.

There are two fashionable Futurist hotspots: The Blitz Club in Covent Garden and Spivz in the East End. Five nights a week, hundreds of young Londoners queue up outside Spivz waiting to see if the owner, a young man called Theodora, will let them in. The dress policy is strict. If you don't look outrageous enough, you won't be admitted.

"I'm not trying to be unreasonable," Theodora insists, "But you must understand that we have to be exclusive or we'd just be normal."

To the Dandies, 'normal' is a dirty word. To be a part of their circle, you have to be as strange as possible. The man who runs the Blitz club even calls himself Steve Strange. But if Steve is strange, Theodora is plain weird. With a chalk-white face and clown-like makeup, he struts around in baggy white trousers and a huge, billowing silk-shirt decorated with brightly coloured pompoms.

"Our tastes are eclectic," says Theodora, "There are no boundaries in music, style or life. In fact, as far as I am concerned, music and style are life. If you don't understand what that means then you aren't one of us."

On the outside, Spivz looks like any number of old London buildings. Once inside, you are in another world. It started life as a Victorian music hall. But now the seats have all gone. Where the stalls used to be, there is now a dance hall. In the last century, people sat there watching pantomime dames on stage. Now the dames are in the audience.

Men in makeup and outrageous hairstyles dance with women – and sometimes with men! – who take glamour to new extremes. Some of them look like Sophia Loren and Jayne Mansfield in their heyday.

"It's true," says Theodora, "There are no sex barriers at Spivz. We have straight people, we have 'gay' people, we have people whose sexuality has no name."

Theodora's girlfriend, a stunning Lauren Bacall lookalike called Velma, agrees: "Spivz is like Berlin in the '30s," she says, "It's like Cabaret. You know, the film. Outside everything is s***. Inside everything is beautiful."

"That's right," agrees Theodora, "The world outside is dark and depressing. What we are doing is making our own world. Spivz isn't just a club. It's a way of life."

Chapter 1

The sour taste in my mouth was all that was left of 1979. I vaguely remembered seeing out the night, the year and the decade in a blaze of luminous cocktails that were still throbbing somewhere at the back of my skull. And now, here I was on the first morning of the '80s. So far, I couldn't see anything special about them. I was lying in the same unmade bed in the same squalid room in the same damp, depressing, undersized and over-priced flat that I'd been living in at the fag end of the '70s.

There was just one thing that was different. There was something in my ear. It felt suspiciously like a tongue.

At other times, on other mornings, I might have found the sensation of a tongue in my ear moderately pleasant. Those were mornings on which I could remember going to bed the night before and on which I might even have hazarded a guess as to the identity of the person I had gone to bed with and who might, therefore, be the owner of the tongue in question. This was not one of those mornings. I couldn't remember getting home the night before, let alone getting into bed. And if I'd brought someone with me, I shuddered to think who it might be.

I decided the mystery could wait. For the time being it was enough to know that I was at home, in bed and that there was a tongue in my ear. I turned over, buried my face deep into my pillow and went back to sleep.

Let me be honest with you. I was not feeling at my best. The night before had flown by in a neon blare of music, cocktails and drugs. I had vague memories of bumping into Steve Strange somewhere and of bumping into the Kemp brothers somewhere else. Steve was too busy being admired by the masses to waste any time talking to me but the Kemps were more forthcoming. They've formed a band with a silly name and they wanted to know if I could get them an interview with one of the more up-market magazines. I suggested 'Jackie'. I got the impression this wouldn't have been their first choice but they put a brave face on it, smiled at me and told me they thought that sounded like a great idea.

At some time in the early hours of the morning I remember being in a taxi with a whole load of people I'd never met before (there was somebody called Zena who was wearing pink eye-shadow and a gold lamé boob tube but of whose gender I am not entirely certain) and we were all heading towards a club in Archway or some such godforsaken hole. No idea why we were going there and I can't recall a single thing about what we did once we got there. Apart from drink. We did a lot of that. I'd been down at Spivz earlier in the evening, which is Theodora's new nightclub ("Divine decadence, my darling, abso-fucking-lutely divine!") and I remember there was a bit of a flap going on when Lala Los Alamos, the synth-player from The Sexteens, collapsed — for the usual reason, or so I assumed at the time (incorrectly, as I would soon discover), by which I mean: coke, booze, smack and speed. Anyway, it must have been about twenty-past twelve when I left Spivz or maybe a bit earlier because I remember having to step over Lala's lifeless body on the way out. And since Spivz is down the East End, mid-way between Shadwell and Whitechapel, and we were up at the club in Archway, I couldn't have left much later than 12:20. I'd already had a few daiquiris at Spivz and when I got to the place in Archway I started hitting the zombies pretty hard. I had no idea how or when I got back home again. And, come to think of it, I also had no idea whose tongue it was that was once again exploring the inner reaches of my ear.

Somewhere just beyond the boundaries of my headache, I was dimly aware that birds were tweeting, the sun was shining and the tongue was on the move. There are probably people who like the feeling of a tongue slopping around inside their auditory crevices but I am not one of them. On the whole, I should very much have preferred to remain silently embracing my pillow without any unnecessary disturbance. However, my curiosity finally got the better of me. If you have ever found yourself in a similar situation you will understand what I mean. Headache or no headache, if an unknown tongue keeps thrusting itself into your ear there comes a point when you start wondering to whom the tongue belongs and how he or she came to be lying in your bed in the first place. I spent some moments racking my memories before coming to the inescapable conclusion that I had no memories to be racked. There was no alternative for it but to go through the painful manoeuvre of opening my eyelids and having a look.

That was when I saw the tongue. It was closely followed by a nose, a pair of eyes and a face bristling with whiskers. I closed my eyes again and turned over. This was a problem that could wait till later. I snuggled back into my pillow and began drifting to sleep. Alpine meadows beckoned in the distance, little skipping sheep frolicked amongst cascading drifts of daisies, Julie Andrews came prancing over a hilltop, her arms flung wide, skipped merrily in my direction and stuck her tongue deep inside my ear.

Damn blast! That was the final straw! I leapt from my bed, raised myself to my full height, shouted "What the bloody hell!" and immediately fell back onto the bed again. When you have a hangover, it is always a bad idea to speak in anything louder than a whisper. When you have the hangover of a lifetime and Julie Andrews has just stuck her tongue into your ear it is playing fast and loose with life and death to leap out of bed and start shouting at the top of your voice. Dizziness and palpitations are the inevitable consequences. And thus it was that I now found myself sitting upon the mattress, clutching my head between my hands and looking into two big, brown, soulful eyes that were staring back at me.

I have, it is true, found myself sharing a bed with some strange people in my time. But never before had I found myself sharing a bed with a strange dog. To whom the dog belonged and why and how it was in my bed I had not the slightest idea. I have never owned a dog, I have never wanted to own a dog and even if I had wanted to own a dog this sad specimen would certainly not have been the dog of my choice. It was a smallish, scruffyish sort of dog with a distinctly dog-like smell. It was not the sort of dog any sane person would want in their house and it was certainly not the sort of dog you would want lying on your bed sticking its tongue into your ear.

For a moment, I wondered if the creature's owner might be lurking about the house somewhere. Might it be possible that I had picked up some dog-walking stranger on the way back from the club in Archway in the dark, early hours of the morning? Under the influence of strong liquor, I have occasionally been known to be bring back persons who, in the harsh light of day on the morning after, have caused me some regret. Sometimes, they are much older than they had seemed the night before, often they prove to be considerably less good-looking and, on at least two occasions, they turned out to be of entirely an unexpected sex. But could it be that even I would be so desperate as to waylay a random dog-walker and bring him or her back complete with random dog?

I shuddered at the thought. Then I shuddered at a cold breeze that happened to waft through the bedroom door. Cold breezes do not generally waft much through the bedroom door unless the living room door which leads into the passage (shared with the flat upstairs) and front door beyond that, both happen to be open. I do not generally make a habit of leaving every door in the place open but I am not generally as blasted out of my mind as I had been the night before so anything was possible. I walked from my bedroom, through my tiny kitchen, into the living room and out into the passage. Sure enough all the inner doors were open and the front door was distinctly ajar. Thus the mystery was explained. I had arrived home at some ungodly hour, had failed to secure the doors and, seeing its opportunity for a bit of extracurricular ear-licking, this unprepossessing specimen of doghood had scampered into the house, through the living room, past the kitchen and into my bedroom whereupon it had availed itself of my aural orifices with fervour.

The dog had to go.

All I had to do was to locate the creature's rightful owners and give them a phone. They would then hotfoot it over here at breakneck speed, tears of joy coursing down their faces, and they'd whisk the aforesaid mutt back to its natural abode which, if my luck was in, would be at a considerable distance from my flat.

I searched about the beast's neck for some signs of a collar and associated name tag. For some reason, this caused the mutt lick me with even greater abandon. The collar I eventually found lurking in the matted fur but of a name tag there was no sign. Oh well, if the owner was so foolish as to let the mutt go about the streets unannounced, so be it. I would get out of bed, bounce the smelly creature down the passage with the assistance of a well-aimed toe applied to the tail-end and off it could go. It was then that I noticed a small red plastic capsule dangling from the collar. I popped this open with a thumbnail and out fell a faded and dirty scrap of paper upon which was written the word "Scruffy" (which was either an unbiased description of the animal or its name) and a telephone number. This, I felt, was good news. I headed towards the telephone with a happy heart and the intention of imparting the good news to the grieving owners, for which I would no doubt receive their undying gratitude with the added possibility of a reward in the form of a used five pound note.

I was about to pick up the phone when the blasted thing rang. If you've ever heard a phone ringing when you have a hangover you will know that it echoes through the skull with the same joyous tone as a dentist's drill. I staggered across the room, then staggered back again in the general direction of the phone. I picked up the handset and mumbled something that was intended to be "Hello," but was probably closer to the groan of a dying rat and then I sat down on the floor. It was the shock, you see. I had been expecting someone to exclaim "Happy New Year!" or something similarly vacuous, instead of which a half hysterical voice was screaming, "He's dead!"

"Who's that speaking?" I mumbled, for I have never been good as recognising screaming voices on telephones when I have a hangover.

"It's Zipgun," he screeched.

For those of you who do not keep up with the comings and goings of the London's fashionable demimonde, I should explain that Zipgun Dandy was the fairly fashionable partner of the more fashionable Theodora: style icon and owner of the not-quite-as-fashionable-as-he-would-have-liked, Spivz Nightclub.

"Ngghhhhh!!!" he screamed, or noises to that effect, "I don't know what to do! You have to help me!"

I momentarily considered whether now would be the right moment to wish him a Happy New Year but there was something about the hysterical edge to his screaming that made me think it might not be.

"So," I said, "Is something is the matter, then?"

"Haven't you heard?" he screamed, "He... he's..."

Whether he paused at this point to choke back a tear or merely for dramatic effect, I could not say. At any rate, I took advantage of the moment of silence to speculate upon the nature of the calamity which had occasioned Zipgun's hysteria. My thoughts floated back again to the curious spectacle, the night before, of the deathly pale, unmoving body over which I had been obliged to step on my way out of Spivz: Lala Los Alamos, the slim, effete, blonde-haired synth-player with the up-and-coming electro ensemble, The Sexteens. At the time I had assumed he had merely fainted under the influence of an excess of artificial stimulants. But now, I toyed with more fatal possibilities.

"You mean...?" I said, cutting my words off suddenly as though to leave three dots and a question mark hanging in the air.

"Yes!" Zipgun screamed, "He's dead! And they think I killed him!"

Chapter 2

I have no idea which end of a stick is the right one but whichever it is, I have a habit of not getting hold of it. Having ventured out into the dismal, wintry streets of Kentish Town, I hailed a passing minicab only to discover that its driver had but a passing familiarity with the English language which, however, considerably exceeded his familiarity with the streets of London.

We were halfway to Brighton before I realised that this was not the most direct route to Bayswater. Luckily I had brought with me a copy of the *London A-To-Z* and, communicating via arm movements and grimaces, I eventually managed to guide him back to where we should have been an hour or so earlier. I don't know what he said when he pulled away after dropping me off in the cobbled backwater of Mingely Mews, W2, since the language in which he said it is not one with which I am familiar. From the redness of his face and the elaborate gesture he made with his fingers, I suspect he was attempting to convey to me his opinion that, having treated me to an unexpectedly compendious tour of the outer reaches of Metropolitan London, he had every right to expect from me a generous tip. I affected not to notice, turned my back on him and rang the bell of the bilious green door of Number 22a.

When the door opened, I staggered back, gasped, staggered forward again, propped myself against the doorpost for added support and exclaimed a coarse expression which might be more politely paraphrased as: "Good Heavens! It's you!"

This was the moment at which I realised that the end of the metaphorical stick that I had been grasping was not the one that nine out of ten cats would have recommended.

In my already frail state, all this staggering and gasping had caused me to feel giddy and so I clung to the doorpost as though it was the last doorpost in the world and I was the last doorpost fetishist. In my defence I may say that I think I had very good grounds for staggering and gasping. It is, after all, not every day that a dead person opens the door for you. The person standing before me, in that open door, was the very one whom I had expected to be solidifying somewhere at that very moment on a mortuary slab. But how, you might wonder, could I be so certain of the person's identity when he was, at the time, wearing dark glasses? I shall tell you. Nobody else would have had the exquisite bad taste to wear silver-lacquered blonde hair, a pink double-breasted suit and a white satin shirt with frilled cuffs. The moment I set eyes on him I knew that, dead or alive, it was quite definitely Lala Los Alamos.

"What's up?" he said in that whining accent of his which somehow manages to blend Wolverhampton with California, "You look as though you've seen a...."

"Ghost?" I suggested, "That's just about what I have seen. You're supposed to be dead."

"Me?" he said, "Dead? That's the first I've heard of it. Come in. Zipgun's expecting you. You're late. Have a cup of tea?"

I took off my fedora, undid the top two buttons and the belt (knotted, not tied) of my Burberry trench coat and glided in through the linoleum-covered hallway – "He's in the front room," Lala said, "Have a cup of tea?"

The front room was elaborately Victorian in decor. The walls were covered in a red-and-green-striped paper, the floor was covered in a moth-eaten floral carpet which might once have been a deep burgundy. Against one wall stood a big carved sideboard sort of thing with huge barley twist columns that made it look like a hybrid of a mausoleum and a cinema organ. A stuffed owl stared out through an inverted glass bell jar. There were big, tatty armchairs everywhere and, sitting cross-legged on a beanbag in the centre of the floor, there was Zipgun Dandy.

Zipgun was wearing his trademark cowboy jacket. You probably know the one I mean. He's worn it a couple of times in magazine photo-shoots – I'm pretty sure he wore it in Smash Hits and maybe for Record Mirror? – anyway, it's the one with all the fringes hanging down the sleeves. To be honest, I'm not sure how practical a jacket like that would be if you were riding horses and herding steers or steering herds or whatever it is cowboys do all day on the lonesome prairies. Suffice to say, it's not the sort of thing you'd have seen John Wayne nancying about in!

Complementing the tasselled jacket was a pair of blood-red, silk-effect, very tight trousers that stopped just below the knee at which point the ensemble was completed by a pair of white knee-length socks. He looked fabulous and I told him so. Well, apart from the mascara which was running. I gathered he'd been crying a good deal as his eyes were watery and their rims were red. Frankly, this troubled me. Zipgun may not be the brightest banana in the bunch, but I should have thought that even he would have had sense enough to wear waterproof mascara if he'd felt a weepy-fit coming on and this I told him.

"It's all I could find," he said, "Normally, I'd use Theodora's but his mascara was in his pocket when they..." and at that point he began blubbering incoherently.

While this was happening, Lala had entered the room silently behind me. "I was wondering," he said, "If you'd like a cup of tea?"

There is, in my view, something unwholesome about the English obsession with drinking tea at every occasion possible and I was starting to think that Lala might be suffering from a fixation or a mania. I declined the tea and asked Lala what exactly was going on – "First I thought you were dead and now I find you are alive. And, that being so, why is Zipgun blubbering?"

"Theodora," Lala said.

"Theodora?" I said.

I waited.

"Yes," Lala said.

I waited some more.

"What about Theodora?" I said.

"Dead," Lala said, "As a doorknob."

"Doornail," I corrected.

"We have Chinese, Indian and Ceylon," he said.

"What?" I said.

"Tea," he said.

"Tea?" I said.

"There isn't any coffee," he said.

I was confused. Not about the tea. I am well acquainted with the full range of teas on offer from Mssrs Twining, Williamson, Jacksons of Piccadilly and other fine purveyors of the dried leaf of *Camellia sinensis* but that was not the subject rattling away at the forefront of my mind.

"Theodora can't be dead," I said, "I saw him last night. I was talking to him. He was fine. Positively bubbling. Full of life, in fact. He can't possibly be...."

"Murdered," said Lala.

"And I'm the main suspect," Zipgun blubbered.

I felt tied in knots. This made no sense. It had most definitely been Lala who'd been lying lifeless and cold as I stepped over his recumbent body the night before (he had been wearing a powder blue suit at the time, with a black lace cravat and co-respondent shoes – moreover, he hadn't been wearing sunglasses at the time so there was not the slightest possibility of mistaken identity). Now I was being asked to believe that Lala had made a full recovery while Theodora had been bumped off.

I looked around the room. This was Theodora's house; the house he shared with Zipgun Dandy. There was a photograph of them – smiling, arms around each other – in an ornate gilt frame propped up on the mausoleum-sideboard, next to the stuffed owl. There were traces of Theodora everywhere – the black velvet tam o'shanter hanging from a hook of a bent-wood hat stand, the screen-print picture hanging over the fireplace: Theodora's face looking like a porcelain Victorian doll with two perfect red circles highlighting his cheeks. It felt as though he had just popped out and would be back at any moment.

Why anyone would want to bump off Theodora was beyond me. He might have been a bit of an idiot – no, let me be frank about this, he definitely was a bit of an idiot – but he was quite harmless, really. Everybody liked him. Besides which, Spivz was his club and it seemed improbable to me that anyone fashionable enough to be allowed admittance would harbour a grudge against him. There was, of course, the possibility that someone who had been refused admittance might have been a bit miffed. But, by definition, someone who hadn't been admitted wouldn't have been there and so couldn't have been the murderer. But the least likely person of all to want to kill Theodora was Zipgun Dandy. They were partners – in every respect. They ran the club together and they lived their lives together. They always seemed happy. As far as one could tell.

"How was he killed?" I asked Zipgun.

Zipgun put his hand over his eyes and shook his head, desperately fighting back sobs, "It was horrible, horrible. Strangled."

"With his own scarf," Lala added.

I thought back to the night before. Theodora had been dressed to the nines or, possibly, to the tens, in a top hat, white tie and tails with all matching accessories, including a silver-topped cane and a long white, silk scarf.

"Strangled?" I said, "Where? By whom?"

"In the bog," Lala said, "By him," and he nodded towards Zipgun Dandy.

"You can't believe that?" I said. Then, just to make sure I wasn't getting the wrong end of the stick yet again, I turned to Zipgun and said, "You didn't do it. Did you?"

"No," he said, "No, of course I didn't. With a *scarf?*"

He said the word 'scarf' with distaste, suggesting that, as a murder weapon, a scarf was simply not à la mode. I momentarily wondered how he would have responded had the weapon been a bit more exotic – a stiletto, say, or a poisoned skull.

"But if you didn't do it," I said, "Why on earth would anyone think you did?"

"He was Tyrone's partner, he was at the scene of the crime, who else is there to suspect?" Lala said, smiling merrily, "We have Earl Grey or Lapsang Souchong if you prefer."

It was with some difficulty and the aid of a stout oak door that I finally managed to persuade Lala that I wished to speak privately with Zipgun Dandy, free from the distraction of pink double-breasted suits and gratuitous offers of hot beverages. In the circumstances, I felt that a drink of somewhat greater potency was called for. My keen eye had spotted a large bottle of ten year-old Laphroaig standing next to a china spotted dog on the mausoleum-sideboard-thing and I wasted no time in rustling up a couple of hefty glasses of the stuff with which to calm our nerves.

Zipgun, who was now sitting in one of the more elaborately moth-eaten armchairs, affected a Pre-Raphaelite pose of aesthetic despair. His face, turned towards the vast bay window, was silvered by the cold winter light. The fingers of his left hand toyed dejectedly with the some strands of his jet-black hair which fell stylishly over his forehead, leaving his right hand free for the whisky.

"I loved him," he said, "I know what people said. They said I was only in it for the money. They said we had arguments. They said I had affairs."

"Did you?"

"What? Have arguments or affairs?"

"Well, both."

"Yes."

"Yes to which? The arguments or the affairs?"

"To both. But that's beside the point. The point is that some people say I didn't love him. I know they do. But they are wrong."

"So what exactly do you want me to do?" I said.

"I just thought, well, you've always been the clever one. If anyone can figure out who killed him, it's you."

I was flattered. I also knew he was wrong. I'm clever in trivial ways. I can use undergraduate rhetoric to tie people in knots, I can come up with tired metaphors that fool people into thinking I'm witty. But I can't write operas or make head or tail of quantum mechanics and, most of all, I can't solve murders. I told him so. But he wouldn't believe me.

"Surely the police are in a better position to find the culprit than I am," I said.

He shook his head: "They don't know the scene. they don't know what we are about. They wouldn't understand someone like Theodora."

I was about to point out that it was a bit late to worry about understanding Theodora but he went on before I had the chance – "The thing is, Theodora had a habit of getting himself into situations."

"What kind of situations?"

"All kinds of situations. He was no kind of businessman. He could never tell the difference between money that belonged to the club and money that belonged to him. And he had expensive tastes. You know, clothes and..."

"Drugs?"

"Clothes and – other things. And he made enemies. He had a cutting tongue. he didn't mean any harm, really. But sometimes he'd say things. Get people against him. There are a lot of people who...."

His voice faded out. I could see tears welling in his eyes. I poured him another whisky. That bucked him enough to continue: "A lot of people will be glad to see him gone," he said, "But the police, they can't see that. All they can see is that Theodora and I lived together and we ran the club together. They can see that Theodora's lifestyle was eating into the profits and that I stand to gain by his death. I don't mean a will or anything. He didn't have a will. But the club. They think that I can make more money from the club without him."

"Can you?"

He shook his head. "What do you think?"

"I think he was the reason people came to the club."

Zipgun smiled. there were tears rolling down his cheeks now but he smiled anyway. "I knew you'd understand. I tried explaining to the police but they didn't believe me. That's why they'll never find who killed him. They don't understand. You do."

I wasn't sure I deserved the confidence he placed in me. Even so, my curiosity and – let me be honest – my pride, got the better of me. I realised that I stood on the brink of a great and terrible mystery. Theodora, doyen of London's fashionable demimonde, nightclub owner, style icon, artist and would-be musician, had been brutally strangled to death by person or person's unknown. In a toilet. And now I found myself in a uniquely privileged position. I had direct access to the person closest in all the world to the murdered man. He was asking me to delve into the mystery and see what I could find. For a writer like me that would be the scoop of a lifetime. There really was no way I could refuse.

"You'll have to tell me everything," I said, "And I really mean *everything.*"

I sat upon a saggy satin-covered armchair facing Zipgun and arranged my features in such a way as to convey a shared sense of loss discreetly mingled with an urgent desire to hear the details of the murder in all its grisly detail. At first he was reluctant to talk, unwilling to remember the horrific details of the night before. But with my encouragement and the assistance of a couple of generous tumblers of Laphroaig, he gradually, haltingly, recounted the events that led up to the dreadful discovery of the Theodora's hideously staring corpse in the executive toilet of Spivz Nightclub, London E1. And then he told me the name of Theodora's killer.

Chapter 3

I was still reeling from the impact of Zipgun's story when I left his house as twilight was beginning to fall. He was reclining in his armchair as I opened the door and walked out of the room. I ran straight into Lala. I had been under the impression that he had been ensconced in the kitchen at the far end of the hallway engaged in a comparative tasting of the various blends of tea on offer. I was, therefore, surprised to find him lurking at the other side of the door and I could not help but wonder how long he had been there.

He looked flustered. "I wondered if you might...?"

"I don't want tea," I said, "I don't want Earl Gray nor Lapsang Souchong, nor Broken Orange Pekoe nor even P G Bloody Tips."

I paused.

So did Lala.

I paused again.

"I wasn't going to offer you any tea," he said.

"Oh no?" I said.

"No."

"Then what?"

"I wondered," he said, "If you might like to know who killed Theodora."

"That," I said loftily, "Is a matter for the police."

He took off his dark glasses, stared at me and raised one finely plucked eyebrow. In spite of the fact that the hallway was dimly lit by a single light-bulb inside a red silk lampshade, I could not help but notice that the rims of his eyelids were bright red.

"You've been crying too?" I said.

He looked surprised. "Me? No. I barely even knew Theodora. And what little I did know I didn't much like."

"I can't help noticing..."

"Oh! My eyes! I'd forgotten! An allergy, I think. Mascara."

"You have an allergy to mascara?"

"Well, no, not normally I don't. Just to Theodora's."

I wasn't following the thread of what he was saying and I told him so.

"Last night," he said, "At the club. Theodora didn't like the colour of his mascara so we swapped. End result is what you see before you. Red itchy eyes. They are quite sensitive, I can tell you."

"What exactly happened to you last night?" I said, "The last I saw of you, you were lying, dead to the world, on the carpet in the foyer of Spivz."

Lala smiled, "Oh that! Well, I think I must have overdone it a bit really. Cocktails. What are they called – tequila something."

"Tequila Sunrise?" I suggested.

"Could be. They were bright orange with ice cubes and umbrellas. I don't normally drink more than half a shandy at a time so it went to my head. Suddenly I came all over faint. If it hadn't been for the smelling salts, I'd still be lying there."

"Smelling salts?"

"Yeah, someone stuck them under my nose. No idea what's in them but whatever it is, it's got quite a kick. Brought me back to life, as you might say."

"Extraordinary. And do you remember who gave you the smelling salts?"

"No idea. There was loads of people there. Pete, Adam Xeon, Squirrel. All I remember is Adam taking me off into a corner and getting me some water to drink. Then I came home and was flat out to the world. Next thing I knew the phone was ringing and it was Zipgun. Me and Zipgun, we're old mates. Both from Islington. I mean, I'm from Wolverhampton originally. But me mum and dad moved to Islington when I was a kid. Zipgun used to live just around the corner. When he called me this morning was the first I heard about Theodora. Being, you know..."

"Bumped off."

"So, naturally, I came over here right away and found Zipgun, well, much as you see him. A couple of bobbies were here at the time. Interviewing him. He's convinced that he's their chief suspect. They interviewed me too but not so much as him. They were very close, you know, him and Theodora. Though, personally, I don't know why. If you want my opinion, Theodora was nothing but a talentless, gold digging cow and the world is better off without him."

"Really?" I said, "And is that what you told the police?"

He laughed. "Course not. I said we all loved Theodora. What, do you think I am – stupid or just a bastard?"

I did not answer the question.

"You said a moment ago that you know who killed Theodora?"

"Not for sure. It's just what I heard."

"From whom?"

"From Pete. You know Pete, I suppose?"

"Only slightly," I said. He was referring to Pete de Gré, the lead-singer of a group called The Sexteens. I had interviewed him once for My Guy magazine but apart from that our paths had not much crossed.

"Yeah, well it was Pete what told me," Lala went on, "He reckons it was Dave Buzzard."

Dave Buzzard had formerly been the lead singer of The Sexteens, the same group for which Lala played keyboards. And then, about three months ago, Dave been replaced by Pete. I wondered if there might be some degree of professional jealousy between the two of them.

"And why," I asked, "does Pete believe that Dave Buzzard did it?"

Lala shrugged his shoulders. "Don't know. You'd have to ask him."

"Yes," I said, "I shall."

Chapter 4

When I had arrived at Spivz Nightclub, the night before, there had been nothing to suggest that anything was amiss. Theodora himself had been in high spirits and was playing the jovial host with his usual panache.

Just in case you've never been there, I should explain that Spivz is not at all like a normal nightclub. The club is constructed inside an old and only partially renovated Victorian building. Apparently it was a music hall in the 19th Century and, in spite of being used for all kinds of other activities in the intervening period (everything from a Gospel Mission to a warehouse) there are still numerous traces of its former glory. From the outside it doesn't look much at all. It is located down a narrow cobbled street of very ordinary two-storey terraced houses. About midway down the street the houses suddenly cease to have any visible windows and this windowless facade continues for the equivalent of four houses. At the approx-imate middle of the windowless area there is a set of double doors over which there is a neon sign showing the club's name. Spivz lies behind the faceless walls and it is entered, if Theodora approves of you, through the double doors.

Once you are through the doors you stand in a small carpeted lobby to the left of which is the cloakroom; to the right is the main bar which is called "Harlow's". Immediately in front of you there is an small open wooden staircase leading up to the floor above which, as a sign over the staircase informs you, is known as "The Gallery". The staircase itself is about five feet wide and it occupies the centre of the lobby leaving a three foot gap on either side.

Staying on the ground floor you may walk to either side of the staircase in which case you will immediately arrive at the end of the lobby. Here a corridor runs to your left and to your right. The lobby and the corridor form a sot of T-junction: the lobby is the stem of the T and the corridor is its crossbar. There is nothing of any significance at either end of the corridor, unless you happen to have been drinking in which case the presence of the Ladies' toilets at the left end of the corridor and the Gents' at the right end might be of passing interest.

Standing now at the end of the lobby just beneath the wooden staircase, you will see two sets of double-doors in the wall facing you: one set of doors is to your left, another is directly in front of you. These doors are the entrances to what would once have been the stalls of the music hall but is now the dance floor of the nightclub.

On New Year's Eve 1979, I arrived at Spivz a bit before eleven o'clock, having spent an hour or so prior to that at a bar called The Pink Pussycat in the company of Sanford Bouche-Torrington, editor and publisher of Great Hits magazine which is so named, as Sanford keeps telling me, for its attraction to "Spotty Herbert boys who will pay good money for the chance to go into a newsagent and ask a woman employee if they have Great Hits (said without aspirating the 'h')". My evening with Sanford in The Pink Pussycat is irrelevant to the events that followed, though it was undoubtedly a contributory factor both to my advanced state of inebriation and to my relatively late arrival at Spivz.

Brigitte was on the door when I arrived which was fortuitous since Brigitte knows me pretty well and, I think, rather likes me, so I was waved in without requiring to prove my identity, pay an admittance fee or go through the humiliation of having my attire assessed, criticised and (as all too frequently happened) rejected as unsuitable. Brigitte, as you probably know, is one of the more glamorous adornments of the Futurist movement: slim, blonde, immaculately made-up and invariably glittering in costumes of a magnificence that would make Joan Collins envious. She (or rather 'he' – to be honest, where Brigitte is concerned, I have never been entirely certain which is the more appropriate personal pronoun) has already received widespread coverage in pop music magazines which is an extraordinary feat given the fact that, as far as anyone knows, he has no musical talent of any description. But he does look fabulous in photographs.

From the moment I entered I could hear booming bass notes coming from the direction of the dance floor. I walked along the lobby, past the stairs and entered via the set of double-doors facing me. The dance floor was crowded with a bewildering collection of exotically dressed people dancing to the thunderously amplified sounds of (if my memory serves me well) Moskow Diskow by Telex, a Belgian electro-group which is, in my view, considerably over-played at Spivz. It was hard to see what was what and who was who in the whirl of people moving through the kaleidoscope of coloured light flickering through the pulsing darkness. This is not helped by the fact that the favoured dance style at Spivz is of a strangely athletic variety, typically with partners holding one another at arm's length before springing into and then away from one another as though their arms were elasticated. From a distance it is an almost impossible task to identify anyone in the swirling blur of movement .

Having entered by the right-hand doors I turned to the right and walked towards the stage. Here the venue's original purposes is self-evident. The stage takes the form of a proscenium arch with a wooden-boarded floor recessed twelve or fifteen feet. This is where the DJ sits, surrounded by three record decks and a mixing board. At either side of the stage there is a large stack of speakers while other, smaller speakers are wall-mounted throughout the remainder of the building. Skirting the mass of dancing people, I walked to the other side of the stage. Here there is a staircase that leads up from the dance floor to the Gallery. The staircase goes up ten steps until it meets the wall at the edge of the proscenium arch. Then there is a small platform at which point the staircase turns back upon itself to continue the ascent to the Gallery.

The Gallery is what most modern theatres would call "the circle". It is a balcony shaped like a horse-shoe that runs around three walls of the building, terminating on either side of the stage. I suppose that, in years gone by, the Gallery might have held two rows of seats at either side and maybe six or seven rows at the back where the seats would have faced directly towards the stage. The original seats have long ago been removed and, in their place, each side of the Gallery now contains a row of small circular tables with three or four chairs around each. At the back, there is a cocktail bar with a number of tall bar-stools set before it. It was towards the cocktail bar that I headed. The cocktail bar was usually the gathering place for Theodora's exclusive circle of friends, acolytes and hangers-on.

I tried to make my way in that direction but I soon met with a barrier of people all gathered together and craning their heads to get a look in the direction of the bar. There was a sudden flash of white light. At first I thought it was one of the disco lights, possibly a flash of the strobe lighting which they sometimes use. But several seconds passed before the next white flash and several more seconds passed before there was a third. If there is one thing Theodora liked even more than cocaine and cocktails it is the inebriation that only publicity brings. So, when the crowd finally began to disperse, allowing me to move towards the cocktail bar, I was not in the least surprised to see that a photo session had just come to an end and that the bright white light had been produced by the photographer's flashgun.

Theodora was looking even more astonishing than usual. When last I'd seen him, over two weeks ago, he had been dressed like a harlequin. I'd met him in a cafe in Soho to do an interview for 'Star Beat' magazine. Well, to be honest, at the time I'd thought he was dressed like a clown but he had been quick to correct me: "Comedia dell'arte, my dear," he'd said, "Arlecchino, Scaramuccia, Pulcinella. It's absolutely the coming trend, my darling." Whether, in the intervening fortnight he had revised his opinion or whether he had deliberately encouraged lesser mortals to copy "the coming trend" slavishly so that, when he changed his own style he would be able to scorn their lack of originality is a matter of conjecture. All I can say for sure is that, while a large number of the Spivz clientele were dressed in motley, Theodora was not among their number. He was, in fact, dressed in what might be regarded as a remarkably conservative style: top hat, white tie and tails. Not to mention white gloves, a silver-topped cane and a white silk scarf draped loosely over his shoulders. If it hadn't been for the stark white grease-painted face, the heavy mascara and the vermillion lipstick, one might easily have assumed he was dressed for a night at the opera or, possibly, a twirl around the ballroom with Ginger Rogers.

Tonight the closest approximation of Ginger Rogers was a girl called Velma. Theoretically, and for the benefit of the press, she was Theodora's girlfriend and she would occasionally turn up at Theodora's side when cameras were in evidence. Velma was a nice girl who, in spite of her rather exotic appearance (Siouxsie Sioux makeup with Lauren Bacall accessories), was really very down-to-earth. By day she worked at a checkout in a supermarket. By night she was a glamorous and mysterious femme fatale. Theodora kissed Velma on the cheek and she teetered off on her hazardously elevated stilettos to do whatever it is that femme fatales do when not being photographed.

I waited on the sidelines until the photographer packed his equipment into his camera case and Theodora had shaken his hand, told him how much he had enjoyed the photo session and offered him the freedom of the cocktail bar which the photographer declined. It was only then that I recognised the photographer. His name is Kev (I've no idea if he has a last name – Kev is the only name he's ever admitted to). He is a biker and Heavy Metal fan which probably explains why he was in a hurry to leave. Neither the clientele nor the music at Spivz would have been to his taste. When Kev had left, Theodora noticed me, beamed broadly as though I were the one person in all the world he was hoping to see and embraced me cautiously so as to avoid any risk of rumpling his clothes or smearing his makeup.

"What was the photo session?" I asked.

"Oh, one of the newspapers," he said, "The Sunday Times I think."

"The photographer seemed in a hurry to leave," I said.

"He has someone else to photograph, apparently," he said, "One can only hope it's not that Strange person."

Theodora liked to pretend that a "friendly rivalry" existed between himself and Steve Strange who has recently opened a ("deeply unfashionable" according to Theodora) rival club called Blitz somewhere in the purlieus of Covent Garden. However, if you'd heard some of the things Theodora has said about Strange, you might conclude that the word "friendly" applies to "rivalry" in much the same way that it applies to "fire". In either case, you wouldn't want to get in the way of it.

I don't recall exactly what happened next. I remember drinking a bright blue cocktail in a large glass shaped like a dish. I don't recall buying it so I guess it must have been on the house. I remember staring down at the dance floor trying to see if I could recognise anyone. Theodora had wandered off to mingle, no doubt, with the famous and the fashionable. I think I went downstairs for a while. I remember noticing Pete de Gré dancing at one point. I couldn't see who he was with though. And then I went for a look in Harlow's Bar. It's even darker in there than on the dance floor. Lots of tables with candles for illumination and the bar set at one end of the room. I remember talking to Brigitte for a while. She'd finished her stint on the door and was preparing to have "the night of my life, honey, know what I mean?" She winked broadly and I laughed though I didn't really know why since I had no idea what she was talking about. Then I went into the dance floor again and had a dance with Adam Xeon, one of the synth players with The Sexteens. Then I went back to the bar upstairs via the open wooden staircase in the lobby. The staircase leads up to a corridor on the first floor that lies directly over the corridor on the ground floor. When you get to the top of the stairs you face another blank wall with a single set of double-doors just in front of you. These doors lead into the left-hand balcony of the Gallery.

If, instead of going into the Gallery, you were to turn left and walk down the length of the corridor you would pass some decrepit-looking walls covered with flaking paint (the upstairs corridor is definitely one of the unrenovated parts of Spivz) and a couple of locked doors one of which leads to a store room and the other of which contains equipment related to the lighting system.

If, on the other hand, you were to turn right and walk down the corridor in that direction (which, according to a sign hanging from the ceiling, you should not do since the area is 'Private') you would first pass the manager's office which is the sole preserve of Theodora and Zipgun Dandy. Beyond the manager's office a tiny passageway opens up on the right. At the far end of this passageway there is a door to another storeroom. Next to the storeroom, on the corner where the passageway meets the main corridor, is the managerial toilet.

Having climbed the stairs from the lobby, I moved directly towards the set of double-doors leading onto the Gallery. As I was about to open the doors, I happened to notice Theodora standing just outside the toilet at the private end of the corridor. Dave Buzzard was with him. I thought I saw Theodora hand something to Buzzard which I thought I saw Buzzard put into an inside pocket of his jacket. Although I only saw Theodora and Buzzard for a few seconds, I got the distinct impression that all was not sweetness and light between them. As Buzzard turned away from Theodora I caught the look on his face. If looks, as they say, could kill, then the look on Buzzard's face could have depopulated a room. Behind Buzzard's back, Theodora gave him a two-finger sign. At least, I think he did. When he saw me he seamlessly turned the gesture into a friendly wave. Buzzard walked past me without saying a word and went downstairs, Theodora went back into his office, I went into the Gallery and made my way back to the cocktail bar.

That fleetingly glimpsed incident between Theodora and Dave Buzzard would have seemed entirely insignificant but for the fact that, less than one hour later, Theodora's dead body would be discovered inside the toilet at the private end of the corridor.

It must have been about twenty to twelve when I arrived at the cocktail bar. I noticed that, sitting at a table on the opposite balcony, were Lala and Pete de Gré. I quite like them both and if they'd been alone I might have joined them. However, they weren't alone. Clifton Chuttle was with them. I've always found Chuttle a bit on the creepy side. To be honest, my experience of rock group managers in general is that they are singularly predisposed to creepiness. Typically they present themselves to the world as devil-may-care rock music anarchists while lurking, just below the surface, is a hard-headed businessman whose only interest in anarchy is how much it could earn in royalties. Chuttle insisted on wearing tight, black leather jeans and far too much mascara in spite of the fact that this was appropriate neither to his age nor his waistline (something over 40 in both cases). I was also suspicious of Chuttle's effusive good humour: in public he was always excessively pleased to see anybody and everybody at all times. In private, I suspected that he was a much less good-natured creature who would think nothing of turning his grandmother's pet Chihuahua into sausage meat if there was money to be made from it.

Chuttle's "stable of artistes", as he pompously liked to call his two bands, were fully represented tonight: Chuttle himself was sharing a table with two members of The Sexteens while, at the next table, there were three members of Mascara Addiction: Dusty Evsky, Anvil Evans and Joe Jonson; only Dave Buzzard was missing from the band and I'd seen him heading downstairs a few minutes earlier.

Closer to hand, I noticed that Zipgun Dandy, Brigitte, Adam Xeon and Velma were sitting at a table on the nearside of the cocktail bar. I got myself a cocktail – pink this time, no idea what was in it – and went to join them. "So what's happened to the time of your life?" I shouted at Brigitte. I had to shout in order to be heard over the sound system. The DJ was playing hard-core electronic stuff that night – Fad Gadget, The Normal, The Human League – and the bass was turned way up high. Brigitte raised a well-plucked eyebrow, stuck out the tip of her tongue and ran her index finger down it. I don't know what the gesture was intended to mean but it looked vaguely obscene. Velma ignored Brigitte studiously. I got the feeling there was some sort of style rivalry going on between the two: there was Brigitte, ostentatiously beautiful in her gold-sequined blouse and blonde peek-a-boo hairdo; and there was Velma looking like a Lauren Bacall dressed immaculately in black with a small pillbox hat and a black net trimming pulled down over the eyes. If this were a movie, Brigitte would be the tart who leads the hero astray and Velma would be the girl who gets him back on the tracks again. Brigitte was made for one-night stands but Velma was for life.

The music was so loud that there was no point in trying to hold a conversation so I went to the balcony and leaned over to gape at the dancers below. Then I saw the balcony double-doors swing open and Theodora came in. No, let me rephrase that. Theodora didn't just "come in" – he made an entrance. In his white tie and tails, he cut a striking figure. The stark whiteness of his made-up face contrasted with the black of his clothes, making him look positively vampiric. At several tables, heads turned to look. There was no doubt about it: Theodora had succeeded in out-glamming everyone. A dozen Pierrots and Harlequins tried to pretended they hadn't noticed him or, if they had, that they didn't care. As Theodora once told me, "The plain truth of the matter, darling, is that they *follow* the trends. I *set* them."

Theodora swaggered over to me and shouted into my ear, "Having a good time, darling?" I mimed back, "Great". Then he walked over to the table where Brigitte, Adam, Velma and Zipgun Dandy were sitting. He leaned over and spoke into Zipgun's ear. I could see Zipgun saying something like "Oh no, not again!" then Theodora said something else to him and Zipgun said something back. I couldn't make out what he was saying but, as he said it, he made a sharp hand gesture with his thumb pointed towards the double-doors. It was the sort of gesture you might make if you were telling someone to "Get out of it! Clear off!". He obviously wasn't telling Theodora to clear off so I assumed they must talking about someone else. After what I'd seen out there in the corridor a few minutes earlier, I assumed they were talking about Dave Buzzard. Maybe Dave had been cadging money off Theodora? Or drugs? Everyone knew that Theodora indulged but was he supplying too? Now Theodora was shaking his head and Zipgun Dandy was shrugging his shoulders. So whatever they'd been discussing, it seemed they had decided to take it no further. Then Theodora went to the bar and came back with a martini.

At some point I noticed Dusty Evsky, the keyboard player with Mascara Addiction. He had left the table where he'd been sitting with Clifton Chuttle and he was now leaning on the balcony on at the opposite side of the Gallery from me. Whatever else you might say about Dusty there is no getting away from the fact that he is an exceptionally good looking young man. He has something of James Dean about him, or Marlon Brando. That's the young Marlon Brando, I mean, the sexy Marlon Brando of On The Waterfront and The Wild One not the old, mumbling Marlon Brando of The Godfather or Superman's dad. People like Brando shouldn't get old. Just as James Dean didn't and Dusty always claimed he wouldn't – "I'll never be forty," he'd say, "I'll live fast and die young."

Dusty always wears the same clothes, or anyway, clothes that are similar enough to *look* the same: faded blue jeans, classic black leather biker's jacket. This contravenes the strict dress code of Spivz in every respect. Nobody else wearing an outfit like that would stand a chance of being allowed inside (unless they were journalists or photographers in which case they could wear greasy boiler suits or come stark naked – Theodora was always ready to make exceptions for the gentlemen of the press). But Dusty was Dusty and Dusty always got his way. He could break a heart with a wink or a smile, so getting into a nightclub was child's play. Dusty was staring fixedly in the direction of the cocktail bar. I turned to see what he was looking at. Brigitte was standing there, smiling and looking at Dusty. I turned back to look at Dusty but he was gone. Then I saw him again. He was walking nonchalantly past the cocktail bar, then past me and finally through the double-doors that lead out of the Gallery and into the first-floor corridor. A few moments later Brigitte left the same way. I went back to sit at the table with Theodora, but it was just about impossible to have a conversation so I decided to go downstairs to the Harlow's Bar instead.

Harlow's Bar is located off the lobby and it is quieter there than anywhere else in the building. It must have been a few minutes before twelve by then, I suppose, which was around half an hour or so before Theodora's body was found. When I last saw him, Theodora looked happy enough. He was sitting at that table near the cocktail bar along with Zipgun Dandy, Velma and Adam Xeon. To look at him, you would have thought he didn't have a care in the world.

Harlow's Bar was almost empty. I supposed everybody had gone inside to get ready to see in the fast-approaching new decade. I knew that at twelve o'clock sharp there would be some kind of celebration that would probably involve balloons, streamers, the singing of Auld Lang Syne and quite possibly a conga around the club, none of which appealed to me. I ordered a daiquiri at the bar and went to join Squirrel, who was sitting at a table in the corner under a big black and white poster of Jean Harlow. Squirrel is a bit of an oddity. He's the fourth member of The Sexteens and doesn't exactly blend in with the others. Pete de Gré, Adam Xeon and Lala Los Alamos are all young, slim and more or less good looking. Squirrel on the other hand, is at least a few years older than the others, distinctly on the porky side and completely bald. To compensate for these disadvantages, he wears more mascara and eyeliner than the other three put together. The end result is that he looks a lot like a giant panda.

While the low noise level in the bar was conducive to conversation, Squirrel's low intelligence is not. My best efforts to engage him in discussions of politics, religion, the invasion of Afghanistan, the wit and wisdom of Mother Teresa and the hunt for the Yorkshire Ripper all fell on stony ground. "Yeah," or "Is that right?" are about the most penetrating observations I was able to elicit. Only when I chanced to mention drumming did he show any real interest. Squirrel is a drummer of the old school. He likes the feel of wooden sticks banged against dead animal skin. Which is something he never gets to do in The Sexteens. At Chuttle's insistence they don't do anything that isn't synthetic which means that 'drum machines' are now the nearest that Squirrel ever gets to percussion. Once he gets started on his pet subject, there's no stopping him. Five minutes of "hi-hats" and "rimshots", "snares, toms and rides" is about four and a half minutes more than I can take and at some point I must have wandered off because the next thing I can remember is chatting to someone called Zena who was wearing pink eye-shadow and a gold lamé boob tube. I think it was Zena who suggested we all go up to a club in Archway which was "ten times better than this dump". It was as Zena, I and a few other people I'd never met before, were on our way out of Spivz in search of a cab that we encountered pandemonium in the lobby because Lala had fainted and was surrounded by crowds of people most of whom were dressed like extras in a provincial pantomime, gawking, talking, laughing and telling each other to stay back and give the poor guy some air. We forced our way through the crowd and stepped over Lala's unmoving body on our way to the exit.

And that is all I can remember of that fateful New Year's Eve in Spivz. I don't even recall the moment at which 1979 turned into 1980. It was as though the new decade had crept in without bothering to tell me.

January 1st, 1980

Chapter 5

But you are no doubt wondering what had become of the scruffy dog whose cold, wet tongue had been my first conscious experience of the new decade. You may recall that I was in the process of devising a stratagem for liberating myself of the unwanted mutt's presence in my hitherto dog-free life. Having discovered a telephone number on a piece of paper inside a red plastic capsule attached to the mutt's collar, I had been about to phone the creature's tearful owners and claim what no doubt would be a generous reward for its return when my plan had been dramatically interrupted by Zipgun Dandy's phone call. After dealing with that, it took me a few moments to gather my thoughts together. I then revised my strategy in regards to the mutt and decided that a more direct solution to the problem would be to open my front door and apply the toe end of my boot to the mutt's rear end. I was about to do so when the aforementioned mutt happened to glance up at me with its big, sad soulful eyes, proffered a winsome paw, lolled its tongue out of the corner of its mouth and proceeded to make a strangely pathetical huffing sound.

My experience of dogs is somewhat limited and so I cannot say if this behaviour is common to all members of the species or is unique to this particular individual. What I can say is that when confronted by big, sad soulful eyes, a winsome paw, a lolling tongue and a pathetical huffing, it becomes remarkably difficult to apply one's boot to the animal's rear end. This, I imagine, is something to do with evolution and would cut no ice at all with a fully trained evolutionary biologist. Unfortunately, I am not a fully trained evolutionary biologist and so the mutt had an unfair advantage over me. Instead of kicking the animal up the backside as I had intended, I patted it on the head, scratched it behind the ears and (I am ashamed to confess) I went so far as to give it a saucer of milk.

I then set off on the visit to Zipgun Dandy about which I have already written, deferring a decision on the dog's future until later in the day. Upon my return, I discovered that the creature had mistaken my small kindnesses for moral weakness. It had brazenly determined to take advantage of all that my home had to offer. The beast was stretched out, fast asleep and snoring, on my settee. It lay on its back with its paws in the air and digestive biscuit crumbs scattered profusely over the cushions around it. I shall skip quickly over the sad history of the biscuits. Suffice to say my plans for them had not involved the fattening up of scruffy dogs.

Looking at the brazen creature, I could barely believe how weak willed I had thus far been. Well, no more would I be swayed by its soulful eyes and winsome paws! I was resolved that it should no longer avail itself of my settee, digestive biscuits and saucers of milk. The ungrateful cur already had a home and the sooner it returned there the happier I would be. I dialled the phone number which I had extracted from the capsule attached to the dog's collar and was preparing for the sounds of rapturous joy which would soon be zinging down the phone line when I informed the grieving owners of their beloved pet's recovery.

The phone was answered with a grunt. With all the happiness I could stuff into my voice, I informed the grunting person that I had discovered their dog and that, should they wish to come and collect it, there was no time like the present. I paused to allow for a bit of joyous rapture, the odd cry of "Halleluiah!" and, quite possibly, the offer of a substantial reward. No such rapture, cry or offer forthcoming, I was forced to ask, "Um, are you still there?"

"Yeah, 'course, I'm 'ere," came back the unhelpful reply.

The thought occurred to me that I had dialled the wrong number. I unravelled the scrap of paper carefully and read back the digits for verification. "Yeah, that's our number," the loquacious grunter confirmed. This was followed by a rustling sound such as might be caused by a large and meaty hand being placed over the mouthpiece of a telephone followed by a muffled conversation which, in spite of the meaty hand, was nonetheless entirely audible. It went along these lines.

"Who is it?"

"Don't know."

41

"What's he want then?"

"Says he's found a dog."

"Scruffy?"

"Didn't say."

"How d'e find our phone number?"

"Says it was on the dog's collar?"

"You didn't put our phone number on his collar, did you?"

"Don't know. Must have."

"You bloody idiot."

"Why?"

"Putting our phone number on Scruffy's collar. That's how he knew he was our dog, I 'spect."

"Yeah, I 'spect."

"So what you gonna do now then?"

"Nothing."

"What'cha mean, 'nothing'?"

"What I said. Nothing."

Then there was a sound as of a large and meaty hand being removed from a telephone mouthpiece followed by a grunt and – "Nah, there ain't no dog here, mate."

"No, I realise that," I said, "That's my point. The dog is not there. He's here."

"No, he ain't mate," came the reply, "There ain't no dog here."

I felt that the complex logic of this discussion might be causing some confusion and so I changed tack – "His name, I said, is Scruffy."

"Nice dog, is he?" said the grunter.

"I don't know," I said, "I mean, I haven't enough experience of dogs to make a comparative assessment."

The grunt down the telephone suggested to me that my comment was not advancing our discussion so I tried again: "Yes," I said, "He's a lovely dog."

"Nice," said the grunter, "I'm sure you'll be very happy together" – and he put down the phone!

The dog was staring at me. Recumbent on the sofa, among the crumb-infested cushions, it was looking up with its big, soulful eyes and I could have sworn that it was smiling. I suppose I may have been mistaken. Possibly the expression was not so much a smile as a slackening of the jaws accompanied by a curling of the tongue. But the impression it gave was one of a poor, unloved dog, cast out into the cold, cruel world to fend for itself with no one to look after it, doomed to a life of misery and destitution. Until, that is, the person glowering at it from the direction of the telephone had taken it in with blandishments of saucers of milk, digestive biscuits and ready access to a settee. I was torn between booting the damn' brute out into the frosty darkness and giving it a cuddle and a pat on the head. I shall leave you to surmise which course of action I pursued from the fact that the small, scruffy dog is still here and my settee is now covered with a fine coating of small scruffy dog hairs.

I don't know what one is expected to do with small scruffy dogs that suddenly turn up on the doorstep and, what's more to the point, I don't know what small scruffy dogs expect you to do with them. The one in question was still doing the big soulful eyes thing: the one that makes the hardest heart melt and inspires an irresistible desire to reach for a can opener. This gave rise to another question: what does a small, scruffy dog eat? My cupboards were stocked with foodstuffs intended principally for consumption by beings of the human variety. Dog food did not feature large among them. The dog's eyes took on a more desperately pathetic look of the sort one imagines in the eyes of starving orphans who've been heartlessly refused a spoonful of congealing gruel in the works of Mr. Charles Dickens. That was when my eyes fell upon a tinned steak and kidney pudding which I had been saving for the weekend. I don't know how closely a tinned steak and kidney pudding resembles dog food but, when heated in an oven and deposited into a dish, it appears to form an acceptable substitute. Scruffy polished it off with alacrity then rolled over on his back, consented to a little light scratching of the tummy, and scurried off into the living room to continue his snooze on the settee. I meanwhile contented myself with a cold collation comprising two pieces of bread and a tinned pilchard. To be honest, my stomach was not yet fully recovered from the alcoholic exertions of the night before and even the pilchard required an effort of will.

Having eaten my fill of pilchard, I turned my attention back to the events that had led up to Theodora's murder. I took an A4 pad of narrow-lined paper from a drawer and placed it before me on the kitchen table. I quickly jotted down such details as I knew in order than I should not forget them.

It, frankly, didn't make much sense to me. I'm not sure I'd say that many people really liked Theodora, but then again, as far as I was aware there weren't many people who particularly disliked him either. Mind you, I can't say I was a close friend of Theodora's; I occasionally saw him at Spivz and I'd done a couple of interviews with him (once for 'Great Hits' magazine and another for 'Jackie') but on those occasions it was as though he had been on stage, playing the 'role' of Theodora. I didn't really know what he was like when the makeup and the costume came off and he was just Terry Binton, the son of a TV repair man and a freelance chiropodist from Pudsey in West Yorkshire. I don't even know if he answered to that name any more. He had certainly worked hard at losing the accent. There was barely a trace of Yorkshire left in his voice, apart from the soft Northern "u" sound which, try as he might, he could never quite eradicate.

It is, I suppose, quite possible that the amiable personality which he presented to the public was just a thin facade over a much tougher and less likable character. If so, the only glimpse I ever had of that character was the strange encounter between Theodora and Dave Buzzard in the upstairs corridor close to the toilet in which Theodora's body was subsequently discovered. I had no way of knowing whether they had been having a minor disagreement over, say, the price of the salt and vinegar crisps or whether the argument was a symptom of a deeper rift.

That argument wasn't much to go on but, even so, it was enough to make me think that Dave Buzzard might have some reason to harbour a grievance against Theodora. In fact, as far as I was aware, Dave Buzzard was the *only* person who might harbour a grievance against Theodora. Well, apart from Steve Strange, I suppose. I wrote down the heading 'Suspects' on my A4 pad and, beneath it I wrote the names 'Dave Buzzard' and 'Steve Strange'. Over the past few months, Steve Strange had become an increasingly well-known and fashionable figure in the London music and club scene – a fact that Theodora seemed to take as a personal affront. On several occasions, Theodora has been extremely incautious in the things he's said about Strange and, on one occasion at least, one of his comments (potentially libellous, in my opinion) made it into a published interview. But was that kind of bitchiness really a motive for murder?

Needless to say, Theodora never went to Strange's club and Strange never came to Theodora's so, unless he was in disguise (which is certainly not impossible), Steve Strange would not have been in Spivz on New Year's Eve. Grasping at straws, I considered the possibility that Strange might have hired a professional assassin to do away with Theodora. But the more I thought about it, the more preposterous it sounded. I put a question mark alongside Steve Strange's name and then, after thinking about it some more, I took an eraser and rubbed his name out – which left just one name, Dave Buzzard, listed under 'Suspects'.

So far, I'd only been considering events I'd seen with my own eyes and, frankly, they didn't amount to much. But I also had the testimony of someone who'd known Theodora much better than I had, someone who had probably known him better than *anyone* had. Zipgun Dandy had been both Theodora's lover and his business partner. They had met four years earlier when the young Terry Binton had arrived in London with no greater ambition than to get away from Pudsey. At the time Binton had been a punk. He'd worn torn denim and latex clothes and, for a while, had sported a pink Mohican hairdo. But even then he had never been wholly committed to the punk ethos – he absolutely would not consider having his nose or (as some of his friends had done) his nipples and penis pierced and he had a horror of being spat upon. In short, he'd been a punk in Pudsey because it has been shocking. In London it wasn't shocking and so he quickly decided that the time had come to move on. He met Zipgun Dandy in a pub in Earl's Court and, as though in a sudden flash of enlightenment, he immediately felt that he had seen his future.

By Theodora's own account (see my interview for the November 1979 edition of 'Great Hits') Zipgun Dandy had been wearing green satin trousers and a loose white shirt with huge, billowy sleeves on the occasion of their meeting. It turned out that he'd bought the shirt in a second-hand clothes shop and it had originally been intended for a ballet dancer. Terry Binton had never seen anyone like Zipgun Dandy in Pudsey and whatever subculture Zipgun was a part of, Terry wanted to be a part of it too.

In the officially-sanctioned version of his life, the transformation of Pudsey punk, Terry Binton, into London trend-setter, Theodora, gets a bit vague at that point, mainly because Theodora claimed to be one hundred percent heterosexual which made it difficult to explain why he and Zipgun Dandy were living together. Anyway, one thing that both the official and unofficial versions of Theodora's life story agree upon is that he and Zipgun Dandy began DJing one-off 'Futurist' nights, first at a pub in Vauxhall ,then later at a nightclub in Notting Hill. And finally, they opened Spivz ("The London Futurist Club") in August, 1979.

When I'd spoken to him earlier that day, Zipgun Dandy had been convinced that he knew the murderer's identity – and it wasn't Dave Buzzard or Steve Strange.

I hefted my trusty old Imperial 66 typewriter out of a cupboard and onto the kitchen table. If you have ever hefted an Imperial 66 you will be aware that this is practically worthy of the status of an Olympic sport. The Imperial 66 is not one of those flaky modern typewriters that you can carry in one hand and will break down after a year of hard use. It's a vintage model made of solid iron. If you dropped it on your foot, it would not be the typewriter that ended up broken. After taking a few moments to recover from the typewriter-hefting, I plugged in my cassette recorder, wound back the tape and prepared to transcribe my interview with Zipgun Dandy.

The transcript is reproduced here in a slightly edited version. On the tape, there are lots of digressions, repetitions and hesit-ations. These I have removed. I've also cut a number of passages that have no bearing on the events of New Year's Eve and I've omitted my questions.

Chapter 6

The Testimony of Zipgun Dandy

We got there, Spivz, about, I'd say, yeah, about half past eight. We got a cab, me and Theo, Theodora I mean, we booked a cab for ten to eight but it was late. I said, "You're late. This could be an emergency, mate!" and he says – the cabbie, I mean – he says, "It's New Year's Eve, guv. What's the rush, you expecting a baby?" and Theo says to me, "It's only a few minutes. Not worth arguing about," he says. But me, I'm thinking, "Well, I don't know. Late is late, know what I mean." But, so anyway, that's how we was late. And when we got there Lady Vlad was there already, waiting. Lady Vlad's the DJ? You know her, yeah? No? I thought you did. Well, so anyway, she says, "You're late," and I says, "Yeah. The cab was late," and she says, "Yeah, well, New Year's Eve," and then I unlocked the doors and we went in and I turned the lights on and Vlad went off to sort out her records, and me and Theo went up to the office.

And then. Well, then, Brigitte turned up.

Must have been, what, ten, fifteen minutes after we got there, yeah I'd say maybe about quarter an hour, and Brigitte comes up to the office. And. What? No, we, no, we don't let... I mean, not many people come up there. Not the office. The office is for me and Theo. There's a sign up there says it's private. We don't want people wandering about. It's not safe for one thing. The building, you know, it's not what-do-you-call it, repaired or something. What? Renovated? Yeah, it's not renovated up there. It's an old building. 1850 or something. But yeah, we let Brigitte up there. Well, we known her for, you know, years. We always thought.... *[Can't make out what he says here]* Sorry, I'm still, I mean I think I must be still in shock or something. I can't seem to get used to thinking that Theo is... What was I...? Oh, yeah, Brigitte. Well, she was, like I was saying, she came up to the office...

Anyway, then I went to check on the lighting and stuff and I had a word with Lady Vlad and I asked her what stuff she was going to play and that. She's into a whole load of weird disco type stuff. You know, French, Italian and stuff. I told her to keep it electro. I keeping saying, How can Spivz be a Futurist nightclub if she keeps playing Italian bleedin' disco? So she says, yeah, ok. She said she had an advance copy of something by some bloke who used to be in Ultravox. I said, Ultravox isn't Futurist but she said "Just wait till you hear this. It'll freak you." She was right.

[Here there follows a discussion, lasting about five minutes, of trends in electronic music. I have omitted this from the transcript]

So, anyway, it must have been about five to nine when I went to have a look if there was anyone waiting to get it. There's a window in the first floor toilet. It's right over the alley. D'you know where I mean? There this alley that runs along the side of the club, on the right-hand side and when there's people queuing, when there's a long queue, that's where it goes. They queue outside the front doors and then we get them to go down the alley, down the side, so they don't block up the street. Like I say, you can see them from the toilet window. You can't hardly see the window from downstairs because we painted it the same colour as the bricks. But if you want to have a look outside that's where you can do it. So I open the window a crack and I can see that there's maybe already about fifty people out there so then I go back down to the foyer and I get Bad Tommy set up on the door. Tommy and Brigitte was doing it in turns. Tommy was on for an hour, then Brigitte took over for an hour, then it was Tommy again. Do you know Tommy? No? Well, you haven't missed much. He's a bit of an idiot, really.

So anyway, the doors opened at about nine. No, not 'about' – dead on nine. And Tommy was left on the door, in charge of admissions and stuff and The Ape was there in case of trouble. The Ape is what we call our 'security officer'. He's about six-foot-two and built like a brick shit-house. I think he's a boxing champion or something. Or wrestling. I don't know, but whatever it is he's not the sort of guy you'd want to mess with. We get trouble sometimes but it's never a problem. If anyone starts causing problems The Ape just picks them up and chucks them out. No, we didn't have any trouble last night. I don't think so, anyway. Nobody mentioned any and I think I'd have heard about it.

Dusty arrived pretty early. I remember that because I remember being surprised because I thought he'd be coming with the band.

Mascara Addiction. Have you heard them? They are pretty good, actually. Well, I mean, they're ok. A bit rough around the edges maybe but, you know... They're sort of slipstream – kind of Futurist but not hard-core. Not like Kraftwerk or Telex or The Normal or whatever. Kind of hard rock-Futurist, if you know what I mean. Dusty does synth, Joe Jonson's on bass, Dave Buzzard's guitar and vocals and I think maybe he does a bit of synth too. And Anvil Evans is on drums. Real drums, I mean. They've got an interesting sound, actually. We was talking about getting them to do a gig as a matter of fact.

[Discussion about music here... omitted from transcript]

Anyway, as I was saying, Dusty arrived at maybe quarter-past nine. Not sure when Dave Buzzard, Anvil and Joe arrived. Later, I know that much. A lot later, I'd say. I was just mingling most of the night, you know, meeting and greeting, smiling and making sure everything was ok. Then that photographer comes and does a photo shoot. Theodora. Up in The Gallery. By the cocktail bar mostly. Wanted to get some shots with the club in the background. You know, so you could see down onto the dance floor and that. One of them lenses he had, what d'you call them. Telephoto or something. Or wide-angle or something. Wide-angle I think. And he did some with Velma too, who was supposed to be…

[here he mutters something which I can't make out on the recording]

I read in one magazine Theo was engaged to her! To Velma. For Christ's sake, how stupid would you have to be to believe that?

Anyway, later on I came up to the Gallery and sat there for a while – well, you saw me, didn't you? I was with Adam Xeon and Brigitte. And then Brigitte went off somewhere. Then, at midnight, we let off a whole load of streamers and stuff and some people did the conga and then I remember I started wondering where Theo was. He'd gone off at about five to twelve I reckon. I suppose I'd been expecting him to say something, you know, at midnight, to go on stage and wish people Happy New Year or something. Happy New whatever you call it, decade, or something. I don't think he had anything planned but even so I sort of thought that'd be what he'd do.

So then I started looking around for him but I couldn't see him anywhere. Not on the dance floor, not in Harlow's, not in the office. Then I went back to the cocktail bar and I saw Adam there and he said he hadn't seen Theo since before midnight. He thought he must have locked himself in the toilet. Not sure why he said that. It didn't cross my mind to ask him. Not at the time it didn't. And later, I was... Yeah, yeah, you should ask him. But I was just starting to panic a bit, I suppose, so I dashed straight to the toilet, the one upstairs, next to the office and I banged on the door but there was nothing, no answer, no nothing.

Someone said I should kick it down. No, I can't remember who. Adam, Adam Xeon, was with me, I know that, but there was a few others too. Must have seen there was something wrong and they just, I don't know, they just turned up, I guess. I remember the doors to the Gallery opening, some time, not sure when, I wasn't thinking straight really, and some people came out, carrying someone out. Well, not 'carrying', not like off the ground I don't mean, just sort of holding him upright. I thought it was, you know, someone who'd had a few too many daiquiris. But I suppose it must have been Lala. You know Lala fainted? Yeah, weird. But I wasn't really paying attention. I was just worried about Theo. I was afraid he might have, overdosed, or something. So anyway, we keep a key in the office, to the toilet I mean, so I went there which only took a few seconds and then I came back but the toilet door was already open. Apparently it had been open all the time. Not locked, I mean. For some reason, Adam thought it was locked and I'd believed him but it wasn't. And that's when we found Theo. He was stretched out on the floor with his eyes were staring and... *[Here he says something but I can't make it out. His voice breaks up a bit and he takes a while to recover before carrying on]*

The police think I did it, I'm sure they do. They talked to me, you know. Last night and again today. They said I was at the scene, I was Theodora's business partner, they wanted to know what stake I had in the club. I said, "What d'you mean, 'what stake?'" It's like as if they think we was making a ton of money out of it or something. I tried to tell them we wasn't making money but I don't think they believed me. And they wanted to know if we'd, if I'd had arguments, if I'd had any arguments with Theo. I'm sure they think I killed. Him. I mean, anyway, what do they mean did we have arguments? Christ sake! How can you not have arguments? Everyone has arguments. And now there's the business of the key. Adam swears the door was locked a few minutes earlier and... well, anyway, I had the key. In the office. I just know they're trying to pin it on me! For Christ sake, they say we had arguments, I locked him in or something, I had the key. They think that means I... Christ! Why would I, of all people, why would I...?

Besides which, I know who did it. I know who killed Theo.

I heard them. They was arguing. Going at it hammer and tongs. Must have been about half past nine I'd say. They didn't know I was there but I heard them clear as day. I was outside the office. I was going to come in but when I heard all the screaming I decided not to. I thought, well, I can just ask Theo about it later on. But I never had the chance. Never will have the chance now. But I heard her clear as day screaming: "I'll kill you! I'll kill you, you bastard! I'll bloody kill you!"

And she did, didn't she? You saw for yourself. She'd been up in the Gallery for ages. Then about ten to midnight she suddenly ups and leaves. And a few minutes later, Theo leaves. And that's when she killed him. It's obvious, isn't it? It was that twisted mad bitch, Brigitte.

Chapter 7

That evening, I had arranged to meet my old friend, Tyrone, at the Pineapple public house in Leverton Street which is at the northern end of Kentish Town, just beyond the underground station. Tyrone is of middling height, with dark, slightly curly hair and a what you might call a 'chunky' physique. His eyes, which are hazel in colour, burn with what might either be the light of a penetrating intelligence or a fierce stupidity. Tyrone is a freelance physicist. Or, to be more precise, he is a physicist by training and a computer programmer by profession. He signed on as a theoretical physicist at the Kentish Town job centre but the vacancies proved to be thin on the ground.

What precisely he does for a living I could not say. I did ask him once but his answer didn't make much sense. All I know for sure is that it involves a great many two-syllable words that end with the letter "L" – Algol, Cobol and Pascal are among the names I've heard him bandy about pretty freely.

Tyrone not only works with computers, he even has one at home. He keeps trying to convince me that one day everyone will have one. When he tells me this I laugh. Once I asked him how much he paid for his home computer. When he told me I laughed again but louder.

After transcribing my chat with Zipgun Dandy, I put the typewriter back into its cupboard, took a quick shower and prepared myself to leave. Unfortunately, my departure was delayed. I had, for some twenty minutes or so, been aware of a pathetic squeaking noise coming from the direction of the aforementioned scruffy dog but, being unfamiliar with the ways of dogs, I had not taken this to be of any consequence. When I returned from my shower, I discovered my error. The scruffy dog was sitting in a corner of the kitchen with its head dropped between its shoulders and its eyes taking on that sad and soulful look which I have had occasion to mention previously.

Positioned immediately in front of the dog, on the attractive red terracotta tiles of my kitchen floor, was a large puddle and a considerable pile of what I can only imagine to be the end results of the tinned steak and kidney pudding which he had consumed earlier. I shall not go into the details of the cleaning procedure that followed. Suffice to say, it did not increase the overall joviality of my mood. It suddenly occurred to me that a feature of dog ownership is the requirement to take the animal for walks, presumably with the associated requirement of removing from the public highway any detritus which might be deposited as a result. I must confess that the attractions of dog ownership were not obvious to me and I was starting to understand why Scruffy's former owners had gone to such lengths to get rid of the beast.

When I finally arrived at The Pineapple, I discovered Tyrone solving equations at a corner table and chuckling merrily to himself. I do not understand the mathematical mind but I am told by those who do that the humorous possibilities of a good equation are greatly underestimated by the population at large. Tyrone had obviously struck upon a particularly juicy one as he was verging on the hysterical.

Having dispensed with the preliminaries (namely, buying a round of drinks and a packet of pork scratchings) I took out the notes which I had made earlier and, using them for reference, I narrated the events leading up to the murder of Theodora including such facts as I had gleaned that afternoon from Zipgun Dandy and Lala Los Alamos. I had clearly grabbed Tyrone's attention for during the whole of my narrative he barely took more than a fleeting glimpse at the equations scrawled upon the notepad in front of him.

At the end of my story, Tyrone leaned back in his chair, took a long gulp of beer, balanced an equation abstractedly, looked me in the eye and said: "Why didn't he mention the argument?"

I should explain that Tyrone often speaks in a manner which might be characterised as 'elliptical'. He states what he considers to be the salient details without bothering with any extraneous material. This leads to a great economy of speech but it can produce problems of comprehensibility.

"Why didn't *who* mention the argument?" I asked.

He raised his eyebrows – an expression intended to convey his astonishment that I was unable to understand a simple question which had been expressed with perfect clarity.

Speaking rather more slowly and loudly than was entirely necessary, as though he were addressing a partially deaf idiot, he filled in the gaps: "You said you'd seen A have an argument with B, and that C had suggested to A that B should be removed. But when you spoke to C, he didn't mention it. That is curious."

I am convinced that Tyrone regards conversation as an intelligence test. On this occasion, I managed to scrape through with a pass grade. I had initially thought that he'd been talking about the argument between Theodora and Brigitte which had been overheard by Zipgun Dandy. The A, B and C matched; but the agreement of C and B to remove A did not. I suddenly twigged. I had seen Theodora arguing with Dave Buzzard, out in the corridor. I'd later seen Theodora talking (I assumed) about the argument to Zipgun Dandy. So, substituting Theodora for A, Dave Buzzard for B and Zipgun Dandy for C, what Tyrone was saying was that: I had seen Theodora have an argument with Dave Buzzard, and Zipgun Dandy had suggested to Theodora that Dave Buzzard should be removed. But when I spoke to Zipgun Dandy, he didn't mention it. And Tyrone found that omission to be curious.

I had to agree. It did seem curious. But was it just an oversight or did Zipgun deliberately avoid mentioning it in an effort to conceal something of importance from me? I jotted down a note to remind myself to make further enquiries on the matter.

"And another thing," Tyrone said, "The smelling salts. Who takes smelling salts to a nightclub?"

He was talking about the person or persons unknown who had administered smelling salts to Lala Los Alamos when he had fainted in the lobby.

"Then there's the odd circumstance of Brigitte leaving the Gallery minutes before Theodora."

"That must be significant," I said, "Zipgun is convinced that Brigitte is the killer."

"If Theodora had left first and Brigitte had followed, the logic would be sound," Tyrone said, "But the other way around – first Brigitte then Theodora? That doesn't make much sense."

"Maybe they'd arranged to meet, had an argument and..."

Tyrone interrupted me. "But the fundamental problem is the coincidence. It's too big a coincidence. The chances against a coincidence like that are astronomical. Let's see, assuming that one person in a thousand is likely on any given night to be strangled in the toilets of a nightclub..."

"One person in a thousand!" I sputtered.

"What? You think that's an over-estimate?"

"Just slightly."

"Well, it's close enough. As an approximation. Now let's assume that one person in a hundred is likely to faint at any given moment. Again, that's just an approximation..."

Here he paused to jot down some calculations while muttering to himself things such as "Let 'm' represent murders and 's' represent strangulation." There were a few tens to the minus this-that-and-the-other, the probability of fainting set against the probability of strangulation and some factoring in of toilets, nightclubs and mascara. He concluded by writing the number 1 over a horizontal line. Beneath the horizontal line he wrote 1 again but this time followed a very large number of zeros.

"So there you have it," he said, "For these two events to happen coincidentally, you would probably have to wait about one thousand times longer than the life of the Universe."

"Which is a long time," I said.

"A very long time," he agreed.

"Of course," he added, "Just because it's improbable that doesn't mean it's impossible. Those two events could happen coincidentally at any time."

"But," I said, "That's not very likely."

"Not very likely at all," he agreed, "In fact extremely, incredibly, astonishingly, almost inconceivably unlikely. So unlikely in fact that the chances of you suddenly turning into a pink butterfly and flying around the room singing The Halleluiah Chorus, in Serbo-Croat, are of approximately the same order of probability."

I conceded that he had a point. What that point was I didn't know but I thought it better to concede it anyway. I think the general gist was that Lala's fainting must be connected in some way with Theodora's murder. But, for the life of me, I couldn't figure out what the connection might be. Could Lala be implicated in some way? After Lala fainted, a small crowd gathered around him which meant that he was surrounded by people at precisely the time the body was being discovered. That gave him a pretty plausible alibi. And since he was also surrounded by people, as he sat up in the Gallery of the club, before and during the time of the murder, his alibi wasn't just plausible – it was rock solid.

"Could have been a deliberate diversion," Tyrone suggested, "Lala causes a scene. And while everyone's concentrating on him, an accomplice goes and throttles Theodora."

My main objection to this theory was more emotional than logical. I know Lala Los Alamos pretty well and, to be honest, I like him. I couldn't bring myself to believe that he would get involved in a murder.

"Or maybe somebody had a reason to bump off both Theodora and Lala but for whatever reason, they failed with one and succeeded with the other."

I made a note of that as a possibility. But it raised even more questions: Why would anyone want to kill them both? We didn't have a workable motive for Theodora's murder, let alone for an attempted murder of Lala. And how could anyone try to kill Lala when he'd been in full sight all evening?

"Poisoned cocktails?" Tyrone suggested.

I made a note of that too.

"And what about the mascara?"

"I beg your pardon?"

"You said that Lala Los Angeles..."

"Los Alamos," I corrected.

"...was suffering from a hitherto undiagnosed allergy to mascara. Is there such a thing as an allergy to mascara?"

I confessed that I had never heard of one but there were probably thousands of allergies I'd never heard of.

"And the mascara that brought on the allergic reaction had been borrowed from..."

"Theodora," I said, "That's what he told me. He said they'd swapped mascara."

"Why would anyone swap mascara?" Tyrone asked.

"I don't know. Maybe Theodora's mascara wasn't waterproof, or maybe it was the wrong colour, or maybe he was allergic to it or... Hell, I don't know."

"Then you should find out," said Tyrone, "Find the mascara and you find the murderer!"

I made a note of that. My notes were starting to get complicated. One on page, I'd written out a timeline of the events I'd witnessed. On another page, I'd written out a timeline based on what Zipgun had told me. On another page I'd started jotting down suspects (currently these were Dave Buzzard, Brigitte, Lala followed by a question mark, Steve Strange crossed out and Zipgun Dandy – It was Tyrone who'd suggested adding Zipgun's name "As he was Theodora's lover and his business partner who knows what kinds of disagreements they might have had? Plus the fact that he's already tried to incriminate Brigitte and he's left gaps in the story he told you?") and on another page I was making random notes.

Tyrone looked at my notepad and tutted. "What you need," he said, "Is a spreadsheet."

I had no idea what he was talking about. Apparently it's something to do with computers. He tried to explain but I couldn't really figure it out. The gist of it seems to be that it's like a big sheet of graph paper and it's just the thing for balancing your accounts and solving murders. I wasn't entirely convinced.

I had a feeling that Tyrone wanted me to think that his interest in Theodora's murder was purely academic – an intellectual exercise which was, in some tawdry way, beneath his dignity. He isn't a good actor, however. I knew that he would have given anything for a chance to do a bit of amateur investigation. This impression was further confirmed when he wrote down a phone number on a scrap of paper, gave it to me and told me to call him if there were any further developments. I pocketed the scrap of paper and said I would.

And then I mentioned my other problem. The dog. Tyrone became unusually animated. To my astonishment, he loves dogs; he babbles, coos and drools at the very mention them. Even the mention of the piles of poo and pee on my kitchen floor didn't diminish his enthusiasm (though I couldn't help thinking it might have if he'd been the one who'd had to clean it up).

"The problem," I explained, "Is that I don't know what you are supposed to feed a dog."

"Bones!" he said.

"Bones?"

"Bones!" he repeated, "That's exactly what a dog needs. Bones and plenty of them."

"I was thinking," I said, "More along the lines of dog food. That is, food made for dogs. In tins."

Tyrone gave me another one of his scornful looks, raising his eyebrow to a height that bordered on the offensive.

"The dog," he said, "In all important respects, is a wolf."

I tried to visualize Scruffy roaming the Steppes, terrorising sheep and eating villagers (or vice versa) but found the task beyond the limits of my imagination.

"Would you feed dog food to a wolf?" he asked.

"I don't think the circumstance is likely to arise," I replied.

"You would not!" he snapped, blatantly ignoring my witticism, "Certainly not in tins! The wolf is a proud and savage beast with a lust for bones. And meat, of course. And that is what you must give to your dog."

"What sort of bones and meat?"

"Preferably venison. And a few chickens. Though chickens can be noisy and the neighbours might object to their screams."

I smiled. Tyrone did not. Tyrone does not tell jokes. He always says precisely what he means. This can, at times, be quite disturbing.

"On the whole," I said, "I think it would be more practical if the meat were no longer mobile. Dead would be my distinct preference."

"Then beef should be an acceptable substitute. Rump is probably best. Or sirloin."

There are times when I wonder if Tyrone's advice is as good as he believes it to be. I certainly wouldn't challenge his opinions on matters pertaining to quantum physics or computer programming. But I am by no means convinced that the dietary requirements of the dog are among his areas of specialist knowledge.

When I got back to the house, the dog was asleep on the sofa and the red light on my answer machine was flashing. I pressed the playback button. there was a whirring of tapes and then the recorded message. It was Lala's voice: "You said you wanted to talk to Pete. Clifton just phoned. He wants us down the studio tomorrow.

We'll be there from ten. But we're breaking for lunch at one. That would be a good time."

Lala had told me that Pete de Gré was convinced that Dave Buzzard had strangled Theodora. The recording studio was down Brixton way. There was still the mystery of the argument between Dave Buzzard and Theodora. I wondered if Pete would have any light to shed?

January 2nd, 1980

Chapter 8

The following morning, out of curiosity, I called into a chemist's on the Kentish Town Road and asked if he had any smelling salts. He looked at me blankly and said that he did not. I tried in a second chemist's and received a similar reply. Finally, I found a chemist in Camden Town who knew what I was talking about. "Sal volatile!" he said, "We don't get much call these days but I believe I may have some." He went into a back room and returned with a small screw-top bottle, "For sports, is it?"

I had no idea what he was talking about so I said, "Do many sports people use smelling salts?"

"Oh," he said, "Not so many these days. Boxers sometimes. I think long-distance runners maybe?"

"To bring them around?" I asked.

"When they feel faint," he said, "Or get knocked out. Boxers, that is. Not long-distance runners. As far as I am aware."

I bought the bottle, telling him I had an elderly aunt, which seemed to satisfy him. Out on the street I unscrewed the bottle, took a good, deep sniff and immediately wished I hadn't. It smelled like the sort of thing you'd use to clean drains which is not surprising since, when I read the label, I discovered that its main constituent is ammonia. When the coughing had subsided to a manageable level, I wiped the tears from my eyes with a handkerchief and assured the small crowd which had gathered around me that, in spite of all evidence to the contrary, I did not require the services of an ambulance.

I was, I confess, surprised not only by the odour and the effect of the salts but also by their form. On the whole you expect salt to be salt. You don't expect it to be liquid. I had imagined that smelling salts were granules of some sort, possibly in various pleasant hues like multi-coloured sugar or sherbet. That they were, in all obvious details, much closer to an industrial cleaning fluid was news to me.

Who, I wondered, would be in the habit of carrying such a thing about their person at a nightclub? The chemist had mentioned boxers and long-distance runners. I would obviously have to seek out any of Lala's friends who might be of an athletic disposition.

The phone had rung just as I was leaving the house that morning. It was Sanford. He wanted to rush through a special one-shot edition of Great Hits. 'One-shots' are what the trash journalism industry calls one-off magazines aimed at turning a fast buck from whatever mindless tripe the Great British public can be persuaded to fork out their hard-earned cash on at any given moment.

Previous Sanford one-shots had included '*Blonde Ambition (the Debbie Harry Story)*', '*The Gary Numan Compendium Of Fun*' and '*Margaret Thatcher, Warrior Queen*' (that one sold very disappointingly). Sanford was convinced he was onto a winner this time: '*Tribute To Theodora – Martyr Of A Doomed Generation*'. Where tragedy is concerned, Sanford never lets sentimentality get in the way of business.

Today was Wednesday and he wanted all the copy by Friday. "Ten thousand words of your most gushing prose." Normally I would have dashed that off in an evening, culled together from random snippets of information in other magazines or from my own old interviews padded out with meaninglessly mawkish waffle. But on this occasion, I thought I might be able to do something better – original research, as you might say, which could also be a handy excuse for making a few enquiries for my own purposes. I was still keen on the idea of writing a book that would be regarded as the definitive 'inside story' of the celebrity murder of the decade.

In Camden Town I bought a newspaper, went down into the underground and waited in the soot-and-oil smelling gloom. There was nothing about Theodora on the front page or page 2 or page 3. In fact, it wasn't until page 11 that I came across this tiny, and not very informative, mention of the murder:

*

A man has died following an incident at a trendy London nightclub last night.

Police were called to the Spivz Night Club in E1 at about 12:30 in the early hours of this morning. A murder investigation has begun. Detective Chief Inspector Alan Manfreds said there were a number of possible witnesses and appealed for information.

Police have not revealed the cause of death.

Mr Manfred added: "I'd like to reassure members of the local community that there is no cause for alarm as we have reason to believe that this was an isolated incident. We are actively pursuing a number of lines of inquiry and we are confident that we will be able to bring the person responsible to justice."

*

From Camden I went straight down the Northern Line, changed at Stockwell and then took the Victoria line to Brixton. It was only about a ten minute walk from there to the studio. I'd been there a couple of times before so I had no problem finding it. It's an old building that used to be a car repair-shop and it's surrounded by about an acre of waste land which is just as well because I don't think neighbours would have put up with the racket unless they were stone deaf.

There is one main room (the 'music room' they call it) which is where the band plays and, adjoining this, there is another small room behind a pane of glass which houses the mixing desk. There is also a small and tatty sitting room containing two tatty armchairs, a tatty sofa, a sink, a fridge, a metal filing cabinet, a scabby-looking coffee table and a kettle. This is where anyone in the band sits when they are not needed or (as I've done in the past) where visiting journalists and photographers are made to wait if the band isn't ready to see them yet.

I arrived at about ten to one and, seeing that the door to the music room was shut, I went into the sitting room. Janis was sitting there reading Melody Maker. Janis is Chuttle's 'personal assistant' which, in the music business is often a euphemism for 'live-in lover' but, in Chuttle's case, it wasn't. It's common knowledge in the business that Chuttle's sexual preferences lie in other directions:

mainly in the directions of the boys in his bands. He is always discreet about it, of course, and nothing has ever been mentioned in the press. But, you can take it from me that everybody in the music business knows that the main talent that Chuttle looks for in his bands has nothing to do with music.

"I'm here to see Pete," I said.

"Better make yourself comfortable, then," said Janis, "He'll be a while."

"He said they'd be done by one."

"Some hopes!"

"They running late?"

"They're not running at all yet. Pete only got here a few minutes ago. Cliff's been going mad. Given them a right bollockin'."

Janis is the only person I've ever heard calling Chuttle "Cliff". Everyone else called him either Clifton or Mr Chuttle. "You here to do an interview?" she said.

"No. More of a social call. I was in the area."

She laughed. "You've seen this area. Nobody's just 'in' it. People only come here if they've got a very good reason. Fancy a cup of tea?" – she waved her hand towards a shelf filled with boxes of Broken Orange Pekoe, Darjeeling, Assam, Lapsang Souchong, Russian Caravan and other fragrant blends.

"Lala's tea collection?" I said.

She nodded. "All a load if rubbish if you ask me. I bring me own. A fine choice of Typhoo or P G Tips. I can spare you a tea-bag if you like."

I shook my head. "So how long before they'll be done, d'you reckon."

"He might let them off after a couple of hours. If they're good. Otherwise, who knows, they could be here all night."

"I'll come back," I said, "I'll go for a walk, take in a few of the sights," (Janis laughed), "And I'll call back at about three. Tell Pete to wait."

"Ok," she said.

Outside, the day was cold but clear. I was walking towards the shops with vague thoughts of taking the tube back into town and getting an ice cream in Bourne's on Oxford Street and I was wondering why Pete de Gré was so convinced that Dave Buzzard was the killer when I noticed a familiar figure walking towards me. At first, from a distance, I didn't recognise him. He looked like so many people – a young man in his early twenties with unkempt, collar-length dark hair, Levi jeans, trainers and denim jacket, he walked towards me with his gaze cast down and his hands in the pockets of his jeans, looking oblivious to everything around him. It was Dave Buzzard.

"Hi, Dave!" I said.

He looked up but didn't seem to recognise me. But he smiled drily and not very convincingly and said, "Hi. How's things?"

"I've just been to the studio. That where you are going?"

"Yeah, I... you did the interview didn't you?" recognition was breaking in upon him like light through a cloud, "For NME was it?"

"Blue Jeans, I said."

"You what?"

"The interview I did, on Mascara Addiction. It was for Blue Jeans magazine."

"Oh yeah? Nice one." (I could tell he had never heard of Blue Jeans magazine) "How are you, mate?" He put out his hand and I shook it.

"You heard about...?"

"Yeah, terrible, ain't it."

He spoke so quickly that it gave the impression he'd known what I was going to say before I'd even opened my mouth. "Yes," I said, "It is. Did you know Theodora well?"

"Not really. I mean, you know. Not really. You coming to the studio, you said?"

"I've just been. They're busy."

"What time is it?"

I looked at my watch. "Just gone one."

"Shouldn't be busy then," he said, "Shouldn't have started. Two o'clock we're booked in for."

"He's not in a good mood, I said."

"Clifton, you mean? He's never in a good mood. What's pissing him off this time. Two o'clock we're booked in for. He can't complain I'm late."

"Pete was late, apparently."

"Pete? Bollocks! It's always Pete. He can get away with anything. If it'd been anyone else, he'd have fired us, know what I mean? But oh no, not flamin' Pete! We're supposed to be rehearsing this afternoon. Mascara Addiction. You heard of us?"

"Yeah, I've heard of you. I did an interview with you, remember? For Blue Jeans."

"Oh yeah," he said, clearly not remembering, "You're not telling me he's letting The Sex-fucking-teens have our time, is he?"

"Pete was late, apparently."

"I head you the first time, mate. Repeating it don't make it any better, know what I mean."

"Fancy a cup of tea?" I said.

"I fancy a beer," he replied, "You paying?"

I decided not to commit myself. "Where's the best pub?" I said.

I don't know if it was the best one, but at least the pub we went to did a pretty decent toasted cheese and bacon sandwich. Which, if you've ever eaten a toasted cheese and bacon sandwich, you will realise is not saying much. If you have been fortunate enough to live your life without ever having eaten a toasted cheese and bacon sandwich, let me explain what you've been missing: it's a sandwich of cheese and bacon – toasted. You probably thought there would be more to it than that. Well, there isn't. Unlike a meal at Le Gavroche, for example, which might involve a *coulis* of something in a *millefeuille* of something else, which could mean just about anything, when you order a toasted cheese and bacon sandwich nothing is left to the imagination. You know exactly what you are going to get. You get cheese, you get bacon, you get a sandwich, you get it toasted. Its description is perfect. It's the sort of flawlessly self-describing meal of which the French can only dream. My toasted cheese and bacon sandwich filled a greasy little hole somewhere deep inside me and had the beneficial side-effect of taking away the taste of the flat, insipid beer.

Being of a less adventurous taste in gourmet pub nosh, Dave Buzzard didn't bother with a sandwich. He was content to give his full attention to the beer. We sat in a dark corner next to an electric fire that was designed to look like a coal fire, complete with lumps of fake coal and a flickering red light which was designed (I'm guessing) to convey the impression of warmth and cosiness. In fact, it radiated nothing but depression.

If Futurism was the face of modern music, the pub jukebox was living in the past. The nearest it came to electro was "Day Trip To Bangor" and the Nolans' "I'm In The Mood For Dancing". My heart skipped an excited beat when, in a fleeting brush with the world of modern music, the jukebox played Madness's "One Step Beyond" but, as though to make up for this momentary lapse in taste, it immediately followed this with Peters and Lee's wailing dirge, "Welcome Home". I contemplated my tepid beer sadly and took consolation from the last remaining cold and congealing crumbs of my toasted cheese and bacon sandwich.

Unless you've ever tried it, you may not realise how tricky it can be to strike up a conversation about a murder, especially when you happen to be talking to one of the main suspects and you don't want him to know that you suspect him. Columbo makes it look easy. He turns up at the villain's Malibu mansion, admires his fine collection of African fertility masks, turns to leave and then suddenly turns back to ask him "one more thing" which stops the murderer right in his tracks because he didn't know that Columbo knew that his glamorous wife was having an affair with a Hollywood director and she was at a party on the night of the murder which meant she couldn't have been on the murderer's boat with him, so his alibi is worthless and suddenly everything falls into place – case solved.

"You ever watch Columbo?" I said.

"No."

I decided I would need to approach the matter more circuitously. I asked him about the band. "What are you doing today. You recording an album?"

"Nah, not yet. We're rehearsing. Well, supposed to be. If that lot of useless twats can get finished in time."

By "useless twats" I took him to mean The Sexteens. Until a few months ago, Dave Buzzard had been the lead singer with The Sexteens. I had a distinct impression that there was some festering resentment between Dave and his replacement, Pete de Gré. Maybe that was why Pete was, according to Lala, trying to pin the murder on Dave. Even though I had my own reasons to suspect Dave, I wasn't prepared to take Pete's word for anything. Pete was only a kid, after all.

"How's the new band going?" I asked.

"Mascara Addiction is great. I'm not just saying that 'cos it's my band. You follow?"

"Hmmm-mmm," I mumbled into my beer.

"We got something special, you know. Clifton still thinks The Sexqueens can make the breakthrough. The Sexqueens, that's what I call them." He laughed. I tried to force a smile but it died on my lips. "I keep telling him, synth bands are ten a penny. Six months from now, nobody'll be interested. The '70s was synth. In the '80s, synth is dead. You agree with that, don't you?"

I did my beer-mumbling thing again.

"I mean, so yeah, ok, we got a keyboard player, Dusty Evsky – that's not his real name, you know."

I expressed surprise.

"But we also got a real drummer, Anvil Evans, who's like, you know, a classic drummer. As good as Philthy Animal Taylor, if you want my opinion, maybe even better."

As you probably know, Phil "Philthy Animal" Taylor is the drummer with Motorhead. I'm not an expert on drummers so I couldn't tell you how good he is in the great pantheon of rock drummers. All I know for sure is that he's what's known in the business as "a drummer's drummer". That means he's loud. And he does not use a drum machine.

"What's the nearest the Sexteens've got? A fuckin' Roland CR-78, that's what? That's not drumming. It's more like a shortwave fuckin' radio. I tell you, Squirrel's sick as a parrot. You know Squirrel? He's what passes for a drummer in The Sexteens. He's a good bloke really, old mate of mine, but lumbered with a lousy group. In the old days, he was a proper drummer. He used to be with a ska band. You know that? Now all he does is stand at the back messing about with a shortwave fuckin' radio! Kids don't want that stuff no more, you know. They want classic rock. That's drums, bass, guitar. You seen my Gibson?"

I shrugged.

"Fantastic guitar, man. Don't even talk about Stratocaster. You can't beat a Gibson. I mean, if it's good enough for Clapton and Sumner..."

"Sumner?" I said.

"Joy Division, man. Joy Division. I thought you was a rock journalist. Great guitarist, man. Clifton tried to palm me off with some piece of Japanese Fender-ripoff tat. I said, no way, man. It's got to be a Gibson."

"How did you get involved with Clifton Chuttle?" I asked.

"What?"

"Clifton Chuttle, I was wondering how you..."

"I heard you. You got this habit of repeating yourself, you know that. Gets a bit fucking irritating after a while."

"Sorry."

"What was it you said? You was asking me something."

"I was wondering how you..."

"How me and Clifton met up?"

"Yes."

"I was a photographer, mate. Sold some stuff to Record Mirror and Sounds: Bowie, Roxy, Mott The Hoople. My mate, Squirrel, was doing some session drumming for Clifton. You know Clifton was in some Glam group in the early '70s, then later on he went into management and production, tried to cash in on the teenybop thing, pretty-boy groups and crap like that, like The Bay City Rollers and stuff. Started a band called The Atlantic Village Skaters. But he left it too late. By '78 The Rollers were old hat. Punk was the big thing. He'd missed the wave, know what I mean. So anyway, he had this idea that all he needed was some good publicity shots so Squirrel got me the job. I took the shots and they were good but that didn't change the fact that the band was bleedin' rotten.

"And then Clifton had this idea for a synth band and he recruited some new people. Squirrel was the only one he kept from The Atlantic Village Skaters. He advertised in Melody Maker and that's how he got Adam Xeon and Lala Los Alamos. They had the look he wanted. That's always the main thing with Clifton. They got to look good. Except for Squirrel. Not sure how he ended up with Squirrel. He's fat, old band and ugly. Maybe that's why Clifton likes him. He knows that Squirrel is no competition."

"Competition?" I said, "How d'you mean?"

"You really are naive, aren't you! Clifton has a taste in chicken flesh, know what I mean? The old casting couch thing."

"And that's how you got the job?" I asked.

"Nah, I don't think I ever was his type really. But he had this idea that I'd be a contrast. That's what he used to say. He reckoned I had 'masculine good looks' that contrasted with, well, Adam and Lala."

"Who have...?"

He laughed – "Not such masculine good looks, I guess."

"So why did you quit The Sexteens?" I asked.

My question was too blunt. Dave's expression told me that.

"Did I jump or was I pushed is what you mean, ain't it? I jumped, ok. I left them 'cos I'd had enough of them. I'm a rock singer, man. You know – rock. Jerry Lee, Gene Vincent. Little Richard. You heard the way Pete 'sings'? A short-wave bleedin' radio could do better. Everything they do sounds like a short-wave bleedin' radio. I keep telling Clifton. It's dead, man. All that synth stuff. Nobody wants it any more."

"You and Pete don't get on, do you?"

"I don't give him a second thought, mate. That's the honest truth."

"Did you get on ok with Theodora?"

Again, the question was too blunt but there was no alternative. Believe me, if you want to ask somebody about a murder, there really isn't any easy way to lead up to the subject gently. I'd expected Dave to clam up or tell me it was none of my business or just refuse to answer. What I wasn't expecting was for him to laugh. But that is exactly what he did.

"No, I fucking didn't," he said, "I hated the rancid old queen. I'm glad the old bugger's dead."

"Why did you hate him?"

"How long have you got, mate? It'd take me all day and I'd hardly even have started. Did you know Theodora?"

I admitted that I only knew him slightly. I'd interviewed him twice, I'd met him a few times at Spivz, but that was about it.

"So you thought he was an ok kind of guy, did you? No way. He was bloody poisonous. Everyone hated him. He used to badmouth everyone. He sent a card to Clifton once. Like a card you'd send if someone had died. It said: *Deepest Sympathy For Your Sad Loss.*"

"I don't get it," I said.

"Neither did Clifton. He went apeshit. I asked Theo about the card once. He said it was supposed to be funny. See, Theo was always trying to get a record deal. God knows why. He couldn't play, he couldn't sing and he was ugly as hell. Clifton told him to piss off. So that's why Theo sent him the card. It was supposed to be a joke. Clifton didn't see it that way, though. Said he'd tear the bastard's head off if he ever got the chance. But that was just how Theodora was. Slagged off everyone. He probably slagged you off behind your back. That's the way it was with Theodora. Nice as pie to your face and slag you something rotten behind your back."

"You think Theodora had enemies?"

"Too many to mention. But what you mean is was there anyone who hated him enough to kill him? I could think of a few. He even slagged off David fuckin' Bowie. Can you believe that?"

"You think David Bowie killed him?"

He thought about it a few moments before arriving at an opinion. "Nah. I doubt if Bowie has even heard of him. That's why Theodora slagged him off. Bowie is like some kind of god. Theodora was nobody. He couldn't stand that. He was just a nobody in a swanky outfit and mascara. He collected people, that's what he did. Hangers on, like that tart, what's her name, Brigitte? I always said them two was like some kind of cheap double act like, what's their names, you know...?"

"Cannon and Ball?" I suggested.

"Hilda Baker and Arthur Mullard," he said, "You ever hear that song they did, you know the one from Grease, the one Olivia Newton John and that other fellah did?"

"John Travolta?"

"Fuckin' brilliant. Hilda Fucking Baker and Arthur Fucking Mullard. That's what them two should have done, Theo and Brigitte, they could have been the new Hilda Baker and Arthur Mullard, don't you think?"

"Which would be which?" I said.

"Fuckin' obvious, mate. Brigitte's a dead fuckin' ringer for Hilda Baker." He laughed a bit then drank some beer and the he said, "What's this all about, anyway? You writing a book or something?"

I smiled. "Not exactly." I told him about the Great Hits Theodora Special. He told me it sounded like a stupid idea. "Who'd buy a magazine about that old twat?"

There's a difference between a twat and a dead twat, I told him. In terms of magazine sales, death can add on anything from 50 to 80 per cent.

"Ok, sounds like the old bugger made a good career move then. He's finally getting the publicity he always wanted. So what do you want from me, then?"

"A few quotes from you would be handy. You know the angle, 'Theodora's close friend, lead singer with up-and-coming Futurist band, Mascara Addiction, had this to say...' And then some stuff about what a great guy Theodora was, how he'll be a loss to the world of music and fashion, etcetera, etcetera. You don't have to mean it, you just have to say it. I can write it for you if you like."

"Yeah, I suppose," he said unenthusiastically, "All a lot of bollocks. But good publicity for the band, I suppose."

"Exactly."

"But miss out the Futurist stuff. Mascara Addiction ain't Futurist."

"No? What are you then?"

"Nouveau Expressionist."

"Oh really? I've never heard of that. So who are the other Nouveau Expressionist bands?"

"There ain't any. We're the first."

"Ah."

"I tell you another thing about Theodora. He hated Zipgun. They was always having fights."

"I thought they were..."

"Close? Nah, they hated one another's guts. I mean, take the club. People think it was Theodora what did all that. That's a laugh, I tell you! Theodora couldn't organize a piss-up in a brewery let alone a club like Spivz. Zipgun's the brains – always has been. Theodora just takes all the credit. And the drugs."

"What was he on?"

"What *wasn't* he on? He was 'on' just about everything. Don't tell me you didn't know! And then there was all the shagging. Affairs and stuff."

"Theodora?"

"Well, he had some. But it was mostly Zipgun. A lot of people think he's good looking. Can't see it myself but that what a lot of people say. They was always having arguments about Zipgun's affairs."

"I didn't know he had affairs."

That was a lie, but then I hadn't sworn to tell the truth.

"'Course he had affairs. Everybody knew."

"I didn't."

"Everybody but you then."

"So why were you arguing?"

"Me? Not me. It was Zipgun and Theodora. It was them that had the arguments."

"In the club, I mean. I saw you in Spivz. Upstairs. Near the, you know, the toilet where..."

"Where his body was found? Ha! You think I bumped him off! Give me a break! If I'd have bumped him off I wouldn't be trying to hide it. I'd want the world to know. If I'd bumped the old queen off I'd probably be selling my story to The Daily Mirror."

"So what were you arguing about, then?"

"Can't remember. Oh, I don't know, I think it was... Yeah, it was something to do with the gig. He'd booked a gig, that must have been it. He wanted Mascara Addiction to do a night at the club but he was too bleedin' mean to pay us. I said, 'We're not amateurs, man. We are not doing this for charity' and he says, 'This is your spotlight to the world' – Silly old bugger! That's what he said – 'your spotlight to the world'. Like we was supposed to be grateful to him or something for the privilege of being chosen to perform in his poxy nightclub."

"So is the booking is still on? The gig, I mean?"

"Depends if Spivz ever opens again, I suppose. But anyway, we're starting rehearsing. Zipgun's a top man, you know. He's letting us use the club to rehearse. Which is a lot better than Clifton Chuttle's poxy studio. We're taking our gear down there tomorrow. You should come along. See us rehearsing, I mean. You could write something about us, maybe. Get an exclusive or whatever for – what magazine did you say you write for...?"

"There's a few."

"Well there you go then. Come down the club, see us in action like, and then write something."

"Yeah, I might just do that. Look, I don't want you to think I'm prying," I lied, "But what did he give you?"

"Theodora never gave me nothing in his life. What you talking about, man?"

"I thought I saw him, in the club, I thought I saw him hand you something."

"Nah, not him. He never gave me nothing. Here, none of this, what I'm saying, none of it's on the record, ok?"

I smiled in what I thought was a reassuring way without actually committing myself one way or another but what I was thinking was: "Look, I'm a journalist. If it's a good story, there's no such thing as 'off the record'."

When we left the pub, the jukebox was playing Johnny Nash's "There Are More Questions Than Answers" – I had a feeling that just about summed up what Dave Buzzard had told me.

Chapter 9

I was wishing I hadn't had the second pint as we made our way back to the studio. It must have been about half past two by then and I was busting for a pee. We heard the studio before we saw it. Either they were spending too much on amplifiers or too little on insulation. By the time the waste ground surrounding the studio hove into sight it felt as though someone was rhythmically thumping me in the stomach with a large cuddly toy. It's the bass notes that do it. I don't know what song they were playing since the bass was all I could hear. Maybe you can recognise it. It goes: *Dah-du-du-du-Daaaaaah-du-du-du-du-du-daah-du-du-du-du-du-Daaaaaah...*

"Prodigy," said Dave.

"What?"

"Moog Prodigy. The bass. Great little synth."

"I thought you didn't like synthesisers," I said.

"Great little synth if you like that sort of thing," he said, "That's Squirrel. On the Moog."

"I thought Squirrel played the drum machine."

"He's versatile," said Dave.

By the time we got to the front door (painted in dark green, flaking paint with a narrow vertical strip of wire-reinforced glass at its centre), the music had stopped. This was fortuitous as it gave me the opportunity to ask Janis for directions to the toilet which turned out to be tucked away at the far corner of the sitting room just beyond the fridge. Once I'd availed myself of its services I felt in a more positive frame of mind. Janis was no longer alone in the sitting room. Lounging on the tatty chairs and sofa were the other three members of Mascara Addiction: Dusty Evsky, Anvil Evans and Joe Jonson. It was Dusty I wanted to talk to; I was curious about the way that he and Brigitte had been looking at one another so meaningfully on that night in Spivz. I also wanted to know if there was anything more than coincidence in the fact that they happened to leave the Gallery at more or less the same time, just before midnight – just minutes before Theodora left, which was the last time that he was seen by anyone other than his killer or killers.

I was about to broach the subject when the doors to the music room flew open and Lala came out. He was, as ever, done up to the nines. Today he was wearing a powder-blue double-breasted suit with extensively padded shoulders and a shirt as frilly as a pair of Victorian lady's bloomers. I was impressed by the fact that, even in a tatty recording studio he had put so much effort into his appearance. He told the assembled masses that The Sexteens were done for the day and the music room was ready to be turned over to whomsoever might want to use it. Dusty, Anvil and Joe pushed themselves, half-heartedly, out of the tatty three-piece suite and, together with Dave Buzzard, made their way, grumblingly, into the adjoining room.

"You may as well come through too," Lala said, "It'll be ten minutes or so before we clear out of the place."

The music room felt distinctly overpopulated. Lala and Squirrel were moving their synthesisers to the side of the room. Anvil's drum kit was in more or less permanent residence there – it just got moved against a wall whenever The Sexteens came in and back into the main studio-space when Mascara Addiction took over. As the singer, Pete de Gré didn't have an instrument – just his mike stand, which he left where it was ready for Dave Buzzard. Lala's synthesiser (a Yamaha CS-5) was, in fact, owned by Chuttle and it was shared between Lala and Dusty Evsky. Lala had once asked Chuttle what they would do if ever The Sexteens and Mascara Addiction had a gig on the same night. Chuttle had told him "We'll worry about that when it happens." So far the circumstance had not arisen.

I turned to look through the glass window that separated the music room from the mixing room. Chuttle was in there, pressing buttons and twisting dials. To this day, I have no idea what all the buttons and sliders on a mixing desk actually do but they look damned impressive.

The contrast between the appearance of the two groups was interesting. Mascara Addiction (Dave, Joe, Anvil and Dusty) were all wearing jeans and tee-shirts. In terms of their clothing, there was little to tell one from the other. Dusty Evsky was, as always, set apart by the 'attitude' – the James Dean 'rebel without a cause' pose which I suspect he cultivates deliberately. I noticed his black leather jacket on a hanger at the side of the studio: a Schott Perfecto – the classic biker jacket. I've never worn a leather jacket myself but were I ever to do so, that would be the one.

The Sexteens, by comparison, looked, well eccentric. I've already mentioned Lala's power-blue suit and frills. While Lala was explosion of colour, Adam Xeon was entirely monochrome. He was dressed, as always, in black: black shoulder-length hair, black tee-shirt, skinny-fit black jeans, black mascara and black nail varnish. This is pretty much the school uniform of the "gothic punks". To my eye, Adam looked totally out of place in a Futurist band, which was maybe the idea. Squirrel, meanwhile, looked like Squirrel: bald, fat and weighed down by black mascara, eye-liner and eye-shadow which he seemed to have applied with a trowel; he looked like Uncle Fester in a tee-shirt.

And then there was Pete de Gré. He wasn't wearing makeup at all. In fact, he was wearing almost the same outfit as Dave Buzzard: Levis, denim shirt and trainers. Pete would have looked ordinary but for the fact that he was quite astonishingly good looking. Even though he was the newest member of The Sexteens, it was pretty obvious that, if the group ever managed to make it big, it was Pete who would be the pinup: naturally blond hair, smooth skin, perfect teeth, doe-like eyes and a disarmingly boyish smile – he'd look terrific in photos and even better on TV. If he could sing too that would be bonus but, given his other advantages, hardly a necessity.

As Pete wasn't doing much other than standing around looking decorative, I struck up a conversation with him. Although we'd met before a couple of times I can't say I know Pete well. The longest conversation I'd ever had previously was an interview I did for 'My Guy' in which he told me such fascinating details as the name of the first girl he'd kissed (Helen Brown), his favourite colour underwear (white) and his favourite school meal (steak and kidney pudding). But Pete is one of those rare people who make it easy to strike up a conversation. You start talking and he talks back. 'Happy go-lucky' is probably a phrase that describes his outlook on life.

I began the conversation with a few platitudes about Theodora. We agreed that his death was sad though he didn't look in any mood to shed tears over it. Then I moved onto some specifics.

"How well did you know Theodora?"

"Not very."

"Did you like him?"

"Never gave him any thought. Clifton didn't like him, I know that."

"Oh, really?" I paused to check that Chuttle was out of earshot, locked away at the mixing desk behind the glass window, "Why was that?"

"Theodora was always pestering him. Wanted Clifton to record him. But he wouldn't. Said he was too old, too ugly and couldn't sing."

"And you?" I said, "Can you sing?"

Pete laughed. "You didn't hear our last single then?"

I confessed I hadn't.

"Nah," he said, "Don't think anyone did. Not that it'd have answered your question. Dave Buzzard was the singer on that. I only been the lead singer since September. But, yeah, I can sing. And anyway, I'm not old and ugly. Would you say?"

"How old are you?" I asked.

He smiled. "Don't be cheeky."

"Too young to be in Spivz?" I suggested.

"To young for lot of stuff," he said, "But that don't stop me."

"So you're recording a new single now, are you?"

"Will be. Put down some tracks but Clifton's not happy with them yet."

He nodded his head towards the door – "C'mon. It's a bit stuffy in here."

We walked out into the passageway. Pete nodded towards Janis who was watering a plant on the filing cabinet in the sitting room. She waved at us. Then Pete pushed open the front door and we went outside into the cold, crisp afternoon air.

"You know what they say about the last single, don't you?" Pete said.

"What?"

"That Dave didn't really sing on it?"

"I hadn't heard that."

"That's a rumour Theodora was putting around anyway. He had it in for Dave. I think Theodora was jealous – that Dave had a deal with Clifton but Theodora didn't."

"Was Theodora jealous of you?" I asked.

"I just told you. I hardly even knew him. He told a journo once that Dave was a junky. Dave went ballistic. Said if Theodora ever badmouthed him again, he'd kill him."

"Maybe he did?" I said.

"What, Dave Buzzard kill Theodora? Yeah, possible, I suppose. Here, have a sniff..."

Pete had taken a small silver coloured jar from his pocket and was holding it out to me.

"No thanks," I said.

He unscrewed the cap, put an index finger against his left nostril and held the bottle beneath his right nostril. He took a good, long sniff then repeated the operation with the other nostril. Then he screwed back the top onto the bottle, put it into a pocket and began laughing uproariously.

Suddenly he looked up, sheepishly, staring towards the door of the studio. Clifton Chuttle was standing there, glowering at Pete. Pete blushed slightly. Chuttle went away, glowering still.

"What was that you sniffed?" I asked, "Smelling salts?"

"Don't be such a twat," he said, "It's poppers, ain't it."

"Oh," I said, "Of course."

I must admit that, while I'd heard of poppers, I didn't know what they were. "Can I have a smell?" I said.

Pete took the bottle from his pocket again and, checking first to make sure that Chuttle wasn't watching, he handed it over to me. It was a small bottle whose external surface was decorated in a mix of intense yellow and red colours. On the top of the label there was a warning stating that the contents were flammable and may be fatal if swallowed. It claimed to be a 'liquid aroma' and it suggested that a few drops might be placed in a saucer in order to perfume the room. I unscrewed the top and sniffed cautiously. It smelled revolting. Not quite as revolting as smelling salts, but close. But the for the label's assertion to the contrary, it wasn't the sort of thing I'd have thought of using to perfume a room.

"Take a good one," he said, "You won't get a hit if you take baby little sniffs like that."

"No, it's ok," I said, "I try not to when I'm working," and I handed the bottle back to him.

"You didn't happen to give Lala some of this on New Year's Eve, did you?"

"You bet I did! He fainted. He was flat out on the floor and people were poncing around like idiots. I thought to myself: a good whiff of this'll bring him around. And I was right, wasn't I!"

There was a soft rat-tat-tatting noise behind us. I turned and saw Janis tapping on the window pane inside the sitting room. The she gesticulated for us to come inside.

"Must be time," Pete said, "To start rehearsing or recording or whatever we're supposed to be doing today."

We went back into the music room. As entered, a loud, piercing noise like a buzz saw attacking an electricity pylon suddenly screeched through the air. If I'd been wearing dentures, they would probably have leapt from my mouth in terror. As my teeth are all my own, they contented themselves with rattling pathetically in their sockets. I gathered that the buzz saw noise was being produced by whatever Dusty Evsky was doing to the dials and keys on the synthesiser perched on a stand in front of him and was being amplified through the four huge speakers suspended at head-height from the walls.

That was when I noticed Clifton Chuttle. He had walked into the music room and, in a momentary pause between buzz saw noises, he was telling those of us who were not members of Mascara Addiction to clear the studio, a suggestion with which I was very pleased to comply. As we filed out into the sitting room, I realised this provided me with a good opportunity to have a few words with Chuttle.

I held out my hand, "Hello, Clifton," I said, "Good to see you."

He looked at my hand and grunted. I put my hand away. Its presence was superfluous to requirements.

"I was wondering if I could have a few words."

"I'm busy," he said.

I think I might have mentioned before that Clifton Chuttle is well known to be a man who radiates joy and good humour. He is one of those people who make of politeness an art form. The sort of person for whom any amount of trouble is never too much. At least, that had been my experience up to now.

"Theodora..." I said.

79

He turned his back on me and began walking away in the direction of the mixing room. "I was wondering if you had any memories."

Dave Buzzard suddenly appeared. He went over to Chuttle and had a few words with him which, thanks to the temporary intermission in the buzz saw noises, I was able to overhear: "He's a journalist, man," he was saying, "Great Hits. Be nice to him, man. It could be good publicity for the band."

Chuttle stopped in his tracks. Although he was facing away from me, I had the distinct impression that he was taking a few moments to rearrange his face. When he turned back, the well-known smile was there, the arms were held slightly apart as though he were welcoming a long-lost friend and he was positively oozing with bonhomie: "Theodora," he said, "So, so sad. A tragedy. He'll be sorely missed. You are writing for Smash Hits, are you?"

"Great Hits," I corrected.

"That's our favourite magazine. Isn't it lads?" he looked around for confirmation, received none and continued without a pause, "You writing something about Theodora, are you? We were very close. We talked about doing some recordings as a matter of fact. Here, let's go somewhere quiet. I can only spare five minutes but if that's ok with you...?"

I assured him that five minutes would be plenty. He opened door in the wall to the right of the music room. Once the door was shut, I was surprised to find that the little room was strangely silent. I doubt if it would have been insulated against Mascara Addiction blasting out at full volume. But it certainly kept out all the sounds of conversation coming from the music room. The mixing room was dominated by a huge console – don't ask me to describe it. It had so many buttons, knobs and dials that it would take a leap of faith to believe that any one person could possibly understand what they all did. At the working side of the console was a chair.

There were some hooks on the walls too with set of tools and some little coloured paper bags hanging from them. The tools were things like screw-drivers and wrenches. The bags contained replacement guitar strings.

At the other side of the mixing console was the window looking onto the music room. I could see Mascara Addiction in there, silently tuning their instruments and chatting to one another. I knew they were talking because I could see their mouths moving, but I couldn't tell you what they were saying because I don't read lips. There were two speakers sitting on either side of the mixing console and two more speakers attached to the wall at either side of the window onto the studio. There was also a microphone angled down towards the chair in which Clifton Chuttle was now sitting. He flipped a switch, leaned towards the microphone and said, "Five minutes, lads. Be ready."

Through the speakers I could hear the sound of chatter. Then Dusty Evsky looked towards us and said, "What do we start with?"

"The new song, 'Killing Machine'."

"Fallen Angels," Dusty said.

"I thought it was Killing Machine," said Chuttle.

Dave Buzzard spoke: "We changed it."

Anvil Evans looked up from his drum set – "Judas Priest."

"What?" said Chuttle.

"Judas Priest got a song called Killing Machine."

"Single?"

"It's a song on an album."

"Does it matter if it's just a song on album? Nobody listens to Judas Priest albums."

"I do," said Anvil.

"What's the album called?" said Chuttle.

"Killing Machine," said Anvil.

"I thought that was the name of the song."

"It is," said Anvil.

"Are you sure no one's got a song called Fallen Angels too?" said Chuttle.

"Never heard of one," said Anvil.

"OK, then, whatever it's called. Five minutes."

Chuttle switched off the microphone.

"Frankie Valli did a song called Fallen Angel," I said.

Chuttle groaned. "Just don't tell them, ok?"

I shrugged, "His was in the singular, though," I said, Angel, I mean, not Angels."

"So you are writing about Theodora?" Chuttle smiled broadly then seemed to have second thoughts and adopted a more solemn expression.

"Martyr Of A Doomed Generation," I said.

"You what?"

"That's what we are calling it. The magazine. It's a special issue. As a tribute."

"Ah. So how can I help?"

"You said you were planning to do some records with him?"

"Well, I wouldn't say we'd actually gone that far. I'd just say we'd discussed the possibility."

"When did you last see him?"

Chuttle sighed. "So sad. The night of his death. But I suppose that's when most of us saw him. You too...?"

I nodded.

"I wonder who was the last person to see him?" I said.

"Whoever killed him, I suppose," said Chuttle, "I was in the Gallery, up until just before midnight I suppose. I saw Theodora leave, as a matter of fact."

"So you were in the Gallery all that time? From when you saw Theodora leave until after his body was found?"

Chuttle's expression slipped. For a moment a look of annoyance, anger even, flicked over his face – "That's an odd question to ask," he said. Then the smile came back, "No, I left shortly after Theodora as a matter of fact. I was going to the toilet. The downstairs toilet, that is. The upstairs one is private, of course. And then I bumped into Brigitte and we had a dance. Saw in the New Year together, you might say."

"I didn't realise you knew Brigitte."

"We've been talking about the possibility of recording something as a matter of fact."

"God!" I said, "How many people *haven't* you been talking to?"

He laughed. "He's got the look, Brigitte. Androgynous. Very popular with teenage girls, for some reason. He could be big."

"So you didn't see Theodora after...?"

"Like I say, me and Brigitte had a dance – well, as much of a dance as it's possible to have to that stuff – and then when we finished, that's when I heard about Theodora."

82

"What stuff?"

"I beg your...?"

"I was just wondering what stuff. You know, it would be nice to know, to add a bit of background colour, for the piece I'm writing. You said it was hard to dance to the stuff they were playing."

"Oh, God. You know the stuff. I mean, you were there. You must..."

"I was in Harlow's Bar."

"Not all night you weren't. I saw you."

"At midnight though. I didn't get to see the New Year in with a dance. Sad, I know, but I was just having a quiet drink in the bar. So I was just curious, that's all, about what music they were playing. To see in the New Year."

"I can't recall," Chuttle said, "The usual crap. I kept telling Theodora he should get a proper DJ. I mean, the stuff we are doing, the stuff the Sexteens do, it's got a tune, you know, a beat. Something you can dance to. But Fad Gadget, for God's sake. The Normal! I mean, you can't dance to Fad Gadget, can you? Look, don't quite me on that. Don't make it sound as though I'm slagging off the competition."

"No, no, of course not."

"Look, I don't know what quotes you want from me but why don't you just say that Clifton Chuttle, the manager and producer of The Sexteens, was devastated by the news of Theodora's tragic death and that..."

"Manager and producer of The Sexteens and Mascara Addiction?" I corrected.

He nodded, "Yeah. And if you can give us a plug on the next Sexteens single, that would be great. Released on the independent ChuttleSpinz label at the end of the month. It's a Futurist version of an old '60s hit. Sounds really interesting, actually. It could be huge."

"What's it called?" I said.

"Death Of A Clown," he said. And he smiled when he said it.

83

Chapter 10

It was just after 4 o'clock when I left the studio. As we were leaving, who should stroll up but Brigitte. Well, stroll is perhaps not the most apposite verb to use where Brigitte is concerned. 'Sashay' would be better. 'Explode' would be better still. Brigitte lives his life as though waiting to make an entrance. As soon as he sees a potential audience a spotlight goes on in his head and he is suddenly all arms, eyes, lips and sequins.

"Dahling! How lovely to see you!" – that to me and then immediately turning his attention to Lala, Pete de Gré and Adam Xeon, he was all hugs and air-kisses; the kisses being done at a sufficient distance to avoid any threat to her perfectly applied makeup. Today Brigitte's makeup involved a pale cream foundation with plum-red lips, a cherry blusher, dark eyebrows drawn in a perfect arch and various carefully shaded hues of pink-to-crimson eye shadow; plus of course, the inevitable mascara.

"Dahlings, you aren't *going* are you? But you can't! I've just *arrived*!"

Brigitte is entirely oblivious to the possibility that other people might not organise their lives based on the presence or otherwise of Brigitte.

"He'll be in there another three hours," warned Lala, "Maybe more."

"Dahling," Brigitte simpered, "I really can't think *who* you mean."

Adam Xeon pointed a black-nail-varnished fingernail at me. "Be careful what you say," he warned Brigitte, "He's a journalist."

"I know that, silly," said Brigitte, "Well, dahling, whatever I say is yours to do with as you will."

"He's writing about Theodora," Pete said.

Brigitte rolled his eyes heavenward and angled his head slightly in a manner, if the paintings are to believed, which was much favoured by Saint Teresa of Avila. Except, of course, that unlike Brigitte, Saint Teresa of Avila was not in the habit of wearing black slacks, high-heeled shoes and a golden-sequinned blouse tied in a knot just above her navel, thereby revealing a tantalising glimpse of her firm young stomach. Whether Saint Teresa had long golden-blonde tresses with pink highlights is impossible to know due to the fact that she is usually depicted with her hair tucked up inside a nun's coif and veil.

Having rolled his eyes to a sufficient extent to convey mortification at the death of Theodora, Brigitte looked at me and said, "Where's your photographer?"

I told him I didn't have one with me just at that moment.

"I could give you some very juicy quotes on Theodora," he said, "But what's the point if you haven't got a photographer? I mean, dahling, just feast your eyes on *this*." – He held his arms wide and puckered his lips to indicate that the 'this' upon which he had exhorted my eyes to feast was none other than Brigitte – "This is what your magazine needs. Which magazine is it, by the way?"

"Smash Hits," said Pete.

"Great Hits," I corrected.

"I'd prefer Cosmopolitan," said Brigitte, "But, what the hell, I'm not proud."

"You know Theodora long?" I asked.

"At least several lifetimes, dahling. Or so it often seems."

"Did you get on?"

"Certainly not in *that* way, if that's what you mean!"

"I heard you'd had an argument. On New Year's Eve."

"Who told you that?"

"Oh, I don't know, I just heard."

It was Zipgun Dandy who'd told me but I didn't think that was something Brigitte needed to know.

"Yeah, we was always arguing. Theodora was a bitch. If we wasn't arguing about money or clothes or drugs it was about men."

"Don't listen to her," Lala interrupted, "The only thing she and Theodora ever argued about was men."

"You bitch!" Brigitte screamed, "It's true though. Fact of the matter is, I happened to catch Theodora pawing all over a certain someone – someone rather special in my life, let's say. In her office. And so I blew a bleedin' gasket. As one would, well wouldn't one! I think I may have called her a syphilitic rancid old whore."

"Did you say you'd kill him?" I asked.

"Yeah, probably. Here, what you trying to say? You don't think I...? No, I don't believe it! I mean, don't get me wrong, I hated the bastard's guts but I didn't bump her off."

"Don't worry," I tried to make light of it, "Nobody thinks you did. I mean, for one thing, you were surrounded by witnesses, weren't you."

"Yeah, I supposed I was."

"So where were you between about five to twelve when Theodora was last seen and twenty-five past, when they found his body?"

"I was with Clifton, as a matter of fact. Go on, check if you like, go on, ask him. Ask him!"

I couldn't help noticing there was a slightly hysterical note to Brigitte's voice.

Adam Xeon said drily: "She's lying."

"How d'you know?" asked Pete.

"She's talking ain't she? So she must be lying."

Brigitte did not look amused.

"I've already spoken to Clifton," I said, "He says you had a dance with him at midnight, to see in the New Year."

"Yeah, we did! Exactly, that's right, we did," Brigitte sneered theatrically at Pete, "So I can't have killed him, can I!"

"I didn't notice you," said Pete, "On the dance floor, I mean. Then again, I wasn't really watching."

"Do you remember what you danced to?" I asked.

"You what?"

"What song was being played. When you and Clifton had a dance. At midnight?"

"Can't remember," Brigitte said, "The usual stuff, I think. Electro stuff sounds all the same to me." – he simpered at Adam, Pete and Lala – "No offence intended, dahlings."

By now Adam was looking very pointedly at his watch. He was more interested in catching the train and getting home than in listening to what Brigitte had to say. I told him to go on without me. I just wanted to ask Brigitte a couple more things then I'd catch up with them. Pete lived locally so he headed off in the direction of his flat while Lala accompanied Adam towards the tube station. I wasn't far behind them. They were just buying their tickets when I arrived, a bit out of breath, at the station.

Adam lives in Seven Sisters so he could go directly from Brixton on the Victoria Line. Lala lives in Islington which meant that both he and I had to catch the Victoria Line at Brixton then change onto the Northern Line at Stockwell. As a consequence, the three of us shared a carriage for just one stop. In that brief time, Adam told me something that I hadn't known. I recalled that, on the night of the murder, Adam had been sitting up in the cocktail bar with Brigitte, Zipgun Dandy, Theodora and Velma (Theodora's theoretical 'girlfriend'). It must have been about ten minutes before midnight when Dusty Evsky, who'd been at a table with the other members of Mascara Addiction on the far side of the Gallery, suddenly got up and left and was followed shortly thereafter by Brigitte. I went down to Harlow's Bar so I didn't see anything more of what went on in the Gallery. Adam filled in a few gaps. He told me that Theodora left the Gallery just after me. Theodora had said he was going to "powder his nose".

"And," said Adam, "We all know which powder he meant! Well, when he didn't come back, I assumed he'd gone downstairs. I think we all assumed he would go up on stage at midnight and do a countdown into the '80s or something. It would be just like Theodora to want to be centre stage. But midnight came and went and there was no sign of him.

"Then, a few minutes later, I had to have a pee."

Ignoring the 'Private' signs which strictly forbade it, Adam went to the nearest toilet, in the corridor outside the Gallery; the toilet that is designated for 'management only'. It was locked.

"It was definitely locked," Adam said, "From the inside. I pushed but the door wouldn't budge. I thought maybe Theodora was in there so I shouted, 'Are you in there, Theo? I'm going to bust if I don't have a pee soon.' But there was no answer so there was nothing for it – I had to go to the downstairs bog instead. Only just made it in time. Five seconds more and I'd have pissed meself."

"But everyone says it was unlocked," I said, "Zipgun told me that you told him it was locked which is why he went to the office to get the key. But when he came back the door was already open."

"Yeah. Funny, that. Even so, when I went there, the upstairs toilet was definitely locked. And you can only lock it from the inside unless you got the key. But then later on, when they found Theodora, it wasn't locked. Don't ask me what happened, I only know what I know. When I went there just after midnight, it was definitely locked."

"And you are sure it can only be locked from the inside unless you have the key?"

"Try for yourself if you don't believe me."

"So who has a key?"

"Only Theodora," Adam said, "And Zipgun, of course."

I wanted to ask him more but that's when the train pulled into Stockwell. Lala and I had to get off there to catch a Northern Line train. I wasn't sure if what Adam had told me was important or not. I had a feeling it was. But I couldn't figure out why.

They call it the rush hour but it's more like two hours, or maybe three. When the train pulled into Stockwell a crowd of people like the cells of a gigantic amoeba squeezed themselves through the doors into the carriages while a smaller trickle of people battled to get out of the doors against the prevailing tide. In those circumstances you have no choice but to get into whichever carriage is the closest. It was our bad luck that it was a smoking carriage. The doors closed on us, sealing in the smog. I held my breath between stations. When we arrived at the next station the doors would open so I'd have a chance to lean out and gasp in something approximating to air. It seemed a long way between stations. It felt like I was aiming for the world record for underground station breath-holding but I clearly wasn't a contender. When the train stopped and the doors finally whisked open I took a good lungful of the purest Oval tube-station air and tried to hold my breath again until Kennington.

By the time the train pulled in at Elephant and Castle, my lungs were giving out so I signalled to Lala to change carriages. As the doors opened, we dashed out against the inward-surging wave of people and managed to join another surge moving into a non-smoking carriage. My only consolation was that we were on the City branch-line. If we'd gone via the West End line we'd have had to suffer Waterloo, Charing Cross and Tottenham Court Road. Rush hour on the City branch is relatively civilised by comparison. Not only are the carriages less crowded but the people in them are of an altogether better class: mostly they are young men in dark suits and Givenchy aftershave whose entire conversation consists of the four *B*s: beer, bubbly, bonking and bonuses. Especially bonuses.

When the train pulled into Bank, a prodigy in nature occurred: two seats became vacant. Lala and I immediately took advantage of this opportunity before any women labouring beneath the weight of shopping bags and babies should have the chance to deprive us. That may sound callous, but travelling on the tube is to experience nature red in tooth and claw, survival of the fittest. It is a perfect illustration of why the species Homo sapiens has elevated itself to the point where it can dash off sonnets, write concertos, fly to the moon and make stonking amounts of money from futures, commodities and bonds only to die a bitter and lonely death from alcohol and stress related diseases at the age of 32. Whereas the giant tortoise of the Galapagos for example, has to content itself with lying around in the sun eating weeds and cactuses and dying in bed with a younger tortoise at the age of 170.

Between Bank and Moorgate, we chatted a bit about The Sexteens. Lala told me about the single, 'Death Of A Clown' which, he said, was originally a hit for Dave Davies ("brother of the more famous Ray") back in 1967. I expressed surprise that an old weepy from the Summer of Love was considered an appropriate anthem for the New Futurists.

"Well, it's like making a break with all that Harlequin and Pierrot stuff, I guess," he said, "You know, sweep out last year's fashions of dressing up in frills and makeup and sweep in the New Wave of, well, whatever comes next."

I looked at Lala's frills and makeup and decided not to comment.

"So what is the New Wave?" I said.

"Industrial," he said.

"I thought that was the old wave."

"It's so old it's new again."

"Ah," I said.

I decided to change the subject.

"So who exactly," I asked, "is the 'special person' in Brigitte's life?"

"Oh, come on. You must know. Dusty Evsky. She's wild about him."

I must admit that this information did not come as a complete surprise to me.

"So would I be right to suppose that Brigitte and Dusty may have had some sort of assignation on New Year's Eve?"

"Assignation?" Lala laughed, "I think there are shorter words for what they had on New Year's Eve."

I wondered if he was right. There were enough nooks, crannies and store rooms in Spivz to have a full-blown orgy out of the public gaze.

"Well, they must have been quick about it," I said, "Because Brigitte was with Clifton Chuttle when the bells of midnight struck."

"Really? So that's who he meant. I sort of thought he did but I wasn't sure. You see, me and Pete were with Clifton up in the Gallery until just before midnight. Then, all of a sudden, Chuttle gets up and says 'It's nearly the witching hour, I'd better go and find myself a witch.' He'd been watching Brigitte, I think, and he'd seen her go off just after Dusty left. Clifton has big hopes of Dusty. I think he wants him to be the lead singer with Mascara Addiction, though I'm not sure how he's going to break the news to Dave Buzzard. I mean, Dave took it pretty badly when he was kicked out of The Sexteens..."

"He was kicked out? He didn't leave of his own free will?"

"'Course he was kicked out. Too unreliable, not especially good looking, too old. God knows how he'll take it if Dusty takes over lead vocals in Mascara Addiction! But anyway, suffice to say that Clifton Chuttle does not approve of Brigitte. He especially does not like Brigitte going after Dusty."

"Why not?"

"Dusty is straight, dear. That, at least, is the image Clifton wants for him. Having Brigitte hanging around him sort of gives the game away, don't you think? So what was Chuttle doing with Brigitte? Arguing? Fighting? Were punches thrown?"

"They were dancing," I said.

"Dancing?" Lala gasped as though the concept seemed to be a difficult one to grasp, on a similar scale, I felt, to space-time distortion around a topological singularity, "With Brigitte?"

"Is that so impossible?"

"Unexpected, let's say. Brigitte is not the sort of chick that Chuttle would choose. And I don't think either of them would have wanted to be seen dancing at midnight."

"Why not at midnight?"

"Well, Village People does not score high on the trendiness list among the fashion pack, if you get my drift," he said

Lala had lost me and I told him so. What did Village People have to do with anything?

"That's what they were playing. At midnight."

"Village People?" I sputtered, "You jest surely."

He assured me he did not.

"Village People, " I observed, "Are not generally regarded to be in the vanguard of the Futurist movement."

Lala agreed. For some reason a comment of Tyrone's started bouncing around inside my head: "The fundamental problem is the coincidence." A person collapsing for no obvious reason is unusual. A murder in a nightclub toilet is more unusual still. But for those two events to occur within minutes of one another is so extraordinary that coincidence is not a satisfactory explanation. There was something that united Theodora's murder with Lala's collapse. Tyrone believed that the mascara which had caused Lala's allergic reaction might be important. As Tyrone had said: "Find the mascara and you find the murderer." I couldn't help thinking that sometimes Tyrone oversimplified things.

A we pulled into Old Street I asked Lala about the mascara that has caused the allergic reaction that had made his eyes go all puffy and red. When I'd spoken to Lala at Zipgun's house on New Year's Day, he'd told me he'd swapped mascara with Theodora because Theodora hadn't liked the colour of his own mascara. "But isn't all mascara the same colour?" I asked, naively.

Lala looked at me as though I'd gone mad – "God Good, no!" he said, "Midnight in Morocco is the colour I use."

"And what colour is that?" I asked.

"Black."

"And what colour does Theodora use?"

"Black."

"So?"

"Except not on this occasion. For some reason, on New Year's Eve he had Tropical Night."

"Which is what colour?"

"Blue. Dark blue. Obviously it was the wrong colour because Theodora was wearing all black. Top hat, tails and all that guff. So he asked me if we could swap and we did."

"What time was that?"

"Oh, I don't know. Quite early. Half past ten maybe. I wasn't wearing any mascara at the time but then, later on I thought I'd have a try of the Tropical Night, just to see how it looked."

"What time did you put on the mascara?"

"Not long before I fainted."

"After midnight then?"

"I suppose it must have been."

"And you still have the mascara?"

"You've got to be kidding! After what it did to me eyes. Threw it away, didn't I? From now on, it's going to be Midnight in Morocco or nothing as far as I'm concerned."

"So, when you last saw him, which colour mascara was Theodora...?"

But I never had the chance to finish my question. The train pulled into Angel, Islington and Lala leapt to his feet and dashed for the doors, waving to me on the way out and telling me he'd "See me around."

There was a disturbing anomaly in Lala's story. Village People! I wanted to trust Lala but if he was wrong about that, what else might he be wrong about?

Chapter 11

I decided to get off one stop early at Camden Town and walk back up the Kentish Town Road. On the way out of the tube station I saw a man selling newspapers. He was shouting out something that sounded like, "Evening gertcha, hanya-gurcha murdha". I got "Evening" and "murder" – the bit in between could have been Serbo-Croat for all the sense I could make of it. I suspected he called out the same thing every night irrespective of what the headline was.

I called in at a butchers and asked for some bones. He said he didn't have any! That I find strange to believe. Many are the marvels of modern farming but, as far as I am aware, the boneless cow is not one of them. I settled for settled some steak. The butcher baffled me momentarily by asking which cut of steak I'd like. I asked him what cuts he had. He proceeded to name a bewildering variety. The names meant nothing to me so I just pointed. That one there, I said. I was told this was from the beast's rump. I couldn't remember if, in beef terms, 'rump' was good or bad. This was, after all, only intended for canine consumption. I decided that an animal's backside could not possibly be considered a delicacy so I said I'd take two pounds of it. I am still not sure if I was duped or if cow's bum really does cost that much. If this is really what small and scruffy dogs expect to eat on a daily basis I was starting to understand why Scruffy's previous owners were far from keen to be reunited with him.

I reasoned that if rump was good enough for Scruffy it was probably good enough for me too and so I might as well make a meal of it. I popped across to a greengrocer's and bought some onions and mushrooms. Fried steak à la Scruffy was on the menu tonight. I just hoped the little brute would appreciate it.

When I got back, I opened the door, expecting Scruffy to leap to his paws and come scampering up giving vent to much joyful barking and tail-wagging in celebration of his beloved master's return. It was not to be. He was asleep. On my settee. He opened one languid eye, rolled over, consented to be scratched on the tummy and then rolled over and went back to sleep again.

A second later, he was on his paws, scampering around my feet and doing the joyful barking and tail-wagging bit. Somewhat delayed, I thought, but better late than never. For a few moments he had me deceived. The thought was passing through my mind that dogs as a species were not such bad things after all and that this particular representative of dogdom was by no means as oppressive to the spirit as I had previously taken it to be. Indeed, a bit of joyful wagging and barking to greet its beloved master on his return was, when compared to being greeted by nothing but a cold and silent house, not at all a bad thing.

But then I saw that the dog's attention was not focussed on its beloved master at all, but upon the shopping bag containing two pounds of finest rump steak, hanging from his beloved master's hand. O! Treachery! O! Villainy! That such a small and innocent beast should have so taken me in so callously with its dissembled wags and woofs!

I put the meat in the fridge, well away from prying paws and let Scruffy out into the small paved area at the back of the house which is what passes for a garden in Kentish Town while I took a shower. When I got back, Scruffy was sitting in the kitchen covered in mud. By which I mean, Scruffy was covered in mud and so was the kitchen. I hasn't realised my garden had so much mud in it. Well, it didn't any longer.

I showered Scruffy. This took about two minutes of actual showering and about half an hour of chasing the dog around the house. Having caught the soggy doggy, I dried him off with a towel. It used to be a very nice, fluffy bath towel. It is no longer. Then I cleaned the kitchen by which time Scruffy wanted his food. I could tell that the want of food was on his mind not merely by the big, sad soulful look he was giving me but also by the plaintive howling with which he was letting rip.

I fried the steak with mushrooms, wine, pepper and onions. My half was delicious. Scruffy didn't seem too indifferent to his half either though I think he would have been just as happy without the wine, mushrooms and onions.

I sat and ate my dinner with the newspaper propped up against the Daddy's Sauce bottle on the table in front of me. The news of the murder had finally got out then. "Killers In Mascara" was the headline. There was a photograph of Theodora with a dead white face and what appeared to be black lipstick. He was wearing an inappropriate hat on his head with what looked like artichokes dangling from one side.

Under the headline the crosshead read: "New Year Slayer Could Strike Again, Police Warn".

Then there was a fictionalised account of the life and death of Theodora with hints of depraved parties, kinky sex, weird people and illicit drugs. That wasn't the fictional part. The fiction kicked in when the journalist went on to talk about terror stalking the streets, gangland killings and the curse of Jack The Ripper once again haunting "the blood-soaked streets of Whitechapel."

I flipped through the rest of the paper. There was something about goings on in Afghanistan, steel workers were on strike, there were rumours of a romance blossoming between The Generation Game's Larry Grayson and the star of the Crossroads soap opera, Noel Gordon (I nearly spat out a mouthful of steak when I read that) and a story that Mrs Ethel Smeep of Islington had a remarkable cat which could meow the theme tune to Dallas. A photograph of the pussy prodigy showed it to be a fat, grumpy-looking tabby. I glanced at Scruffy and wondered whether he might have any yet-to-be-discovered musical talents.

Then I noticed the red light flickering on my answer machine. When I played it back there were two messages. The first was from Sanford. He'd had an idea for a one-shot. It had suddenly struck him that it was exactly ten years since Rolf Harris had a number one hit with 'Two Little Boys'. He was sure that there must be thousands of Rolf fans who'd be prepared to lay out good money for a tatty poster magazine to celebrate this notable anniversary and could I manage to throw together about six thousand words by next Tuesday? I pressed the 'Next' button. This was a message from Zipgun. He said that he and Lala were going to be at Spivz the following afternoon. If I wanted to meet him, that was up to me.

I phoned Tyrone. I'd arranged to meet him at the Pineapple pub again that evening. But was going to have to cancel as I was going to be too busy writing the Great Hits Theodora tribute. I asked him if he was free tomorrow. He said he could be. I never could figure out how Tyrone managed to earn a living. He was, in theory, in full time employment but whenever I asked if he was free he always was. Good work if you can get it. We arranged to meet for lunch. I told him I was going back to the scene of the crime in the afternoon and he could come with me if he liked. He made a sterling effort to disguise his enthusiasm but he did not succeed. He was practically burbling with excitement at the prospect.

Finally, I hefted my trusty Imperial 66 typewriter onto the kitchen table, fed in two sheets of A4 with a sheet of carbon paper sandwiched between and began typing up ten thousand finely honed words in sincere tribute to Theodora:

THEODORA, MARTYR OF A DOOMED GENERATION

There are special moments in the history of mankind when a single individual emerges, seeming to capture the very essence of an entire generation. So it was with Theodora. Style guru, Futurist icon, a man who was too beautiful to live and too young to die. But die he did. In the most tragic and bizarre of circumstances.

And so it gushed on. I can do this stuff for hours on end if need be. I turned on my transistor radio (standing on a work surface between the stove and the bread bin) and tuned in to Radio WX22, a pirate station that had a habit of randomly fading in and out in a way that made me feel that the mere act of listening to it must be subversive. They played much better music than Radio One. At the moment they were playing something I'd never heard before but immediately decided I wanted to hear again. It had this really strange bass electronic beat with all kinds of swirling synth sounds weaving in and out and lyrics that simply didn't make any sense at all – "Over all the bridges, echoes in rows, talking at the same time, click click drone." At the end the DJ said it was an advance copy of a new single from John Foxx. I tried to remember where I'd heard of him before then I remembered that he used to be with a group called Ultravox but, for some reason, he'd left them. It happens, I guess. Just the way Dave Buzzard left The Sexteens (or was he pushed?).

I remember Zipgun Dandy telling me that Lady Vlad, the DJ at Spivz, had got hold of an advance copy of a song by someone who was ex-Ultravox. I suppose it must have been the same one. Why did everyone have advance copies except me? I'm supposed to be an influential rock journalist after all. Someone whose every word is analysed and savoured by the great British public.

So why do I end up writing ten thousand words of mindless trash about Theodora?

I got back to the typewriter, turned my brain off and continued until half past eleven. I counted the pages of typescript. There were 39 of them. I generally average about 250 words per page so that must make about 9,750 words. Close enough. If Sanford wanted more, I could easily dash off another 250 tomorrow. But he's even worse at arithmetic than I am so I suspected he wouldn't notice the deficit.

Finally, I got out a bottle of wine, pushed Scruffy to the other end of the settee and wound back the video to watch a programme I'd recorded the day before and which the BBC has been plugging relentlessly for weeks and which turns out to be all about the rib-tickling antics of the employees of a 1950s' seaside holiday camp. Following that I settled down for a nice relaxing half hour reading the latest Stephen King novel which is about a man who gets hit by a car and ends up in a coma (this has slightly fewer rib-tickling episodes), then I decided to switch to the latest issue of Smash Hits wherein I read the traumatising news that Debbie Harry had dyed her hair brown (which made me wonder what colour her hair is when it's not dyed brown or bleached blonde?) and finally, at about ten to one, I patted Scruffy on the head, rubbed him on the tummy, tickled him behind the ears and staggered off to bed.

Chapter 12

I was awakened by a tongue in my ear. The first time it had happened I had disliked the sensation. This was the second time and all I can say is that it does not improve with repetition. If you are curious to know what it feels like to have a dog stick its tongue in your ear, I can suggest two ways in which you can find out. Either: go up to a dog, present your ear to its tongue, grit your teeth and wait. Or: if you can't find a convenient dog, get a slug and stick it in your ear. While I cannot say I've tried the latter, I have every confidence that the sensation will be indistinguishable from the former.

By the time I'd had stuffed down a quick breakfast of muesli and two mugs of freshly ground and filtered coffee, then took Scruffy to inspect the damage which he had done the previous day in my tiny garden, then given him a walk down the street and back again, tied to a piece of string (I decided I would really have to buy a proper dog-lead), it was almost ten o'clock. So I set off to Kentish Town tube station and caught the complicated series of connecting trains (Kentish Town to King's Cross, then King's Cross to Baker Street and finally Baker Street to Kilburn) in order to take me close to the insalubrious side street in which lurks the crumbling wreck of a building that houses the Great Hits publishing empire. To while away the time on the way, I read the latest report on the killing of Theodora in the morning newspaper:

Brutal Nightclub Killing
Jack Smith, Crime Correspondent
3rd Jan, 1980

A 21 year old man who was killed at the Spivz Nightclub in the early hours of New Year's Day has been named.

Terry Binton, also known as 'Theodora', was strangled to death in the fashionable East End club some time after midnight on Tuesday morning. It is understood that Binton was the manager of the club. Detective Superintendent Colin Threep, who is leading the inquiry, said: "A young man lost his life in, as yet, unknown circumstances. We are following several lines of enquiry. There were many hundreds of people on the premises on the night of the incident and we believe there is a very good chance that somebody may know who the killer is.

"We have already spoken to a number of people who have provided us with a great deal of useful information. But, of course, we will always be very pleased to hear from anyone who knows anything which may assist in tracking down the guilty party."

Mr Threep, who is leading a team of more than 50 officers, appealed to anyone who might have information relating to the inquiry to come forward. He particularly wants to hear from anyone who might know the whereabouts of a white silk scarf which it is believed may have been the murder weapon.

Speaking at a press conference, Mr Threep declined to name any suspects or state whether any fingerprints had been found at the scene of the murder.

"This was a busy nightclub," he said, "On one of the busiest nights of the year. It is a very challenging location for my team to investigate. This was a savage attack and it vital that whoever is responsible must be tracked down and brought to justice. I would, however, like to reassure residents and members of the local community that we have no reason to believe that this was anything other than an isolated incident."

The body of Mr Binton was found by revellers in the upstairs toilet of the club in an area which was designated as 'private'. No possible motive for the crime has been revealed but the police have stated that forensic examinations have ruled out a sexual assault.

Some publishers such as VNU and IPC have their headquarters in huge custom-built office blocks. The publishing empire of Great Hits is built on more modest lines: two up, two down, a basement and an outside privy. The ground floor houses a small but plush reception area at the front and a large and squalid office area at the back. The basement is occupied by the art editor, a strange woman named Ingrid of uncertain mental stability. The upper floor is rented out to a person by the name of Madame Sévère who gives French Lessons, a line of business which, judging from the constant stream of gentleman visitors, is more popular than you might imagine.

On entering the building from the street, you find yourself standing in a small foyer about the width of a house door. Well, no, in fact it is precisely the width of a house door. The outer door forms one side of the foyer; the door in front of you which, when unlocked, leads onto the staircase to Madame Sévère's flat, forms the opposite side of the foyer; a wall (just for the sake of novelty) forms the right side and the door to the Great Hits reception is on your left. Should you have no interest in brushing up your French you will at this point, in all probability, choose to open the door on your left.

What you will see when you enter is a smoked glass table, a furry carpet and a G-Plan desk on which sits a phone, a typewriter, a geriatric spider plant and a plastic sign saying 'Reception'. Behind the desk, on a good day, sits a middle-aged woman whose comfortable proportions are at odds with the bosom-hugging floral blouse and tight black miniskirt which she habitually wears. Her turquoise eye-shadowed eyes gaze out from behind a pair of large glasses whose pink frames have dangerous-looking upswept points at their outer edges. The glasses are attached to a gold chain around her neck (presumably in an effort to foil glasses thieves) and her elegant ensemble is topped off with a stack of stiff blonde hair that seems to be living under the delusion that it is still 1966. This, ladies and gentlemen, is Gladys, the office manager, and she is beloved of all who know her.

When I went in that morning, Gladys was knitting something mauve. She looked up and smiled and was about to say something when the phone rang. She picked it up with barely a pause said:

"Sorry, Mr Bouche-Torrington is not in today. He's in conference with EMI. No, I'm afraid he won't be in today. Nor tomorrow. No, I really couldn't say when he'll..."

Somewhere in the course of all this, Gladys nodded her head towards the door at the back of her reception area and mouthed silently at me: "He's in the office."

I recognised Gladys's telephone diversionary tactics from long experience of them. If the call was unimportant she would claim that Sanford was in a meeting. If it was more serious – the bank manager, say, or the accountant – she'd claim he'd just left the office. I'd never heard her say he was away for a few days before so I knew this must be something big.

Sanford Bouche-Torrington was lounging with his feet up on a mound of unopened mail that lay scattered across his desk. He was reading what appeared to be The Daily Telegraph but which, on closer inspection, turned out to be a periodical called "Wild, Wet and Willing" which Sanford had camouflaged behind a copy of The Daily Telegraph. The camouflage was not entirely successful since he had only ever bought one copy of The Telegraph and the headline about the death of Elvis Presley was starting to look a bit faded.

"Come in, come in, my favourite penny scribbler," he said, waving his hand in the general direction of a chair on the other side of his desk, "To what literary masterpiece am I to be treated this fine and lovely day?"

"Gladys has been telling someone you're out of the office until this time next year," I said as I casually swept a heap of magazines from the chair onto the floor, "Who haven't you paid this time?"

"Could be one of innumerable possibilities," he said, "But, in all probability, the printers."

He swung his legs off the desk, stood up and paced around the room with his hands behind his back, Prince Philip-style. "Very common people, printers. All they can think about is base lucre. I tell them, where is your soul, where is your dedication to art and all that is most noble? But my words fall upon stony ground. 'Ere, you done that Theodora stuff yet?"

Sanford has a manner of speaking which can seem strangely disjointed if you aren't used to it. He flits from declamatory oration

101

to banal banter and back again from one moment to the next. It's one of his more charming eccentricities. Not paying his bills is one of his less charming ones.

"That's why I'm here," I said.

"*What's* why you are here?"

"To bring the copy on Theodora."

"Oh, right. Bung it on the desk."

"You'll lose it."

"Don't be bleedin' daft. Bung it on the desk. Now what was I saying?"

"You were waxing rhetorical about your dedication to art and all that is most noble."

The look on his face suggested that he didn't believe a word or it and thought I was trying to pull a fast one.

"You done the stuff about the Queen Mum yet?"

"What stuff?"

"I told you. I'm rushing out a special tribute."

"Rolf Harris, you said."

"What?"

"Rolf Harris. You left a message on my answer machine. It's ten years since Rolf had a hit with 'Two Little Boys'."

Sanford raised an Eton-trained eyebrow. "Has anyone ever told you," he smarmed, "That you don't half talk a lot of bollocks. Who the Hell is going to buy a magazine about Rolf Bleedin' Harris?"

"That's what I thought."

"Never mind Rolf Harris," he said, "The Queen Mum, that's where the money is. I thought I'd call it 'A Loyal Farewell to The Empire's Favourite Granny'. Put a black border around it, Union Jacks all over the place. It'd sell a million."

"But she's not dead," I said.

"True. Do I take it that you think that may be an impediment?"

"Well, black borders, 'farewell'. It sort of gives the impression..."

He sighed and sat down heavily behind his desk. "I suppose you're right. Still, it's always worth being prepared. She could go at any time. How old is she anyway?"

"About eighty, I think."

"Well then."

"She's a tough old bird, though. Could go on for years."

He leaned his head forward and held it in his hands. "There must be someone. How about Cliff Richard?"

"He's even younger," I said, "Only about forty."

"I wasn't suggesting he was about to pop his clogs!" Sanford snapped, "But he's been around so long there must be some excuse for doing a one-shot. Let me see, Cliff Richard, Cliff Richard. If my memory serves me well, Cliff, real name Harry Webb, was born in 1940. Forty years then. That's good. Hmmm, birthday's October. The 14th, I believe. Can't wait that long. First hit, 1958 – that's no good. First number one, 1959, no good either. Ah wait a minute, January 1960 – that's a twenty year anniversary. Hang on, better check the details, make sure I'm not mistaken..." – he pulled down a pop music reference book from a shelf near his desk but I knew this was an unnecessary precaution; where pop music trivia is concerned, Sanford is an authority; he is never mistaken, "Yes, yes. That would be ok. A twenty year anniversary is a nice round number. We could call it 'Cliff Richard – Twenty Golden Years'."

"So what exactly happened in January 1960?" I asked.

"That was when Cliff had his second chart re-entry with 'Living Doll'."

I sucked in through my teeth. Sanford looked at me – "You don't think...?"

"What number did it get to in the charts?" I asked.

"Twenty-eight."

I sucked through my teeth again.

"Oh, bollocks! You're right. As usual. Cliff's no bleedin' good!" – he threw the reference book disgustedly aside, "So what have you got for me today?"

"I just told you. *Theodora – Martyr of a Doomed Generation*."

His face showed no sign of recognition and I was about to essay a choice expletive or two in the hope of jogging his memory when the door opened and in walked Kev.

As you may recall, Kev is the photographer who was snapping pictures of Theodora when I arrived at Spivz on the fateful night. He looks like an unreformed Hell's Angel which makes it all the more odd that his photographs tend to be all romantic and misty. Kev is not want you'd call talkative. He communicates by way of an esoteric code comprising mumbles, murmurs and groans in a variety of expressive timbres. A rising mumble indicates a question, a flat mumble indicates indecision and a low mumble merging into a growl is a good reason to back out of the room quietly without making any sudden movements.

Having entered the room and grunted twice – once to me and once to Sanford – Kev put his metal-covered camera case onto Sanford's desk, flipped open the clasps, pulled out a large manila envelope and slid out two contact sheets showing columns of photos in miniature. Then he pulled out a second manila envelope from which he took an assortment of enlargements of selected pictures.

"These are what?" Sanford asked.

Kev mumbled something incomprehensible.

I glanced at a few of the pictures "They are the photos he took at Spivz on New Year's Eve," I said.

Kev grunted in assent.

"I thought you were doing them for The Sunday Times?" I said.

Kev grunted in a rising tone.

"Well anyway, that's what Theodora told me."

Kev made some rhythmic grumbling noises which I took to be laughter. "Might be able to, well, you know," he said.

Don't get me wrong: Kev does speak from time, just not as often as you might expect, and rarely in full sentences.

I put the contact sheet to one side and flipped through the enlargements. I'm not sure what I was expecting to see. If I'd been hoping to spot a villainous character with waxed moustaches conveniently lurking in the shadows behind Theodora I was dis-appointed. In addition to the posed pictures of Theodora with and without his 'girlfriend', Velma, there were quite a few 'atmosphere' shots of people sitting around drinking cocktails or dancing.

"When did you take these?" I asked, "The ones of people around the club?"

"Before..."

"Before you did the photo shoot?"

"Yeah. Some downstairs. Then some..."

"Upstairs?"

"Yeah."

"How long before?"

He shrugged. "Half an hour. The ones on the dance floor. Fifteen or twenty minutes the..."

"Others?"

"Yeah."

For the benefit of Sanford I translated – "He took the downstairs shots half an hour before the official photo shoot and the upstairs shots about quarter of an hour before."

"Splendid, splendid," Sanford said, "I'll get Ingrid to look at them."

Ingrid is the art editor. She seldom emerges from the basement. It is quite possible that she lives down there permanently.

"Phone me," Kev said, "So, you know..."

"Ok," Sanford said, "If I phone you by two o'clock this afternoon, can you get the prints to me tomorrow morning?"

Kev didn't reply, which Sanford took to mean Yes.

I guess Kev was hoping to sell some photos to one of the style magazines or maybe even to one of the Sunday papers. That would have been nice for Theodora. He'd have loved to have been in a spread of the Sunday Times Colour Supplement even if he'd had to be killed to get there. The London club scene has been getting quite a bit of press coverage lately and the magazines usually like to have photos of the more exotically dressed members of the scene. Which is why, no doubt, Kev's photos concentrated on some of the more outlandishly dressed clubbers. There were a few Regency dandies, someone with green and yellow hair and a pink ballet-dancer's tutu; there was a very sweet photo of two white faced Pierrots and there were about a dozen pictures of Brigitte posing as though she were Marlene Dietrich or Greta Garbo: all lips, cheekbones and backlighting.

Once Kev had left, Sanford quickly flipped through the enlargements and arranged them into two piles. Then he glanced at the contact sheets with the aid of a jeweller's loupe. When he saw a picture he liked he put a circle around it with a wax pencil. Next to some others he put a question mark. I knew that the ones he circled he'd use. The ones with the question marks would be sent down to Ingrid for a second opinion.

I picked up one of the two bundles of enlargements. "So which bundle's for the bin?" I said.

"The one you're holding. Too arty-farty. That's the trouble with Kev. I keep telling him, what we want is movement, energy, bodily fluids."

"Bodily *what?*"

Sanford gave me one of his supercilious looks: "Has anyone ever told you that you have a natural flair for vulgarity?"

"Yes," I said, "You."

"Then I congratulate myself on being right – you have. The body has many fluids and the one I had in mind was perspiration. Otherwise known as sweat."

"I've heard of it," I said.

"How about Princess Margaret then?"

"I fail to see the connection," I said, "With bodily fluids, I mean."

"Tut!" Sanford waved a dismissive hand, "I've moved on from that topic. Why is it you have such difficulty keeping up with me? A one-shot is presently the subject of my discourse. If the Queen Mum isn't suitable, maybe Princess Margaret...?"

"In common with the Queen Mum," I pointed out, "Princess Margaret is alive and is, moreover, not a notable style icon of the younger generation."

"Princess Anne then?"

"Same objection."

"Prince Charles?"

"Well," I hesitated, "Maybe when he gets married?"

"Not *when* but *if*," Sanford said, "Do you think Charles is the marrying kind?"

I shrugged. "What's the sudden obsession with Royals anyway? There must be some pop groups worth a one-shot."

He sighed – "If only. The pop world is dead, that's the trouble. Punk's old hat. There's nothing new on the horizon. Unless this Futurism thing takes off. All we can hope for is a high profile death. Deaths are always good for business. Theodora's ok, I suppose. I'd have preferred a Rolling Stone or a Beatle or a Royal or something, really. Still, you have to work with the material available."

"Is it ok if I take these photos then?" I said, popping the bundle of rejected enlargements into my briefcase.

"Don't let me stop you."

Checking my watch I saw that it was half past eleven. I'd arranged to meet Tyrone in a Greek restaurant in Soho at half-past twelve so I had a bit of time to spare. In spite of all his airs, graces and Eton and Cambridge education, Sanford's special talent is the accumulation of trivial knowledge, most of it in the area of popular music. If he were ever on one of those quiz shows like Brain Of Britain or Mastermind and his specialist subject was The History Of Pop, he'd probably get a perfect score. I've tried to catch him out a few times but have never succeeded. I remember on one occasion I asked him to list all of Tommy Steele's hits and he did so, giving their top chart positions and their B-sides. With a memory like that, I'm surprised he wasn't recruited straight from Cambridge into MI5. If he ever put his mind to espionage, he would be a weapon in human form. He'd be able to waltz into an enemy agent's office, glance at a stack of top secret documents and waltz out again with all the facts committed to memory. Just so long as all the facts were about pop music trivia, that is. His photographic memory doesn't seem to operate on any other areas of human knowledge.

Since I wasn't, at that moment, interested in other areas of human knowledge, I thought I might be able to make good use of Sanford's talents.

"Clifton Chuttle," I said.

Sanford's eyes lit up. He knew I was about to ask him a pop trivia question and the adrenaline was already pumping through his veins.

"Dave Buzzard reckons he used to be in a band. Back in the '70s."

"Indeed he was," said Sanford, "He was actually in two bands. The first was called The Cliff Chuttle Sweet Sound. They were formed in 1968 in an unsuccessful attempt to capitalise upon the success of what one might call the British flower-power groups such as The Move, Traffic and, what was undoubtedly their greatest influence, Simon Dupree and the Big Sound."

I vaguely remembered Simon Dupree's hit, Kites. It was a weird song that began with the sound of wind blowing and a J Arthur

Rank type of gong. God knows what the song itself was all about. Something about someone flying a kite until, half-way through the song, a woman suddenly starts gibbering in Japanese. I decided to air my knowledge. "That's the song with the woman nattering away in Japanese," I said. Airing pop trivia knowledge in Sanford's presence is always a mistake and, no sooner had the words left my mouth than I'd regretted them.

"Japanese!" he sputtered, "Japanese, did you say? Chinese, you mean. The Chinese words were spoken by the very lovely Jacqui Chan."

"The Kung Fu fella!" I said.

"You are thinking of a different chap entirely. Different sex too. Jacqui being a girl. An actress who features in such cinematic blockbusters as 'Krakatoa, East of Java' and 'The World of Suzie Wong'. Legend has it that Chan (the girl not the Kung Fu chappie), who was brought up in Trinidad, could not, in fact, speak Chinese and was taught to recite the words by a Chinese restaurant owner."

"And what did they mean?"

"What?"

"The words. In English. What did the words mean?"

"Probably an order for Number 27, Egg Foo Yong, with a side order of crispy noodles. How the Hell should I know what they mean? The words were spoken in a thick Trinidadian accent and in a Chinese dialect with which I am barely even familiar. But getting back to Chuttle. By 1968 flower power was already a thing of the past, of course, so, in trying to get in on the craze, Chuttle dreadfully miscalculated."

I wanted to find out if Sanford really didn't know the English translation of the Chinese narration in the Simon Dupree record. I've never been able to catch him out on pop trivia and that would be a first but once he's talking it's hard to stop him so I had no choice but to let him rabbit on...

"'67 was the Summer Of Love. '68 was the summer of revolution. Paris burning and all that. All the great flower-power hits were from '67: Traffic's 'Paper Sun' and 'Hole in My Shoe', Simon Dupree's 'Kites', The Move's 'Flowers In The Rain', Scott McKenzie's 'San Francisco'. Nobody was wearing flowers in their hair in '68. The Cliff Chuttle Sweet Sound released their one and only single, 'Sunflower Dreaming', and it didn't even make the Top 100.

"After that. Well, I'm not entirely sure what he did between 1968 and 1971." (For Sanford that gap in his pop trivia knowledge was a monumental admission and I fought hard against the urge to make a face and go 'Na-na-na-na-naaa'. However, that would only have made him sulk so I resisted the temptation.) "But anyway, when glam started happening in the early '70s, Chuttle pops up again, this time in a group called Cliff Edge and The Stardust Warriors. They tried to be a sort of heavy-metal mix of Slade and Sweet but, really, they were more like the poor man's Chicory Tip. At any rate, they put out two singles, 'Silver Slipstream Explosion' in September '72 and 'The Terror Boys' in February '73. The first didn't chart at all. The second made it to number 98."

I interrupted. Once Sanford was in full flow, there is no way of stopping him politely: "In short, what you are saying is that Chuttle was a complete failure. So how did he end up being a record producer?"

"I've hardy even started," Sanford pouted, "I mean, before he was ever in a group he was a solo singer. Rocking Clifton Fierce was his stage name in the early '60s. By the time glam came along, he was already pretty long in the tooth – late 20s or early 30s, I'd say. As far as I'm aware his birth date has never been made public but I think it's reasonable to make a few deductions. He was a rotten front man and a pretty lousy singer but he was a damn' good producer. So by the mid '70s he was concentrating on the production side and he also did some music for TV commercials. You may remember the 'Hedgehog-flavoured Noodle Surprise' adverts? And 'Banish Embarrassing Understains With New Spray-on Pong-go'?

"No? Really? Well, anyway, as far as I can tell, he was making a pretty decent living. But he still wanted to have his own pop band. But by that time even he must have realised that he was too old to be a teen idol so he recruited some teenagers and formed a band called The Atlantic Village Skaters."

"I've heard of them," I said.

"You have?" There was a look of disbelief on Sanford's face.

"Well, not until yesterday. Dave Buzzard told me about them."

Sanford smiled, his smug pride in his unique knowledge of pop trivia fully restored. "But once again," he said, "He'd left it too late. He was trying to capitalise on the success of The Bay City Rollers but the last top ten hit The Rollers had was in '76."

"'Bye bye, baby'," I said.

"'I Only Wanna Be With You,'" Sanford corrected, "'Bye bye Baby' was '75."

"Well," I said, "I was close."

Sanford sniffed dismissively. "Hardly. 'Bye bye Baby' was a number one March 1975, then there was 'Give A Little Love' – another number one in July, then came 'Money Honey' in November, which was the beginning of the end as it only got to number three, then in April of '76, 'Love Me Like I Love You' went to number four. And then they had their last top ten hit with 'I Only Wanna Be With You' at number four in September."

"And that was their last hit," I said, trying to pretend I had known that all along.

"Their last top ten hit," Sanford said, "But not their last chart hit. They got to number sixteen in May of '77 with 'It's A Game' and to number 34 in July with 'You Made Me Believe In Magic.'"

Curious as it may seem, I have only a very limited interest in the hits of The Bay City Rollers and Sanford had exceeded that limit about six hits ago. I reminded him that it was the career of Clifton Chuttle that was of more interest to me.

Sanford gave me a look of withering contempt and got back to the main topic: "Well, as I was saying, Chuttle had missed the boat with flower power, glam and Rollermania. So now he's convinced that he can finally be ahead of the game with this Futurist band of his, The Sexteens."

"Not to mention his Nouveau Expressionist band, Mascara Addiction," I said.

Sanford fixed me with a gimlet stare. "There's no such thing as Nouveau Expressionist," he said, "If there were I would have heard of it."

"They're the only one," I said, "So I am informed."

I may have mentioned his condescending eyebrow before – he gave it me now at full throttle.

It was five past twelve when I left and Gladys was still on the phone: "Yes, that's right, Marseille. It's in France. Yes, at least a week. I'll be sure to tell him as soon as he gets back..."

I waved to her and set off for the underground station.

Chapter 13

Tyrone was already a third of the way through a bottle of Retsina when I arrived at the Athenian Gazebo restaurant. I wanted to be mentally alert when we went to Spivz after lunch so I resolved to drink sparingly, a resolution which, given my strong aversion to Retsina (a beverage which I find only slightly more appetising than mouthwash) would not be difficult to keep. I ordered a meze for two and we picked our way through the various dishes while simultaneously making notes on two A4 pads of paper – one for me, another for Tyrone.

Tyrone had also brought a roll of perforated paper sheets onto which had been printed a grid of little boxes, most of which were empty, but some of which contained words printed in little black dots. This, he told me, was something to do with a spreadsheet which, as I think I mentioned before, is a special kind of computer program. Why there should be special kinds of computer programs for catching killers I cannot say. All I can tell you is what Tyrone told me. Along the top of the grid there were people's names:

Theodora | Brigitte | Zipgun Dandy (and so on)

Down the left-hand column of the sheet there were times entered at five minute intervals. At certain points where the columns of names and the rows of times intersected, there was the name of a location. So, for example, in the column headed with Brigitte's name, 'Cocktail Bar' had been entered into the box on the row labelled '11:45'. I suppose I must have told Tyrone that I'd seen Brigitte in the cocktail bar at that time and he had entered the information into his spreadsheet thing. I wasn't at all convinced that it would be any use but it seemed to please Tyrone and, as we talked, whenever I told him that so-and-so was in such-and-such a place at any given moment, he'd write the location into the appropriate box on his spreadsheet.

We both ate, Tyrone drank and, between mouthfuls of green slimy things with rice and leathery slithery things with olives, I gave him details of all I had discovered from the my visit to the studio the day before. I told him about my talk with Dave Buzzard in the pub and I told him about my meetings with The Sexteens and Mascara Addiction. I tried to remember everything of interest that

Clifton Chuttle and Brigitte had told me and I also went over a few of the more interesting things I'd learnt from Adam Xeon and Lala on the tube journey back.

We were finishing the last of the baby octopus tentacles when I completed my report. Tyrone jotted down a couple more notes on his A4 pad and filled in another box or two of his spreadsheet. Then he sat back, belched, drank the remaining Retsina and, referring to his notes, said: "So, this is how it stands to date. Suspect: Zipgun Dandy. Business partner and live-in lover of the deceased."

"But they got on so well," I protested, "Ask anyone. They were hardly ever apart."

"Relationships," Tyrone muttered as he slurped some tomato sauce from a tentacle, "Messy things. Very stressful. Think of Cora Henrietta."

"Who?"

"Mrs Crippen. Wife of the more famous Doctor Crippen, who bumped her off."

"Ah."

"But with Theodora and Zipgun it's even messier. Business and pleasure. Dangerous mix. Theodora and Zipgun had arguments. According to what Dave Buzzard told you."

"He might have lied," I said, "Dave makes no secret of the fact that he didn't like Theodora."

"But Zipgun admitted they argued. So you tell me."

"Well, yes. But then again, lots of people argue."

"Zipgun had been having affairs and Theodora had been dipping into the club's profits. Why? To buy drugs?"

"Maybe, but even so..."

"And then there's the locked toilet. That's very interesting. Just before midnight, Theodora leaves the Gallery, never to be seen again, except by his killer. Then Adam Xeon goes to the toilet but finds it locked."

"He *thought* it was locked," I corrected, "Maybe it was stuck. Or maybe Theodora's body was wedged against the door?"

"Possible," Tyrone conceded, "But if so, how did the body manage to unwedge itself when the door was opened less than half an hour later? Let's assume that Adam was correct and the toilet door really was locked. You say the door can be locked manually from the inside. And, once it's locked, it can't be opened from the outside without a key."

"That's what I've heard," I said, "I haven't actually tried it."

"We'll try it. This afternoon."

The waiter butted in then to ask if we would like more octopus, more olives, more Retsina or an ash tray. Since neither of us was smoking I thought this was an odd request. I told him we didn't require any of the above but I'd be grateful if he'd bring a glass of fizzy water. Tyrone ordered a bottle of Schlitz.

Once the waiter had sidled off, balancing a stack of greasy places and a precarious Retsina bottle on his arm, I told Tyrone that I had complete faith in Zipgun's innocence. He was a victim, not a villain. And as for the possibility that Zipgun had bumped off Theodora in the bog then locked the body inside and hotfooted it back to the office to hide the key, that was just plain daft.

"That might explain how the toilet was locked when Adam knocked on the door," I said, "But when they found the body later, the door was unlocked. Are you suggesting that Zipgun went back to the scene of the crime, unlocked the door and hid the key back in the desk in his office?"

"Stranger things have happened."

"Really?" I said, "Name one."

"The Bose-Einstein Condensation," he said.

If the Retsina bottle had still been there I would have been sorely tempted to pick it up and give Tyrone a sound smack around the head. As it wasn't, all I can say is that he had a very lucky escape.

"Besides," I said, "When Zipgun arrived and they told him the door was locked, he didn't say 'Oh, not it isn't!' On the contrary, he went scurrying off to the office in search of the key. Why would he do that?"

"Play acting," Tyrone suggested, "Which brings us to the next suspect: Dave Buzzard. You say you saw him arguing with Theodora less than an hour before the latter's dead body was found. You also saw Theodora hand something to him which he later denied."

"I could have been mistaken," I said.

Tyrone smiled. "I have every confidence in your powers of observation. Besides which, by his own admission, Dave Buzzard hated Theodora."

"But would he have admitted that he hated him if he'd bumped him off?"

"Quite possibly," Tyrone said, "To divert suspicion away from himself. On the other hand, from what you tell me, an awful lot of people disliked Theodora, so that alone is not a compelling motive."

The waiter arrived back with a glass of water, an empty beer glass and a bottle of Schlitz. As he poured the beer from the bottle into the glass I was struck by two things: 1) the waiter's uncanny resemblance to the late Bela Lugosi and 2) Tyrone's equally un-canny and enormously irritating ability to consume vast quantities of alcohol without becoming inebriated. The waiter left the beer bottle on the table and I kept it within close reach in case I should feel a sudden desire to bounce it off Tyrone's skull.

"Dave," I said, "had more reason than most to hate Theodora. Theodora was jealous of him. Jealous that Dave had a record deal with Chuttle whereas he, Theodora, didn't."

"By that reasoning, Theodora might have been jealous of all eight members of both the groups," Tyrone said.

"Theodora once told a journalist that Dave was a junky. I doubt if that was calculated to improve their relationship."

"Good point," Tyrone made another note on his writing pad, "And that brings us to Clifton Chuttle. A seedy character from your description. A middle-aged failed pop musician who, according to rumour, adopts the casting couch method of recruitment."

"But he didn't recruit Theodora," I said.

"Was Theodora his type?"

"Not from what I've heard. General opinion seems to be that Clifton likes them young and pretty. Theodora wouldn't score highly in either category."

"So, the position we have is that Theodora wants to be a pop star. Chuttle is his way to the top but Chuttle isn't interested. I suppose that might, just about, be a motive for Theodora to have a crack at Chuttle. But is it a credible motive for Chuttle to bump off Theodora? I doubt it. But then again, we know that Chuttle left the

Gallery, where he had been sitting most of the evening at a few minutes before midnight. Why would he do that? And where did he go?"

"He said he went for a dance with Brigitte."

Just then the waiter came along again, wiped a wet cloth over the table, which only smeared the last sticky remnants of the meze, and asked us if we'd like mint tea, Indian tea or coffee. We ordered mint tea and a dish of loukoumi which Tyrone indiscreetly called 'Turkish Delight' to the undisguised horror of our Greek waiter. By God, he looked like Bela Lugosi! The tea and the sweets arrived and we continued our discussion.

"Brigitte, I would say, is our primary suspect," Tyrone announced.

I nearly choked on my tea. "Really? Have you ever met Brigitte?"

"Is that relevant?"

"Well, let's just say she doesn't strike me as the archetype of a murderer."

"Is there an archetype? By the way, why do you keep calling him 'she' and 'her'? Brigitte is a man, isn't he?"

"Well, yes. But it's sometimes hard to remember. Everybody calls her, I mean him, 'her'. If you see what I mean."

Tyrone sipped his tea and nibbled a corner off a piece of loukoumi. "We know that Brigitte and Theodora had an argument at, let me see... I made a note of it somewhere.... at about half past nine in Theodora's office. You say Zipgun Dandy heard Brigitte screaming the words: 'I'll kill you! I'll kill you, you bastard! I'll bloody kill you!' Brigitte also confirms they had argued."

"Which," I said, "Must go in Brigitte's favour. If she, I mean he, was guilty, then she, I mean he, wouldn't have confessed to the argument."

Tyrone dismissed my conjecture. "Unsound reasoning. Brigitte may have known that the argument had been overheard and attempted to shrug it off, pretend it wasn't important. But the reason for the argument is interesting. Brigitte caught Theodora up to something with somebody. Who do you think the other person was..."

"Dusty Evsky," I said.

116

Tyrone ran his finger down a page of his notes until he found the relevant paragraph – "Ah yes, Dusty Evsky. Not his real name, I suppose?"

"I believe not."

"So, Brigitte says Theodora was having a quick grapple with the person known as Dusty Evsky. And that's why Brigitte threatened to kill Theodora.

"Later on that night at, now let me see, ah yes, at about ten to twelve, Brigitte suddenly leaves the Gallery. He leaves just after Dusty and just before Clifton Chuttle, Theodora and Adam Xeon. Ah, Adam Xeon. He's another suspect."

"Why?"

"He's our only witness to the fact – if it *is* a fact – that the toilet in which Theodora's body was discovered, was locked. But why should we believe him? Nobody else can confirm that. And when some people went to the toilet at 12:25 or thereabouts, the door was open. Since Adam Xeon was seen to leave the Gallery at shortly after midnight, it's possible that he killed Theodora and then claimed that the door had been locked in order to throw suspicion upon Zipgun Dandy who, apart from Theodora, was the only person who had a key. Who was it, incidentally, who mentioned the fact that there were only two keys to the toilet and that Zipgun had one of them?"

"Adam told me," I said, "When I spoke to him yesterday."

Tyrone harrumphed significantly and jotted down a note next to Adam Xeon's name on his pad. "And finally, we come to Lala Los Alamos. Again, not his real name, I suppose?"

I nodded. "Lala's ok," I said, "I don't think there anything to suggest that he could be implicated?"

Tyrone gave me one of his more supercilious looks. "No?" he said, "The coincidence. The fainting. The mascara. Village People!"

"Ah yes, Village People," – that was troubling me too. Village People were definitely not on the regular Spivz playlist. YMCA and In The Navy are not the sort of songs that hard-core Futurists dance to. Bowie, Roxy, The Normal yes. Village People no. So why did Lala tell me that the DJ, Lady Vlad, had played Village People at midnight? Odd. I'd have to look into that.

"And that brings us to the mascara," Tyrone said, "Why did Lala swap mascara with Theodora?"

"The colour apparently," I said, "Theodora wanted black mascara but he only had Midnight Blue. So he swapped with Lala."

"And Lala subsequently developed an allergic reaction and fainted only to be brought around by smelling salts. Have you found who provided the smelling salts."

"Pete de Gré," I said, "And before you ask, no, it's not his real name. His real name is Peter Grey."

"Isn't that what you said the first time?"

"No," I said, "Well yes and no. It's pronounced the same but written differently. And they weren't smelling salts, they were poppers."

"Which are?"

"Amyl nitrite."

"Oh really? That's very interesting." He made another note on his A4 pad.

"I fail to see why," I said.

"So where did Theodora obtain the Midnight Blue mascara which he swapped with Lala Los Alamos and which precipitated the latter's fainting fit?"

"Why are you so convinced that the mascara has anything to do with his fainting?" I asked.

"Surely," said Tyrone, "There can't be any doubt about it."

"I know who gave him the mascara, as a matter of fact. He told me yesterday, just before I left the studio. It was Brigitte."

Tyrone sat back with a horrible self-satisfied grin on his face while my fingers quivered menacingly over the neck of the empty beer bottle.

Chapter 14

I met Theodora for the first time on the night I saw Spivz for the first time. It was a cold, drizzly night in late October, 1979, and I'd trailed along to a dismal side street in east London, trying to persuade myself that I was going to find the pulsing heart of the capital's night life. Even if I failed to find it, it was my job to pretend I had. Nobody wants to read an article about a scintillating world of glamour only to be told it's just a bunch of people wearing Oxfam cast-offs in a cold and crumbling slum of a building in the East End.

Great Hits had commissioned me to do a two-part feature on the emerging 'electro-club scene' (we didn't really know what to call it at the time so we just called everything 'electro-this' and 'electro-that'). I'd been to Blitz in Great Queen Street, WC2, on the Tuesday and on the Thursday I came to Spivz. The contrast between the two venues was striking. Blitz struck me as a bit squalid – a cramped wine bar with a small dance floor overlooked by a ratty little sitting area upstairs. The whole place stank of sweat, booze and stale cooking fat. But, by God, it buzzed! The place was full, the music was non-stop and the people were like nobody I'd ever seen before in my life. Blitz had been going for almost a year by that time and it was the place to be.

Spivz on the other hand, had only been open for a couple of months and when I went there on that night in October, it was almost empty. The trouble with Spivz when it's empty is that there is an awful lot of emptiness. Put a hundred people into Blitz and the place seems crowded. Put two hundred people into Spivz and it seems deserted, with all the ambiance of an empty warehouse. Maybe it was because it was a Thursday, maybe it was because it was a cold, wet and miserable night; whatever the reason, Spivz had all the warmth and glamour of a suburban cemetery.

That was one why Theodora was so keen on getting publicity at all costs. The other reason was that he enjoyed publicity. Theodora gave me a tour of the place. I was introduced to The Ape – a huge bouncer who looked the way that all huge bouncers look only twice as mean – and Bad Tommy who was in charge of the door and cloak room. Bad Tommy is a fairly nondescript character, average height and build, not particularly good looking; he has lank fair hair and, on that night was wearing a semi-transparent cheesecloth shirt and hideous pale turquoise eye shadow.

Theodora took me up to the Gallery so that we could look down on the dance floor. I suppose there must have been twenty or thirty people there, but most of all there was just emptiness. The music was loud (I remember hearing 'Circus of Death' by The Human League and 'No G D M' by Gina X Performance) but the emptiness made the place seem oddly quiet – like a loud stereo playing in an empty room. I would have said at the time that Spivz was in a terminal spiral; that nothing could have saved it from closure. I was wrong. Whether it was due to articles such as the one I wrote or merely by word of mouth I cannot say but over the next few months, Spivz increasingly became the place that the In Crowd wanted to be seen at.

On that miserable night in October, Theodora had worn a grey pin-striped suit (rather moth-eaten, I thought) with a lace cravat and a strange black velvet hat with trimmed with white feathers. Brigitte was wearing tight black slacks, high heels, a white sweater and dark glasses. His hair was wrapped up inside a sort of a loose hairnet which he informed me was called a 'snood'. Now I come to think of it that was the first time I'd met Brigitte. I told him I'd been to the Blitz earlier in the week and Brigitte said, "Poor you. A bit down market, dahling. Was anyone there?"

"Lots of people," I said.

"No, I mean, anyone of *note*?"

I said I'd met Steve Strange and Rusty Egan.

"You didn't bump into George or Marilyn, did you?"

I told him I didn't remember anyone called George but I did remember Marilyn. Once seen never forgotten. Marylyn was dead ringer for Marilyn Monroe and probably the most glamorous man I'd ever met. "Friends of yours?" I asked.

Brigitte made a face as though he'd bitten into an apple and found half a maggot. "You must be kidding, dahling. Miserable cows the both of them! So what did she say about me then? Slagged me off, I bet."

"Marilyn didn't say anything about you," I said.

"What? Nothing?"

"Nope. Not a single thing."

"Ooh! The bitch!" – and off he stomped – in as much as it is possible to stomp when balancing precariously on six inch heels.

Theodora and I sat in a corner of Harlow's Bar with my cassette recorder on the table between us and my microphone resting on an ash-tray pointing in his direction. I kicked off the interview by asking him about the 'scene'.

"Not just a 'scene'," he said haughtily, "That makes it sound like it's just pretending. I don't pretend anything. I am what I am. Take of my makeup and there is another layer of makeup underneath."

I had no idea what that meant but it sounded good so it all went into the magazine.

Then I asked him about the other clubs.

"What other clubs?" he said.

"Well Blitz, for example."

"Oh, I don't think that's relevant. It's just a sort of Top Rank with Bowie records."

I wanted to know if he'd ever been there.

"Certainly not!" he said, "They probably wouldn't let me in anyway and, frankly, I wouldn't want to go in."

"Why not?"

"Darling, let's just say that some of us set trends and others follow. I set trends. I don't wish to slum it with people who just copy me, if you know what I'm saying."

I asked him about his background.

"I'm really very ordinary. I grew up in a working class household in Yorkshire. But I always knew I was different."

I asked him how he came to set up Spivz.

"We found this lovely old music hall," he said, "And I just knew it would be the perfect venue."

So was he the owner?

He laughed, "I like to think of myself as the Master of Ceremonies."

So if he wasn't the owner, who was?

"Oh, it's so vulgar to talk business, don't you think. I really don't even think about it."

Evasive, I thought.

One thing I noticed was that Theodora was a completely different person when the tape recorder was switched on and when it was turned off. When it was on, he reclined, he posed, he waved his hands to emphasise things and he spoke with an oddly affected accent, almost as though he was striving for Noel Coward but only achieving Larry Grayson.

When I turned it off, he instantly became a very ordinary, likeable bloke with a pronounced Yorkshire accent. He seemed pleasant enough. Harmless, you might say. One of those charming, superficial eccentrics that Britain produces so well and whom everybody loves. Except, in Theodora's case, somebody obviously didn't. Not that I could have guessed that at the time.

Chapter 15

I'd never seen Spivz by daylight before. It looks completely different. More squalid. Midway down a narrow cobbled street, the two-storey building has a facade of crumbling orange stucco through which, at irregular intervals, uneven areas of grey cement and brick can be seen. I was surprised to note that the outer walls, which I had hitherto assumed to be completely solid, are, in fact, perforated by several windows. There is quite a big window to the right of the entrance doors. At night this window is covered on the outside by folding wooden shutters and, on the inside, by curtains. But now the shutters were folded back and, peering through the window, I found myself looking into Harlow's Bar. Almost directly above this, on the upper storey, there is a smaller window which is painted to approximately the same colour as the surrounding wall. Even by daylight, this acts as a reasonably effective camouflage, making the window almost invisible.

The entrance to the club is formed by a set of double doors which are in need of a lick of paint. These are big, solid wooden doors which are set into an archway whose two sides are decorated with relief mouldings of flowers and bunches of grapes. These, I presume, were intended to give it an air of luxuriance in its music hall days; in its present decayed state, however, they only add to its appearance of faded desolation.

Lying on the cobbles to either side of the door there were a few bunches of faded flowers. I stooped to read the card attached to a spray of crocuses: "Theo – too beautiful to live, too young to die."

Fixed to the wall, immediately over the doors is a neon sign which spells out the name 'Spivz' in script-like lettering. At Tyrone's suggestion, we walked on past the entrance until we arrived at the narrow alleyway that runs along the side of the building. When a queue of people forms outside the entrance doors, the tail of the queue is directed down this alleyway in an attempt to avoid blocking the cobbled street at the front of the club. The alleyway is bounded, on its left, by the side wall of Spivz and, on its right, by the wall of the adjoining building. The only feature of any note in this alleyway is a small window, the glass of which is once again painted to match the wall, on the upper storey of Spivz. This, I presumed to be the window to the upstairs toilet. The alleyway continues along the side wall of Spivz and then turns sharply left to run along the back of the building, where it finally arrives at a dead end. The only features of note at the back of Spivz are two sets of wooden double doors at ground level and a fire-escape leading up to a door on the upper storey.

Frankly, I couldn't see anything of interest but Tyrone kept making little "Aha!" noises as though his powers of observation combined with his superior intellect were finding clues everywhere he looked. Which, of course, he wasn't; he just likes to give that impression.

We finally made our way back to the entrance doors at the front of the building. Tyrone pushed at the left hand side of the double door. It didn't budge. I saw him raise his left leg with the heel of his foot aiming towards the door.

"What are you doing?" I said.

"The door won't budge," he said.

I realised in horror that he was planning to kick it. Tyrone is what you'd call impulsive. When he has a thought there is often no interval between the thinking and the doing. For all I know, this may be a good thing in the world of theoretical physics. It is by no means as good in the world of practical door opening. I pushed at the right hand side of the double door. It swung open. Tyrone put his foot back on the ground and mumbled something that include the words "I knew that" and "spoilsport". I was already having second thoughts about bringing him. We entered the darkened lobby and the darkness became even darker as the door swung shut behind us.

Suddenly there was a blinding flash of white light.

"What the...?"

"Oh, hi. Didn't see you there."

It was Dusty Evsky. Wearing, as always, his Schott Perfecto biker's jacket, he was kneeling at the foot of the wooden staircase a few yards in front of us. He was holding a camera with an attached flash-gun, its lens angled up the stairs to the floor above.

"What are you doing?" I asked, "Collecting evidence?"

He smiled. "From what I hear, that's more in your line of work than mine. No, I just like old buildings, is all. To be honest, I prefer taking shots without flash. Fast film, good and grainy for atmosphere. But that way you lose out on detail."

"Anyone else around?" I asked.

"I think most of the guys are in the dance hall, setting up the kit. You staying for the rehearsal?"

"Maybe," I said, "Is Zipgun here?"

"Upstairs, I think."

Just then the sound of high heels rattling on wood alerted us to the fact that someone was running down the stairs. Looking in that direction we were greeted with the sight of Brigitte flouncing towards us in a dazzle of cerise sequins, screeching, "I can't stand another minute of that fucking' oh!, I didn't know we had company," – Brigitte segued between a screech and a gush without pausing for beat – "So lovely to see you again, dahling," he air-kissed me on both cheeks, "And who is your *cute* little friend."

I introduced Tyrone and, somewhat to his discomfiture, Brigitte flung his arms around Tyrone and planted a big and noisy kiss firmly on his lips. This left Tyrone with plum-coloured lips but I didn't tell him as I thought the colour rather suited him.

"Sorry for swearing, petals, but it's fucking Zippy. That's what I call him," Brigitte put a hand to his mouth and tittered behind his fingers, "I used to call Theodora 'Bungle Bear'. Well, that's what they were like – Theo all big and stupid and Zipgun all bleedin' mouth. So what are you up to, dearest?" Brigitte had now turned his full attention to Dusty; he flung his arm around Dusty's leather-clad shoulder, gazed adoringly into his eyes and pouted, "Why are you taking pictures of this boring old staircase when you could be taking pictures of me?"

"I've taken loads of pictures of you," Dusty protested.

Brigitte pulled away, posed with hands on hips, shoulders thrust forward and an elaborate pout on his lips. "But dahling," he said, "You can never take too many of me!"

"You don't get along with him?" – this was the first time Tyrone had spoken since we'd arrived, "Why not?"

Brigitte simpered at Tyrone now. "You've got a lovely voice. has anyone ever told you? You're not a radio announcer are you? No. An actor maybe?"

"He's a physicist," I said.

"What's one of those?" asked Brigitte, "Whatever it is, he's got a beautiful intonation. Gravelly, sort of. Butch and yet sensitive."

I don't think I had ever seen Tyrone blush before. He was making up for lost time.

"Don't get along with *who*?" Brigitte said.

Tyrone clenched his teeth which I knew was a sign of irritation. He hates it when people can't make head or tail of what he says. I didn't want things to get off on the wrong foot so I butted in – "I think he meant Zipgun."

"Oh, Zippy!" said Brigitte, "He's ok, I suppose. Usually. Just a bit of a fuckin' idiot, that's all. Ever since Theo got bumped off, he's become sort of unhinged. He thinks I did it! Can you believe that? He hasn't actually said so. Not to my face. But I know what he's thinking."

"Why does he suspect you?" I said, "You've got the perfect alibi, haven't you?"

"Me? Yea, my alibi is that I didn't fuckin' do it. Apart from that, it might as well have been me as anyone. He's got lovely eyes, hasn't he, your friend. What's his name?"

"Tyrone," I said, "And he can speak. I mean, you don't have to talk through an interpreter."

Brigitte wafted a well-manicured hand at me – "Don't be sarcky, you! So what's my alibi then?"

"I mean, you were dancing with Clifton Chuttle, round about midnight and a bit afterwards so you couldn't have been killing Theodora."

Dusty laughed. "She was dancing with who?"

Brigitte simpered, "Yeah, well, that's right, I was. Clifton and me a couple of dances."

126

Brigitte snuggled closer to Dusty and started nibbling one of his ear lobes.

"Why him and not him?" Tyrone said in that oblique manner of his which he alone believes to be a model of clarity.

"What Tyrone means," I said is, "How come you and Dusty didn't...?"

"We're not married, you know!" Brigitte said, pulling away from Dusty and straightening out his blouse.

"So where were you, then?" I asked Dusty, "At midnight, I mean? On New Year's Eve?"

"Why are you so interested? You think I'm the killer?"

"Nobody thinks you're the killer, dahling" Brigitte said, "It's *me* they think's the killer!"

"I was around," Dusty said, "I don't know. Harlow's maybe. Yeah, probably in Harlow's having a few beers. Not," he added, looking me straight in the eye, "That it's any of your business."

"It's posterous," Brigitte continued, "Have you ever heard of anything more posterous, dahlings? Me? Kill someone? How positively posterous. He was strangled, for God's sake! With a scarf! How could I strangle somebody? With *these* nails?"

Brigitte waved his fingernails in front of us. They were varnished the same plum colour as his lips.

"There's one broken," Tyrone said.

"Is there?" Brigitte looked mortified.

"Index finger, right hand."

"Oh yes, so there is. Not surprised, really, in this dump. I mean, have you ever tried running up and down a rickety old staircase in six inch heels?"

Tyrone assured Brigitte that he had not.

"Well, if you had, you'd know. The number of times I've nearly fallen. No wonder I've broken a nail trying to save myself! This place is like a fucking battlefield, dahlings, a fucking battlefield."

We left Dusty and Brigitte in the lobby and made our way upstairs. The staircase itself is uncarpeted and each wooden stair creaked as it was stepped upon. At the top of the stairs we arrived in the upper corridor. The door leading to the Gallery was immediately before us. We ignored it and turned to the right. Just beyond the staircase there is a solid door set in the right-hand wall.

There was a hand-lettered sign pinned to the door saying: "Manager's Office – Private". I knocked. A string of obscenities was shouted from within. Moments later the door was jerked open and Zipgun Dandy appeared, red in the face, and giving forth with a colourful range of expletives some of which were new to me.

He paused for breath, giving his eyes a chance to get us into focus and, "Ah, it's you," he said, wiping some spittle from his lower lip, "I thought it was..."

"Brigitte?"

"Yes. How did you know?"

"Call it a good guess."

"And this is...?"

I introduced Zipgun to Tyrone and vice versa and we all went inside.

The office is fairly spacious but untidy. It is also dark thanks to the fact that the single window is painted over. This makes no difference by night but by the day it adds to the general sense of oppressiveness. The lighting is supplied by a single dismal light bulb inside a paper Chinese lantern hanging from the ceiling plus a brass desk lamp with a green glass shade standing on a large mahogany desk.

The desk is impressive. It is oval in shape when viewed from above and its top is covered in burgundy leather; this rests on two intricate carved pedestals, each of which houses four sets of drawers; an additional drawer spans the 'knee-hole' gap between the two columns. An equally imposing burgundy leather high-back chair was set behind the desk with its seat pushed into the knee-hole. On top of the desk there was an electric typewriter, a calendar, a phone and a small stack of mail. Nothing else. It looked as though someone had been cleaning the desk recently.

The remainder of the furniture in the room was less impressive – merely old rather than antique. There were two faded leather armchairs, two uncomfortable-looking wooden-backed chairs and a moth-eaten green chaise-longue. The floor was bare and the floorboards were stained and rickety. The bricks of the wall were exposed and much of the wall-space was hidden beneath posters: Liza Minnelli in a bowler hat straddled a chair with a black-stockinged leg on a poster for 'Cabaret'; there were several art nouveau posters in brilliant colours and various black-and-white film posters featuring Dietrich, Crawford, Garbo and Bogart. There was even a poster showing an elegant man and women lounging on the balustrade overlooking the sea which gave the impression it might have been painted on Corfu or Capri but was in fact proclaiming the delights of Scarborough.

"Thanks for coming," Zipgun said, "It's been a bit of a nightmare what with the police and the press. Trying to get everything sorted out, I mean. A bit of a... do you want a drink? We could go to the bar if you..."

I shook my head but Tyrone looked undecided.

"You plan on reopening the club?" I asked.

"Yes. Oh, yes. Absolutely. Of course. Life has to go on, hasn't it."

"Have you spoken to the police?" I asked.

"I told you. When you came round the other day..."

"And since?"

"Yes. Several times. They were here for a while. In the club. Well, you know. Fingerprints and stuff. Forensics – is that what it's called? Poking around, anyway. Looking for... well, I'm not sure what exactly. They took a lot of photographs."

"And you still think they suspect you?"

"Yes. But there's no evidence. Well, there wouldn't be, would there. I didn't do it. Trouble is, there's no evidence for anything really. Well, you know what it was like here on New Year's Eve. The place was packed. There was loads of people just milling around, wasn't there."

Tyrone suddenly asked, "What did they take?"

"You what? What did *who* take?"

Tyrone was referring to the police forensics investigators. I could tell that because I know the way Tyrone's mind works but Zipgun wasn't following so I had to fill in the gaps for him.

"Oh them!" Zipgun said, "You want to know what they took?"

Tyrone confirmed that that, indeed, was the gist of his question.

"What, you mean like hairs and fingerprints and stuff? Oh, yes, they got lots of fingerprints. And stuff. Too much, though, that's the trouble. See, even though the toilet is supposed to be private, people use it all the time. They are just too damned lazy to go to the toilets downstairs. So the upstairs toilet's covered in the fingerprints, hairs and, well, other stuff from dozens of different people. Which, if you are looking for evidence, makes it pretty damn' worthless, I gather. One of the police people told me their job would have been a lot easier if only they'd had the scarf. The one Theodora was strangled..."

Zipgun stopped suddenly and turned away. I got the impression that he was clenching his teeth, willing himself not to cry. Or maybe he was just putting on an act for our benefit. After a few moments he continued – "But, there you go, the killer wasn't so thoughtful as to leave the murder weapon behind. So inconsiderate, don't you think!"

"We'd better take a look," Tyrone said.

"What? In the toilet?"

"Everything," Tyrone said.

It was obviously going to be simpler if I did most of the talking. Brevity may be the soul of wit but it can also get people's backs up if they are not used to it. "What Tyrone means," I said, "Is that it might be useful if you could give us a guided tour of the premises so that we may have the opportunity of filing in a few gaps."

"Gaps in what?" said Zipgun.

"In my spreadsheet," said Tyrone.

Zipgun looked blank.

"It's a big sheet of paper with squares on," I said, "Like graph paper, sort of."

"And why is he...?"

"He does things with computers," I said, "It could help. To find the killer, I mean."

"He's a friend of yours?" Zipgun said.

I nodded.

"And he can be trusted?"

I nodded again though with somewhat less conviction.

"And he..."

"And he speaks perfectly good English," Tyrone interrupted, "So if you have anything to say why don't you say it directly to him. Can I ask you something?"

"Fire away," said Zipgun.

"Who has access to this office? Specifically, who, on the night of the murder, had been in here?"

"Hard to say. Well, I mean, Theodora and I were here, 'cos it's our office. Brigitte was here because I heard her shouting at Theodora. Saying she'd kill him. The bitch. I told the bobbies, I said I don't know why you're on to me all the time. They'd be better talking to Brigitte. Cheap bloody tart as she is!"

I found it hard to picture Brigitte strangling Theodora to death. It's true that Brigitte isn't as sylph-like and petite as she might like people to think, but Theodora was no lightweight either. I don't really think Zipgun thought Brigitte was the killer either. But he didn't have anyone else to blame.

"That was about half past nine," he said, "When I heard Brigitte threatening him."

"Did anyone else come up to the office that night?" Tyrone asked.

"I suppose Bad Tommy might have come up. Tommy and Brigitte were taking turns on the door and Tommy was on first so he probably came up to get the book of entrance tickets and the cash box."

"Anyone else?"

"Not sure. It's possible. I mean, anyone who knows me or Theo might have popped up. Oh, and yes, there was someone else. Just before the photo shoot. It might have been about half past ten, I suppose. I went to call on Theodora to tell him the photographer was ready to do the session. You know, in the Gallery, over by the cocktail bar. I was just about to open the door to the office when Theo called out, 'Wait a minute!' so I waited, thinking maybe he was doing something that, you know, he didn't want anyone to see. And almost right away he opened the door and I told him the photographer was ready and he came out and shut the door behind him which was, you know, a bit odd. And I said, quietly like, 'What's up? Anything the matter?' and he said, 'No. It's nothing.' He said he was just putting on his mascara and I said, 'Who's in there?' and it was like he was going to tell me but then he changed his mind and said, 'It's not important. I'll tell you later, ok?' and I said 'Ok' And I went back to the cocktail bar with the photographer. Theo joined us a minute or two later. I remember the first thing he did was go over to Lala and I think that was when they swapped mascara and then Theo went out again to fix his makeup. Then he came back to do the session."

"Let me get this clear," Tyrone said, "When he came to the door he said that he was 'just putting on his mascara'?"

"Yes."

"Was he wearing mascara at the time?"

"I can't remember."

"Was he holding a bottle of mascara?"

"No."

"Have you got any idea who was in the office with him?"

"Yes. I know exactly who was in the office with him. After he shut the door, I stayed there. And I listened. They were having the same old argument. Theodora wanted a record deal. More than anything, he wanted that. But Clifton didn't think he had what it took."

"You are saying it was Clifton Chuttle in here?"

"Yes."

"You are sure?"

"Absolutely."

Just then there was a knock at the door. Zipgun wiped his tearful eyes with his forearm. This has the unfortunate side effect of leaving a streak of eyeliner on the sleeve of his jacket. "Come in!" he yelled.

It was Anvil Evans, the drummer with Mascara Addiction.

"We got all the gear set up now," he said, "We're pretty much ready to start rehearsing. But we ain't seen Dusty. You ain't seen him, 'as you?"

"He was in the lobby a few minutes ago," I said.

"Ah right. I came up the stairs from the dance floor to the Gallery," Anvil said, "That's why I never seen him, I guess."

He was just about to shut the door when Zipgun called out, "Here, can you take this to Brigitte? It came in the morning's mail." He handed over a manila envelope which had been in the stack of mail on the desk, "I'd give it to her myself only I might not be able to resist the temptation of kicking the little whore in the nuts while I'm at it."

Anvil smiled, unsure whether or not Zipgun had made a joke, took the envelope and went out, shutting the door behind him.

"I can't help noticing," said Tyrone, "That the desk looks very tidy. Compared to everything else, I mean."

Zipgun smiled. "Your friend," he said to me, "Doesn't mince his words, does he? What you are saying is that the place is a mess, right?"

Tyrone confirmed that this had been his meaning but added – "The one exception being the desk. Looks like it's had a good clean and tidy. Recently."

"You might be right," Zipgun conceded.

"With the aim of concealing something. You mentioned the police had been here. Inevitable, really. I suppose they might have looked into the desk."

"You suppose right," said Zipgun, "Not when they came first of all. They were only bothered about the crime scene that time."

"The toilet?" Tyrone said.

Zipgun nodded. "The toilet. But the next day they came and had a good scout around all over the place. They didn't find nothing though."

"And what," said Tyrone, "would they have found in the desk if you hadn't already removed it?"

Zipgun looked at Tyrone then he looked at me. I wasn't sure if he was going to bawl us out or throw us out. In the end he did neither. But I sensed that took an effort of will. "I cleaned out the drawers, that's all. Theodora kept a few things in there that the police didn't need to know about. He had a few little habits, let's say. I didn't think it would do his memory any good for anyone to find out about them. And besides it was about time this old desk had a bit of a clean and polish."

"Can I have a look in the drawers?" Tyrone asked.

That was when the screaming began.

Chapter 16

By the time we got to the bottom of the stairs a small crowd had gathered. For a moment, I had an acute sense of déjà vu. On New Year's Even there had been a crowd in the lobby gathered around the stationary body of Lala los Alamos. This time, they were gathered around Brigitte.

Dusty was sitting with his arm around Brigitte on the bottom stair. Anvil Evans, Joe Jonson and Dave Buzzard were there too. Even Lady Vlad, the club DJ, had come to see what the matter was.

Brigitte was sobbing gently on Dusty's shoulder.

"What's going on?" Zipgun said as he trotted down the steps.

Dave Buzzard shrugged – "We know as much as you do."

"Probably saw a rat," Anvil Evans suggested, "There's some big buggers in this place."

"Dusty?" Zipgun said, "What happened?"

Dusty stroked Brigitte's hair – "Don't know. I was only gone a couple of minutes. I was in Harlow's with Brigitte. Then Anvil comes down and tells me the band was ready to start rehearsing. So I go in to get everything set up and then all of a sudden I heard Brigitte screaming the place down and so I ran out and that's all I know."

At the next moment there was a loud creaking noise and a gust of cold air. I turned to look towards the entrance doors which had been opened. Someone was standing there, silhouetted by the wintry light that looked curiously bright by contrast with the gloom of the lobby. It was Lala. He was wearing a Burberry trench coat, a pink double-breasted suit and a pink fedora (where on earth did he get a *pink* fedora?). As he entered, everyone's eyes were fixed upon him. He paused for a second and then said, "Whatever it was, I didn't do it!"

Anvil laughed – "Come on, lads. We've got a band to rehearse."

With some muttering, Dave Buzzard and Joe Jonson followed Anvil back into the dance hall. Dusty told them he'd be along in a few minutes. Lady Vlad said, "They've got rats here the size of cats," and she followed the other three, leaving me in the lobby with Zipgun, Dusty, Tyrone, Lala, Brigitte.

"So," said Lala, "What have I missed?"

"Not exactly sure," I said, "We heard a scream and came running but...."

Brigitte raised his face from Dusty's shoulder and flicked out his hand dramatically. He was holding a manila envelope. It was, in fact the same envelope that Zipgun had taken from his desk and asked Anvil to give to Brigitte a few minutes earlier.

Without waiting to be asked, Tyrone immediately reached out and snatched the envelope from Brigitte's hand. From it, he took a folded sheet of paper which he unfolded. He read aloud what had been typed upon it: "Don't screw with me. You know what I can do."

"There's more," Brigitte said, "Inside".

Tyrone looked into the envelope then turned it upside down and shook something into the palm of his hand. It was a small white silk tassel.

"From a scarf, I'd guess," he said.

"From Theo's scarf," Brigitte said, "The scarf he was wearing that night. The one he was... strangled with."

"That's very interesting," said Tyrone with a broad smile.

There's one thing you have to say about Tyrone: clever he may be; diplomatic he definitely isn't.

*

Call me a stickler for tradition if you like, but I would have said that the letter and the silk tassel were material evidence of an important and sensitive nature; the sort of thing that the police chaps who were investigating Theodora's murder would have wanted to get their hands on with the utmost alacrity. Tyrone, however, as I think I've mentioned before, is a freelance physicist. Freelance physicists are not like the rest of us. With the speed and sang-froid of a conjurer, he slipped the envelope and its contents into an inside pocket, took Zipgun by the arm and, saying, "I believe you were about to show us around the place," led him back upstairs, niftily skirting Dusty and Brigitte who were still sitting – the former providing a cosy shoulder onto which to sob; the latter taking full advantage of the shoulder-sobbing opportunities – on the bottom stair. I followed Zipgun. Lala said he'd hang around with Brigitte for a while and would see us later.

At Tyrone's suggestion we began the tour of the club back in the office. Tyrone was still interested in the desk. He opened each drawer in turn and discovered that they contained a variety of perfectly harmless objects such as papers and pencil sharpeners, a stapler, some notepads (with several moderately obscene doodles but no notes of any consequence), rubber bands, a box of petty cash, some raffle tickets and a well-worn glossy magazine which Zipgun described as a "fitness magazine" but which, based on a cursory glance, contained photographs of young men doing exercises of a nature which would be most unlikely to go down well at the local gym.

"The drugs," Tyrone said.

"What?" said Zipgun.

"What were they?" said Tyrone, "The drugs. In the desk. The ones you removed."

Zipgun muttered something about preferring not to say anything about that and that it would be better to leave bygones be bygones, so Tyrone said: "I'll assume cocaine, heroin and cannabis," and he made a note on the A4 pad which he was carrying around with him.

"And amphetamines," Zipgun added.

"And he kept them in which drawer?"

"The top one," Zipgun said, "Oh, and sometimes MDMA."

"MDMA *is* an amphetamine," Tyrone said, "Methylenedioxy-methamphetamine to be precise."

Tyrone slid open the top drawer. It was a lovely piece of craftsmanship: a hinged brass handle on the outside, red velvet lining on the inside. The movement of the drawer was smooth and silent. And it contained nothing but some small coloured paper packets containing guitar strings and a Yale key.

"The strings are Dave Buzzard's," Zipgun explained.

"And the key?" Tyrone picked it up.

"The key to the toilet."

Tyrone the strode out of the office and turned left. I am used to Tyrone and didn't find anything surprising in his abrupt departure. Zipgun, however, was not used to him and did. He asked me where he'd gone, why he'd gone and was he always like this? I answered: Don't know, don't know and yes and the only way to find out is to follow him which is what we did.

When you leave the office and turn left you either have the option of turning left again, in which case you end up going back downstairs or you can carry straight on in which case you arrive at a door in the left-hand wall beyond the stairwell. The door is painted in flaky green paint. Without asking, Tyrone opened it, walked inside and flicked a light switch on the wall. The naked light bulb that was thus illuminated revealed some stacks of mouldering folding chairs against the far wall of the small room and a big heap of spongy blue gym mats occupying the middle area.

"These are for?"

"The chairs were here when we took on the building," said Zipgun, "Before we arrived it was rented out by a Methodist Ladies' Club. I couldn't tell you what they used the chairs for though."

"Sitting upon might be a reasonable conjecture," said Tyrone.

"The mats belong to a local judo club. We rent them space downstairs on Monday and Wednesday afternoons."

"They were here yesterday?" asked Tyrone.

"No, not since before Christmas. They start back next week."

His interest in the store room sated, Tyrone flicked off the light and continued down the corridor. There wasn't far to continue. The end wall was just a couple of yards away. Before we arrived there, however, a small door opened on our right. Tyrone once again went in and turned on the light. This was another store room with some lamps and metal brackets and various metal boxes and switches on the wall.

"The electrics," Zipgun said.

I thought I caught a hint of a glare flicker over Tyrone's face. He doesn't take kindly to being told the obvious.

"And the murder scene itself?"

There was a catch in Zipgun's voice when he answered — "D'down the other end of th'... the corridor."

We turned around and walked back up the way we'd come. Tyrone paused at the head of the staircase and pointed to the door in the left-hand wall immediately in front of it. "That goes into the Gallery?" he said.

Zipgun said that it did.

We walked on, once again passing the office, until we arrived at a small passageway which turned off on our right. In this passageway there are two doors on the left but a blank wall on the right. Tyrone walked down the passageway and opened the further of the two doors. It led into yet another storeroom, quite small. Its walls were covered with shelves. On the shelves there were plastic beakers, paper serviettes, cloths and brushes, boxes of light bulbs and other run-of-the-mill items. Beneath the shelves, on the floor, there were some buckets and mops and bottles of detergent and disinfectant.

Finding nothing of any interest, Tyrone left that room and walked a few steps back along the small passageway until he arrived to the other of the two doors.

"The murder scene?"

Zipgun nodded. "If you don't mind, I don't want to go in there."

"Why not? It's just a toilet, isn't it?"

Zipgun's face crumpled slightly. For a moment he looked quite pathetic. "I'd prefer not to," he said, "I'll see you later, ok. Back in the office."

Tyrone shrugged and Zipgun left.

"Strange fella," Tyrone said, "Why doesn't he want to see a toilet? Has he got a phobia, do you think?"

"His lover was strangled to death in there," I said.

"I know," Tyrone said, "What has that got to do with a phobia of toilets?"

"He hasn't got a phobia of toilets," I said, "He just doesn't want to see this one."

"Then that's a phobia of toilets," Tyrone said.

"Don't be obtuse," I said, "It's not a phobia of toilets,. There's no such thing as a phobia of toilets!"

A look of manic triumph came into Tyrone's eyes. It's a look that told me he'd set a trap and I'd just fallen into it. "No such thing as a phobia of toilets! On the contrary. There are many and diverse phobias of toilets. For example, there is ablutophobia: the fear of washing; aquaphobia: the fear of water; paruresis: the fear of urinating in public; parcopresis: the fear of defecating; agoraphobia:

the fear of being trapped; claustrophobia: the fear of confined spaces..."

"Yes, yes, ok," I said, "You've convinced me."

"And of course if there are spiders in there we'd have to consider the possibility of arachnophobia; if it is haunted it may be a case of phasmophobia. Then again, if it contains rats, snakes or armadillos..."

Once he gets started on a list the only way to stop Tyrone is to interrupt him. I interrupted: "Are you sure it's ok to go in there? I mean, won't we be spoiling the evidence or something?"

"I can't see any signs saying 'Crime Scene, do not enter'," he replied, "So I think we can presume that any evidence has already been gathered."

Tyrone examined the toilet door. This didn't take long. The door's only notable features were its handle and a keyhole. Tyrone pulled the handle and the door opened. He shut the door. Then he pulled the handle again and once again the door opened; this was no more remarkable the second time than the first. Tyrone looked inside. The toilet was in darkness. There was a pull-string hanging just inside the door. Tyrone pulled it. A light came on revealing a small room with three black tiled walls and a door at the far end.

"Step inside," Tyrone said.

Sharing a toilet is not my idea of a good time and I had no idea what Tyrone was planning. It is, however, usually simpler to do what Tyrone says rather than discuss it in advance. Once we were both inside, he closed the outer door. It was a snug fit. The place was clearly not designed for large parties. On the left-hand wall there was a small wash basin with a mirror mounted over it. Next to the basin there was a metal ring fixed into the wall from which a rather disreputable towel hung. There was no urinal. The room in which we were standing would, I think, be more correctly described as a washroom whereas the 'business area' of the toilet was behind the inner door. Tyrone opened the inner door – just the once this time; it seemed to lack the fascination of the outer door – looked inside and pulled the chain to operate the flush.

"Interesting," he said.

"What is?"

"The flush mechanism."

"What about it?"

"It's an old Thomas Twyford design with a Jennings flush-out siphon."

"Is it significant?" I asked.

"Not at all." He gave me one of those looks that suggested that having to suffer the inferior intellect of others was the great burden of his life, "I didn't say it was significant. I said it was interesting."

He then turned his attention to the lock mechanism of the outer door. There was a sort of little chrome-plated dial on it. You turned the dial and it locked the door.

Abruptly, Tyrone turned to me and said, "Strangle me!"

"What?"

"Strangle me. With a scarf."

"I haven't got a scarf."

"What's that got to do with it? I don't want you to strangle me."

"Then why did you tell me to strangle you?"

"I assumed you'd be able to work out that a pretence of strangulation is all that is required. You are the one who's always telling me I'm too literal. But when I speak figuratively, you are completely at sea."

"That wasn't figurative," I said.

"Well metaphorically then."

"Not metaphorical either."

"For God's sake!" he sputtered, "I don't care what part of speech it is – just pretend, can't you? Pretend!"

So I pretended to strangle him with a scarf that I didn't have. Anything to keep him happy.

"Good, good," he muttered, "Plenty of room to strangle someone. Door securely locked. Excellent. Too small for three people, though. Unless they were midgets. Or contortionists. I don't suppose there were any...?"

"New Year's Eve?" I said, "No. As far as I can recall, homicidal midgets and contortionists were pretty thin on the ground that night."

"Excellent! Then it seems reasonable to assume that the killer was alone. He or she would obviously have locked the door from the inside since he would..."

"Or she," I said.

"Yes, yes, he or she. But for the sake of brevity I shall use the masculine participle."

"Pronoun," I corrected. There are many subjects in which Tyrone's knowledge excels but English grammar is not one of them.

"He or she would have wanted to avoid any risk of being disturbed in the act of throttling. If we can believe Adam Xeon, the door was locked after midnight but it was open again twenty minutes later when the body was found."

"But only Theodora and Zipgun had keys," I said, "Which means..."

"Which means," Tyrone said, "That the killer was, in all probability, inside the locked toilet when Adam knocked on the door shortly after twelve. That's the simplest and most likely explanation: killer goes to toilet, strangles victim and is still there with the dead body when he hears someone trying to get in. All he has to do is remain silent until the person goes away again. At which point he leaves. Once he's left, the door, of course, remains open because it can't be locked from the outside unless you've got a key."

"Sounds reasonable," I said.

"Reasonable," Tyrone agreed, "But not necessarily true. Adam might have been lying."

"If it was Adam who killed Theodora."

"Exactly. We'll have to ask him. But first, let's take a look at the Gallery."

*

The London Broadsheet, Saturday, January 3rd, 1980
Flowers For Clubland Murder Victim
by Ian Jones (staff writer)

Dozens of floral tributes have been left outside the Spivz nightclub near Aldgate with messages of condolence. The club was the scene of the brutal murder of fashion-guru, 'Theodora', early in the morning of New Year's Day.

Police said that many lines of enquiry are being followed but so far nobody has been arrested. Theodora (real name Terrence Binton), 21, was a well-known figure in the London club scene. In December, The Sunday Times named him one of the Top 100 'People To Watch in 1980'. He and his partner, 'Zipgun Dandy', have run the nightclub since August last year.

The nightclub, which was formerly a Victorian music hall featured in a high-profile campaign in 1978, aimed at putting the building in public ownership and renovating it to its former glory. Campaigners hoped to have the building officially listed and reopened as a variety theatre. However, The London Broadsheet understands that the club is now in private ownership.

Over the past few weeks local residents have expressed concerns about the behaviour of some club members. "I knew something like this would happen," shop owner Alfred Green (63), told us, "You should see the people that go there. Some real weirdos. A lot of them are drunk or on drugs. People have complained to the police but they never do anything."

*

We went back to the office to get Zipgun. He had taken the opportunity, I noticed, to refresh his previously tear-streaked eyeliner. Even in grief, he was fastidious about his makeup. The three of us went through the door that led into the Gallery. Leaning over the balcony we could see Mascara Addiction tuning up on the dance floor below.

There was a deafening screech. Dave Buzzard was twanging his guitar directly in front of some speakers stacked on the floor, causing a scream of feedback. Dusty shouted at him to stop it and, after a final screech for good measure, he did so. Dusty, I gathered, was solely doing vocals today due to the fact that the synthesiser which he shared with Adam Xeon was still in Chuttle's studio.

Trying to ignore the discordant noises, I walked around the Gallery, examining it in minute detail. The Gallery is much like the balconies of many old theatres: it is low – ending at about knee height. A metal barrier has been fixed on the inner side with a handrail at about waist height, presumably to reduce the risk of people who, in tripping over someone else's feet, accidentally project themselves over the edge and onto the heads of the people below. The handrail is a modern addition and I can only guess that audiences were either more careful in Victorian days or else the theatre management considered the occasional plummeting patron to be an occupational hazard of no great concern.

Turning to our left, we walked along The Gallery, weaving our way past all the tables and chairs until we arrived at the cocktail bar which is a plain wooden construction painted matt black. There's nothing much to say about this apart from the fact that it's much tattier looking in the light than it seems in the dark.

In the dark, the bar contrives to look glossy and sophisticated. There is a light under the bar itself which shines upward into the bartender's face. The bottles of spirits fixed to the back wall are cunningly illuminated to make them look bright and inviting. When seen by harsh incandescent light, that illusion is shattered.

We moved on until we arrived at the far balcony. Mid-way down this side, there is a set of double-doors recessed into the wall. An illuminated sign over the doors shows it to be an exit. Tyrone pushed the doors. They didn't budge.

"Fire exit," Zipgun explained, "We keep it locked."

"Is that advisable?" Tyrone asked.

"If we didn't keep it locked, anyone would be able to get in or out," Zipgun said, "No problem though. I have a key."

He took a ring of keys from his pocket, selected one and unlocked the door. The three of us walked out onto a rickety metal platform from which an equally rickety set of grid-metal steps descended to the alleyway below. I recognised this as the fire escape at the back of the building which Tyrone and I had seen from ground-level earlier on. It's funny, when you are inside the hall, you tend to think of the back of the building being at the cocktail-bar end, directly opposite to the stage. That isn't the case, though. The wall behind the cocktail bar backs on to an adjoining building. The real 'back' of the building is at the far side of the Gallery and the dance floor which explains why this is the side that has the fire exits. We came back inside and Zipgun locked the door behind us.

"So, let me check this," Tyrone said, "Apart from this fire exit there are only two ways to get from the ground floor to this floor:

143

either by the staircase from the lobby or by the staircase from the dance floor to the Gallery."

"That's right."

 "How many nights a week does the club open?"

"Every night except Sunday and Monday."

"Who was sitting on this side?" Tyrone asked.

I knew the answer to that. People had come and gone throughout the night but, as far as I could recall, for most of the time, at or around midnight, Dusty, Anvil and Joe had been sitting at one table. Lala, Pete de Gré and Clifton Chuttle had been sitting at the next table.

Tyrone glanced at his spreadsheet. "But Dusty left before midnight," he said, "And Clifton Chuttle left a few minutes later?"

"I think so," I said.

Tyrone turned to Zipgun. "Where were you at that time?"

Zipgun pointed at a table just in front of the cocktail bar: "Over there. With Theodora, Velma, Brigitte and Adam Xeon."

"But Brigitte too left before midnight?"

"Yes."

"In fact," said Tyrone, "As I understand it, Dusty left from *this* table," he pointed to a table to his left, "At about ten to twelve. Brigitte left from *that* table," he pointed towards the table immediately in front of the cocktail bar, "Shortly afterwards. Theodora left the same table at about five minutes to twelve. Clifton Chuttle left *this* table," he pointed to the table to his right, "A couple of minutes before twelve? Nobody else left around that time?"

"Not as far as I can remember," Zipgun said, "Except Adam, I think."

Tyrone scrutinised his spreadsheet again – "I have Adam leaving at just after midnight. That's when he went to the toilet and says he found it locked. In the meantime, Clifton Chuttle and Brigitte had gone down to the dance floor. Lala was up here putting on mascara. Squirrel was...?"

"With me," I said, "Downstairs in Harlow's Bar."

"Which," said Tyrone, "Just leaves Dave Buzzard and Dusty Evsky unaccounted for." Tyrone strode towards the staircase leading from the corner of the balcony down towards the stage end of the dance floor. As luck would have it, by the time we arrived downstairs, Mascara Addiction were launching into a raucous song which sounded like a mix of Siouxsie and the Banshees and Donna Summer. Not an obvious blend of musical styles but one which, once heard, is never forgotten.

The band was assembled on the dance floor immediately in front of the proscenium arch that framed the stage. Dave Buzzard was on the left, playing a red mahogany Gibson SG guitar very loudly. Next to him stood Dusty Evsky and next to him was Joe Jonson on bass guitar. Hammering away at the drum-set behind them was Anvil Evans.

Up on stage, I noticed that Lady Vlad, the DJ, was sitting at the record deck sorting through stacks of discs. Lala was sitting on the edge of the stage putting on a fresh coat of nail varnish. Brigitte was lounging against a pillar.

The high volume of the music was not conducive to conversation, so Tyrone mouthed, "I'm going to have a look around," and off he set with me and Zipgun trailing along behind.

The Gallery which overhangs the dance floor is supported by ten deceptively delicate-looking wooden columns carved in a spiralling 'barley twist' design. There are four columns beneath each of the two side-balconies and two at the far end, supporting the cocktail bar area. On the far side of the hall there are two sets of double-doors with 'fire exit' signs over them and a couple of red fire extinguishers standing on the floor to either side. We walked across the dance floor to the area beneath the opposite balcony. Here there are two sets of double doors. Tyrone opened the doors closer to the stage and the three of us walked through.

Now we were back in the corridor near the lobby. Directly in front of us we saw the underside of the wooden staircase which was every bit as decrepit as its upper side. We turned to our left and walked down the corridor in the direction of the stage. At the end of the corridor a small passageway turned off to our right at a right-angle to the main corridor. This is pretty much the same layout as on the upper storey. There were two doors leading off the left-hand side of this passageway. Zipgun used a key to unlock the farther door; it led into an empty, musty-smelling room which Zipgun told us was going to be used for storing the Mascara Addiction drum kit.

"Was this locked?" Tyrone asked, "On New Year's Eve."

"Yes, it was."

"And the upstairs store rooms? Were they locked too?"

Zipgun assured him they were – "If we'd kept them open, we'd have people skiving off to go shoot up or screw. No way. The store rooms were all locked."

"And the room upstairs with the electrics in?"

"Yup. All locked."

"But not your office?"

"No, that's different. Me and Theo, we use that."

The nearer of the two doors had a sign above it saying "Messieurs/Herren" and led into the Gents' toilet.

Tyrone stopped at the door and looked askance at Zipgun. "You'd better stand back," he said.

"Sorry?"

"The toilet. I'm going in. You might want to, you know, stand at a distance."

Tyrone was still convinced that Zipgun was suffering from toilet-phobia. Zipgun looked at Tyrone as though he thought he might be dangerously insane, then he looked at me to see if I agreed. As I've never been entirely certain of Tyrone's mental stability, I smiled noncommittally and shrugged my shoulders. Zipgun pushed open the door and Tyrone congratulated him on his bravery.

This public toilet was more than twice the size of the private toilet on the upper floor but it was no more salubrious or fragrant. The walls were covered with cracked white ceramic tiles, several of which were missing, while the remainder had a good deal of black and green gunge where the grouting should have been. There were two sinks with mirrors over them. The mirrors had seen better days and the silvering had peeled away in several places, leaving ragged brown and green spots. Opposite the sinks there was an ancient urinal. Unlike modern single-user urinals with individual peeing holes set at a convenient aiming level, this one has a communal trough that runs at just below knee height which, in my experience, provides an optimal splash zone. Worse still, whereas modern urinals flush themselves automatically, this one has a cistern set high on the wall at one end. You have to pull the chain to release water to flush down the length of the trough. This provides the user with another opportunity to get splashed should he have missed out the first time around. At the far end of the trough there is a hole through which the flush water enters a downpipe into another trough at floor level which then conducts the water through into its final exit hole.

Tyrone's eye lit up. "Incredible," he said, "A genuine Adams & Co. high-flush urinal. Very rare, you know."

I tried to look fascinated. Finally he pushed open the door to look into the sitting-down toilet. He could not conceal his disappointment. "An Armitage Shanks unit of modern design."

We left the Gents and turned to our right. A short set of steps led upwards and turned sharply left onto the wings of the small stage. Lady Vlad was still sorting through records while beyond the proscenium arch, Mascara Addiction were singing something about the end of civilisation. We retreated down the steps and continued back along the corridor, passing the lobby on our left and continuing to the far end where, on our right, we saw a door marked "Dames/Fraus". This contained a single sit-down toilet which proved once again to be a modern design from Mssrs Armitage Shanks. Tyrone deemed this to be of no interest whatsoever and so we retraced our steps back towards the lobby.

Skirting to one side of the staircase, Tyrone opened a door on the right which led into an empty room with lots of hooks on the wall ("the cloakroom" Zipgun explained, unnecessarily, I thought). There was a door at the end of the cloakroom which, once again, was locked. Zipgun unlocked this and we went into a dank, dimly lit room full of what looked like mouldering curtains. These, we were told, were all that was left of the original stage curtains which were no longer required. It turned out that this storeroom was much bigger than it originally seemed as, at its far end, it turned sharply to the right opening out into a long narrow area. There was no light in this part and nothing much to be seen apart from something scurrying away in the distance which I believe to have been a particularly far and juicy rat.

"Locked too?" Tyrone asked, "On the night in question?"

"The storeroom?" said Zipgun, "Yes, we hardly ever unlock it."

"And the cloakroom?"

"Bad Tommy was in charge."

"He was still on duty at midnight."

"Yes. Well, anyway, yes. I think so."

We left the cloakroom and walked across to the other side of the lobby.

That was where we bumped into Brigitte. He was putting on a black overcoat with an astrakhan collar. It might have been fashionable in the days of Queen Victoria but generations of moths had since had plenty of opportunity to feast upon it.

"I'm off, dahling," he said, "Do I look pale?"

"Attractively so," I said.

He pushed me playfully. Brigitte is stronger than he looks. I nearly overbalanced and it took me a few seconds to recover my breath.

"I meant after the shock," he said, "The murder threat! I'm not sure if I'm safe to be left alone. You can accompany me if you like. Protect me."

"Well, I..."

"Oh no! It's all right. Here's a big butch fella who can escort me home."

"You what?" It was Dusty. He'd just come through the doors from the dance floor into the lobby. He had his leather jacket zipped up, his hands in the pockets of his jeans and a strangely attractive scowl on his face. When he arrived, Brigitte linked arms with him and said, "Now I feel safe. Nothing can harm me!"

They walked together towards the outer doors, Dusty's scowl deepening by the moment. When they got to the doors, Dusty unlinked arms. Brigitte turned to wave – "See you tonight down the Black Cap if you're interested. They got The Trollettes."

"What," Tyrone asked after they'd left, "are Trollettes?"

"I'll tell you some other time," I said and we passed through the door into Harlow's Bar.

Chapter 17

Sitting at a table beneath a black and white poster of Edward G Robinson was a thin, pasty-faced youth with lank fair falling over a pimply forehead. He was holding a magazine called 'Classic Railways' in his left hand and picking his nose with the index finger and thumb of his right hand.

"Hi Bad," I said, "What you doing here?"

"Nothing else to do," he said, "Club's opening next week innit?"

"Is it?"

"That's what they say." He looked to Zipgun for confirmation, "That's right, innit?"

"That's right, Bad."

I introduced Tyrone. Bad Tommy held out his right hand. Tyrone declined to shake it.

"You were on the door?" Tyrone said.

The question was far too oblique to make sense to Tommy so I explained that we were trying to reconstruct the events of New Year's Eve ("Ha! Like Macmillan and Wife!" he said – a cultural reference which clearly meant nothing to Tyrone) and wondered if he could confirm whether he was in the cloakroom as midnight struck.

"Yeah," he said, "I was on the door."

"And nobody else was there?" Tyrone asked.

"Where?"

"In the cloakroom."

Bad Tommy scratched his head, picked his nose again, stuck his finger into his ear and said "In the cloakroom? Nah. Why would anybody be in the cloakroom? There was just me. And The Ape."

"Our head of security," Zipgun said.

"The bouncer," Tommy added.

"You and he were in the cloakroom?" Tyrone asked, "Together?"

I couldn't help feeling the line of questioning was taking an unfortunate direction so I suggested that Tommy might like to go and watch Mascara Addiction commit crimes against music while Tyrone, Zipgun and I had a quiet chat.

"Yeah," said Tommy as he left, "We was in the cloakroom together. I was showing him my Brighton Belle."

When Tommy had gone Tyrone turned to us and explained confidentially, "It's a train. The Brighton Belle. Probably in his magazine. The first all-electric Pullman. Victoria Station to Brighton. Withdrawn in 1972."

There is something frightening about the range of Tyrone's knowledge. "In case you were thinking it might be something else," Tyrone added, "His Brighton Belle, I mean."

Not for the first time in my life, I decided the best way to deal with Tyrone was to ignore him. I suggested that we sit at a table near the door so that Tyrone would have somewhere to arrange his notes. He flipped through his sheaf of paper and brought the spreadsheet-thingummy to the top. He wanted to know how many people had been in Harlow's Bar that night when midnight struck.

"Not sure," I said, "I wasn't paying much attention. Not many though." I pointed to a table next to the shuttered window. "I was sitting there with Squirrel."

It was an old, round-topped stripped pine table stained by the wax drips from the candle that was wedged into the neck of a Pilsner Urquell bottle

Tyrone consulted his notes. "Squirrel being... let me see... the drummer with The Sexteens?"

"Right."

"Whose real name is?"

"Squirrel is his real name," Zipgun said, "At any rate, it's the only one he'll admit to."

"No matter," Tyrone muttered.

"Shall we...?" Zipgun began but immediately Tyrone help up a finger and said "Shhhhh!"

We stood silently for a few seconds. There was nothing to be heard except for the low throbbing of Joe Jonson's bass guitar and the occasional clatter of Anvil's drums.

"It would be difficult to hear the music from here," Tyrone said, "Hard to make out what they are playing, wouldn't you say?"

I told him it would be hard to make out what Mascara Addiction were playing even if you were standing right next to them. Tyrone told me I was being flippant. He hasn't much of a sense of humour.

"So who else was here," he asked me, "Apart from you and Squirrel? There must have been someone."

"There was a girl called Zena," I said, "I remember she had glitter dust all over her hair and she was wearing a gold lamé boob tube. We hired a taxi after we left Spivz and went up to a club in Archway. Actually she might have been a man. I can't be sure on the details. In fact, I don't really remember much after than until I woke up in bed the next morning with a tongue in my ear."

Zipgun smiled. "She had her tongue in your ear and you are not even sure what sex she was! You must have been pretty far gone."

"I was," I admitted, "But it wasn't her tongue that was in my ear."

"If it wasn't her tongue which bit of her was it?"

"No, what I mean is, it *was* a tongue. But not Zena's."

"How many of you were in bed at the time?" Zipgun asked. I felt his interest was unseemly in one so recently bereaved.

"There were just the two of us. Me and a dog."

Tyrone cleared his throat in a meaningful way. "Maybe some other time?" he said.

I realised that my incomplete account might have left the wrong impression. I wanted to clear that up. "I'd never met the dog before," I explained.

"Oh?" said Zipgun.

I'm not completely sure that I had expressed myself as well as I had intended. I was about to have another go when I was distracted by a dazzling vision of pink wafting into the bar. It was Lala. His eyes, I noticed, no longer had red rings around them. I asked him how he was feeling and he said he was pretty much recovered.

Out of the blue, Tyrone asked, "What did it smell like?"

"I beg your pardon?" said Lala, "What did *what* smell like?"

"The mascara. The one that made you faint and gave you red eyes."

"Well, I'm not sure it was the mascara that made me faint."

151

"You may not be sure," said Tyrone, "But I am. What did it smell of?"

"Have you ever worn mascara?" Lala asked.

"Well..."

"No, obviously not. Mascara is stuff that you put onto your eyelashes. With a little brush. Mascara is not something you smell. I have no idea what it smelt like. In fact, I have no idea what *any* mascara smells like. Because, strange at it may seem, I have never smelled it."

By this point, I could tell that Tyrone's attention was starting to wander. I'd seen the symptoms before. You can be half way through a conversation when you notice that his eyes are drifting off and staring at a corner of the room where there is nothing to see apart from the corner itself. When he does that it means he's thinking. And you can bet that what he's thinking has nothing to do with what you are saying. In fact, he won't have heard a word you've said and if you ask him a question he'll ignore you.

The only way to grab his attention at those times is to shake him.

I shook him.

"What?"

I suggested that we go and see the chaps in Mascara Addiction before we leave and he said "Better make it quick then." They were having a pause between songs at that moment so in we went to the dance floor.

Unlike me, Tyrone does not beat around the bush when he's trying to wheedle information out of someone. The first thing he said to Anvil Evans was: "Where were you at midnight on December 31st last?"

Anvil, curiously enough, didn't seem to find the question odd. "Dancing," he said.

Tyrone looked suspicious. "According to my spreadsheet, you were in the Gallery at midnight."

"Anvil and me came down," Joe said, "To have a dance."

"Together?" Tyrone asked.

Anvil laughed – "No, mate. With some girls. We ain't fuckin' poofters. No offence intended, like, to them what is."

Tyrone flipped through the papers in his hand, found his spreadsheet and jotted the new information onto it.

"So Anvil and Joe were down here on the dance floor. As were Brigitte and Clifton Chuttle. Did you see them?"

Joe shrugged. "The dance floor was packed."

"That just leaves Dave," said Tyrone.

Dave Buzzard laughed – "You think I bumped off old Theo? Nah, mate. You're barking up the wrong tree. I was down here too."

"Anyone see you?"

"Loads of people probably. But who'd remember? Everyone was dancing."

"Yeah, Dave was here," Joe said, "I saw him. Remember, you cadged a fiver off me?"

"Oh yeah," Dave said, "I'd forgotten about that."

"I hadn't," said Joe.

"Does anyone recall what record was being played at the stroke of midnight?" Tyrone snapped.

"I can answer that, love," – Lady Vlad called down from the DJ desk up on the stage.

Tyrone put his hand up to silence her. "Just a minute. I'd like to hear what Dave has to say?"

"Don't know what your game is, mate, but yeah. It was some disco crap. 'Hooray for the Fucking 80s' or something."

Tyrone turned to Lady Vlad and magnanimously signalled that she could finally have her say.

"Yeah, well, he's nearly right. I picked it special. Seemed appropriate, like. As we was going into the '80s an' that. Anyway, it made a fuckin' change from all the electro fuckin' stuff. I been telling Theodora, we should do more powerdisco, instead of all this fuckin' techno-crap. Italian disco and that. 'Ere any of you lot know Umberto Tozzi? Fuckin' ace, man. Me fave's 'Gloria' – no idea what the words mean but who cares? Clifton should get The Sexteens to do a cover version."

I couldn't help thinking that Lady Vlad had unusual musical tastes for a goth-punk. God knows how she got a job DJing in Spivz.

Tyrone interrupted her in full flow – "But getting back to the point. The song you played at midnight on New Year's Eve was…?"

"It was this one," Lady Vlad held up a 12 inch disk, "'Get Ready For the 80s'. The extended version. By Village People."

On the tube back home, Tyrone told me the name of the murderer. I was getting used to people telling me the name of the murderer. But this time was different. When Tyrone told me who it was, I knew he was right.

Welcome To Clubland

At the time I had only the vaguest idea about who 'owned' Spivz. I guess I thought that Zipgun and Theodora did. Looking back I can see that would have been impossible. A that date, Zipgun was 23 years old and Theodora was 21. They had barely done a full day's work in their lives. They didn't come from wealthy families. Theodora was the son of a TV repair man and a self-employed chiropodist. Zipgun had been brought up by his mother who ran a dog grooming salon in Putney; he hadn't seen his father in over fifteen years and his mother hadn't made any efforts to find him. In short, Theodora and Zipgun had no money. They couldn't have raised enough cash between them to buy the front door of Spivz let alone the entire building. Which meant that somebody else was behind the business and Theodora and Zipgun were just the front men.

In the '50s and '60s, many of the most exclusive clubs and pubs in London were controlled by underworld gangs. These included notorious gangs such The Krays and The Richardsons. Gangland interest in the profitable nightlife of the Capital didn't end with the '60s, however. In spite of repeated attempts to 'clean up' London clubland, it's an open secret that many of the most lucrative nightspots of London are owned, run, protected and supplied with booze, drugs, slot machines or women by organisations that are distinctly on the shadier side of the law.

This is still the case even now in the 21st Century. In 2007, eight top nightclubs were shut down in an effort to prevent a turf war between rival gangs. Their closure was only temporary, however, and within days most of them were open for business as usual.

Throughout the '80s the gangland involvement in clubs was intimately connected with the flourishing drugs scene. The drugs boom hit a peak in the late '80s with the advent of crack cocaine and the emergence of Acid House. While there was still a demand for 'traditional' drugs such as LSD, cocaine, cannabis and heroin, a number of other drugs were starting to become increasingly fashionable – a fashion that was largely created by the criminal gangs who supplied the drugs. These included PCP (phencyclidine) a powerful hallucinogen popularly known as 'angel dust' which had begun to gain popularity in the late '70s, MDMA (which was to become much more popular towards the end of the '80s by which time it was generally known as 'ecstasy') and a variety of synthesised 'designer drugs'.

To this day, I still don't know who really owned Spivz or what precisely was the nature of their business relationship with Theodora and Zipgun Dandy. What I am pretty certain of, however, is that the club's well-known front-men must have had some delicate dealings with the real powers behind the scenes. I doubt if a murder on the premises went down well with the owners and when Zipgun told me he was afraid of being suspected of the crime, I am not sure whether he was more afraid of the police or of the club owners.

Chapter 18

Tyrone was right about the mascara. He'd said all along that it was the key to the murder. His theory was that the murderer had tried to poison Theodora and only when that had failed did he go back to finish him off by the more certain method of strangulation.

With the aid of his spreadsheet, Tyrone calculated the positions of the main suspects between midnight and about ten past midnight by which time Theodora was probably already dead and the murderer was inside the locked toilet with his corpse: Zipgun, Adam Xeon, Pete de Gré and Lala were up in The Gallery. Adam had left briefly to go to the toilet but, finding it locked, had returned. Squirrel was with me in Harlow's Bar. Dusty claims to have been in Harlow's Bar but I didn't see him there so that was unsubstantiated.

Anvil Evans, Joe Jonson and Dave Buzzard were on the dance floor. Brigitte and Clifton claimed to have been on the dance floor but nobody saw them; neither of them recalled the Village People song played at midnight.

Another puzzle was provided by the note that had arrived threatening Brigitte and containing what appeared to be a silk tassel from the murder weapon. There was no stamp on the envelope so it must have been delivered by hand. "Or written by Zipgun himself," Tyrone said. There was also the possibility that Brigitte had killed Theodora and had written the threatening letter to make it seem that he hadn't – that, on the contrary, he was a victim rather than a villain.

"Brigitte is stronger that he looks," I said, "He could have strangled Theodora."

"And he does have a cracked fingernail," Tyrone added, "Which might have been caused in the struggle."

"Exactly!"

"But which could also have been caused," Tyrone added, "in a thousand more mundane ways. But the crucial thing is the mascara. We know Brigitte gave blue mascara to Theodora and that Theodora swapped that mascara with Lala. It's a shame we don't know what colour Theodora was wearing when he was killed."

"Oh, that's easy," I said, "I have some photographs."

We were travelling home on the Northern Line tube train at the time; Tyrone has a flat in Belsize Park which is on the Western branch leading to Edgware. The train was crowded and I was sitting next to a large blue-rinsed woman who was looking at us disapprovingly as though we might be escaped lunatics which, given the nature of our conversation, was not a bad hypothesis. I took out the envelope of enlargements which I'd obtained at the Great Hits office that morning. Tyrone looked closely at a photo of Theodora. "The mascara is black. Definitely black."

He then found one of Brigitte posing against one of the barley twist columns around the dance floor. "And Brigitte's mascara," he said, "Is definitely blue. So, since we know that Brigitte gave the blue mascara to Theodora and that Theodora swapped this for Lala's black mascara it seems reasonable to assume that the blue mascara being worn by Brigitte is the same blue mascara being worn by Lala. But somewhere between Brigitte putting on the mascara and Lala putting it on, somebody added a few drops of cyanide."

"Why cyanide?"

"Cyanide can be absorbed through moist membranes such as eyelids."

"Which is why Lala's eyelids were so red!"

"And why he collapsed soon after putting on the mascara. Shame he threw the mascara away without smelling it. The bitter almond smell – a dead giveaway. But the clincher is that Pete de Gré brought Lala around with poppers. Amyl nitrite is vasodilator that's often used to counteract the effects of cyanide poisoning."

*

A Side Note On Cyanide...

Just in case you happen to be a bit rusty on the ins and outs of cyanide, its effects and its antidotes, let me take a few minutes to fill you in. After all, you never know when it might come in handy. One of the tragic facts about victims of cyanide poisoning with malice aforethought is that most of them weren't expecting it. By the time they realise what's going on, it's too late to start mugging up on cyanide poisoning and how to treat it. Unless, of course, they happened to have prepared for the eventuality in advance. Alas, so few poisoning victims do! Well, here's your chance to be the exception to the rule.

Cyanide has been used by countless thousands of murderers down the centuries, in all kinds of circumstances. The Emperor Nero used cyanide to bump off various members of his family who'd got on the wrong side of him. Rasputin (the 'mad monk') is said to have been done away with a cyanide-laced cake. Lizzie Borden, the New England axe murderer, is thought to have dabbled in a bit of cyanide poisoning as a sideline. Her preferred tipple was Hydrogen cyanide (HCN), commonly known as 'prussic acid', a naturally occurring toxin that can be found in minute quantities cherry and almond stones, though I am given to understand that the odd slice of cherry and almond cake is unlikely to be a major health hazard. Unless, like Rasputin's, it's been laced with cyanide, that is.

Other varieties of cyanide include Potassium cyanide (KCN), cyanogen chloride (CNCl) and Sodium cyanide (NaCN). The various types of cyanide may be available as gases, solids or liquids. They may be taken into the body via inhalation, ingestion or absorption through the skin. Cyanide is a fast acting and extremely potent poison which works by inhibiting the absorption of oxygen by the red blood cells, causing a sort of chemical asphyxiation – stopping the victim from breathing even though they may be gasping in lungfuls of air.

Symptoms of cyanide poisoning include breathlessness, nausea and fainting. At a lethal dose, gaseous cyanide is instantly fatal. Solid and liquid forms of the poison may take between one and fifteen minutes to result in death. While there is no guaranteed antidote for cyanide poisoning, the inhalation of Amyl nitrite is recommended. This causes the dilation of blood vessels thus lowering the blood pressure and increasing oxygen absorption. Amyl nitrite also induces the formation of methaemoglobin which is an oxygen-carrying form of the haemoglobin protein and this combines with the cyanide to form nontoxic cyanmethaemoglobin.

In addition to its use in murders, suicides, assassinations and executions, cyanide also has a number of non-violent applications. It is used in the mining industry for processing metal ores, it is used in the manufacture of Nylon, textiles, paper and plastics. It is use to colour and clean and electroplate certain metals. It is used in insecticidal fumigants and in photographic development processes. In fact, cyanide also has some medical applications.

While cyanide is not readily available to members of the general public, it is not that hard to get if you put your mind to it. It is stocked in its various forms by scientific supply companies and may be sold, on application and subject to various regulations, for agricultural, medical and manufacturing purposes. If a member of the public needed to obtain cyanide they would probably have to be on friendly terms with a person of dubious moral character who had obtained the chemical through legitimate channels. Given the fact that the manufacturers and processors of illegal recreational drugs are likely to have access to a number of chemicals obtained through dubious means, this is one conceivable route in which cyanide might be obtained. Alternatively, a moderately talented chemist could make 'home made' cyanide from readily available ingredients.

One way of recognising cyanide is by its 'bitter almond' smell but this is not an infallible test since a) some people can't smell it, b) it may be confused with entirely harmless substances such as almond extract (or, indeed, cherry and almond cake) and c) it's not a good idea to smell cyanide – many people have tried and not all of them have lived to tell the tale.

*

"You think Brigitte put the cyanide into the mascara?" I asked.

"Doubtful. He was otherwise engaged at the time of the murder."

"I thought you didn't believe his alibi."

"I don't. But he has another alibi that he isn't admitting to."

According to Tyrone, this is how Brigitte's mascara came to be poisoned: Theodora asked Brigitte for the mascara; Brigitte gave it to him; Zipgun went to the office and found that Theodora was

160

putting on mascara in readiness for the photo session; but when Theodora came to the door of the office he was not holding a mascara bottle; so the mascara bottle must have been inside the office. Whoever was in the office at the time had the perfect opportunity to put the cyanide into the mascara, assuming that Theodora would use it. But Theodora didn't like the colour and exchanged it with Lala. Which explains why Lala was the one who was poisoned.

"Zipgun says Clifton Chuttle was inside the office, " Tyrone said, "QED. Clifton Chuttle killed Theodora."

"But he couldn't have known he'd have the chance to poison the mascara," I objected.

"Maybe he planned to poison Theodora's drink but when he was left alone with the mascara he knew it was an opportunity that was too good to miss. After all, who'd think of checking mascara for poison?"

"But how can you be sure Dusty is innocent?" I said, "His movements are still unaccounted for. Besides which, Clifton Chuttle hasn't got a motive."

"Of course he has a motive!" Tyrone snapped, "We just don't know what it is! And as for Dusty... I find it had to believe that you are so obtuse."

"What do you mean, hard to believe....?"

"Yes, on reconsideration, it isn't that hard to believe. But if you really can't put two and two together and make four, I suppose I'll just have to get them to tell you themselves. Brigitte said he was going to The Black Cap public house tonight. With Dusty, I suppose?"

"I suppose."

"We should go there."

"Why?"

"Apart from anything else, I am curious to know what a Trollette is..."

Chapter 19

The Black Cap is a well-known gay pub on Camden High Street and it should not be confused with the Mother Red Cap, which is not a gay pub, just across the road. In the latter you can sit down and have a quiet drink without the remotest risk of a man in high heels, fishnet stockings and a Shirley Bassey wig disturbing you with a full throated rendition of "Hey, Big Spender"; in the former, you most certainly cannot.

The Black Cap has drag acts. Some of the drag acts are funny with witty banter and rude jokes. The best of them, such as Mrs Shufflewick and the Trollettes are, even on a cold wet night in January, worth taking the trouble to go and see. The worst of them are not. I wouldn't say the acts that were on at The Black Cap on the night of January 3rd 1980 were the worst I've ever seen but they came pretty close. Of The Trollettes there was no sign. I felt that Brigitte had lured us to The Black Cap under false pretences.

It was gone nine o'clock when I got there. I'd gone home first, having stopped off at a pet shop in Camden to buy some tins of dog food and a dog lead. I had a feeling that Scruffy would consider the dog food to be pretty poor fare for a dog that had been used to dining upon choice cuts of rump steak and I was right. When I scooped half a tin of the unsavoury-looking chunks into a saucer, he sniffed them, whimpered and proceeded to turn upon me the full, unrelenting power of his big, sad soulful eyes. But to no avail. I had hardened my heart. After much piteous sobbing and whining, lolling of a pathetic tongue and waving of a pathetic tail, the ungrateful cur eventually consented to eat a few mouthfuls, albeit slowly and reluctantly as though he thought it might be poisoned.

The dog food can't have been so bad really, though, since once he'd eaten the first lot he turned on the big, sad and soulfuls once again until I was persuaded to scoop the remainder into his saucer. After that I gave Scruffy a quick turn around the block on his nice new lead then brought him inside to get forty winks on the sofa while I had a shower. He was still snoozing soundly on the sofa when I crept out of the front door (on tip toe so as not to waken him) and set off for Camden.

When I entered the pub I found Tyrone propped up against a tall blonde transvestite who was propped up against a leather queen who was propped up against the bar. "Fancy a pint?" Tyrone asked and I said I did, so he asked the transvestite to ask the leather queen to ask the barman to get a pint of beer. This done, Tyrone passed some money to the transvestite and, in the fullness of time, a pint of beer and some change was passed back down the queue. The Black Cap, I should say, is often pretty crowded. Getting anywhere near to the bar is a challenge that defeats many. Tyrone had evolved his own system of increasing the odds in his favour.

"Any sign of Brigitte?" I shouted over the amplified sounds of a drag artiste belting out a version of How Much Is That Doggie In The Window with inappropriately altered lyrics in a rich baritone voice.

"Not so far. But I can't see many people. I haven't found any way of moving from where I am currently squashed, eeek!"

The "Eeek!" I should say was accompanied by a startled look in Tyrone's eyes and a big smile from a hirsute man in a checked shirt standing immediately behind him. Tyrone turned and glowered at the hirsute man who, not to be discouraged, gave Tyrone a kiss full on the lips and then moved off to be engulfed in a mass of sweaty bodies further down the pub. This was the second time in one day that I'd seen Tyrone blush. It was beginning to suit him.

By the time we'd finished that drink, the tall blonde transvestite had moved off somewhere and Tyrone was now leaning against the leather queen. This made the transaction between Tyrone and the bar one person faster. By now I was starting to feel uncomfortably hot. Sweat was pouring down me and I realised I'd need another shower by the time I got home and I was starting to get fed up of waiting for Brigitte and frankly wondering whether he was going to turn up or even had any intention of turning up when suddenly there he was!

For a minute Brigitte was all Dahling, so lovely to see you and even lovelier to see your friend again and he was fluttering and air-kissing and generally doing the sort of performance you'd expect from Elizabeth Taylor at the Oscar ceremonies so I didn't even notice that the leather queen next to Tyrone was giving some serious attention to Dusty who had trailed, in clouds of glory, behind Brigitte.

Against the background of the show (a tear-jerking rendition of D.I.V.O.R.C.E was currently assailing my eardrums) I tried to make small talk with Brigitte. How was he feeling, had he got over the shock of the death threat, did he think the murderer would come after him next and so on? I was discovering that it is surprisingly difficult to make small talk about death threats. Behind Brigitte, I noticed that Dusty was saying something to the leather queen and he was saying it with a vengeance. The leather queen looked sheepish and moved away which had the beneficial consequence of putting Tyrone bang up against the bar. Brigitte told him he'd have a Blue Desperation (no, I don't know what that is either), Dusty said he'd have a lager and I said I'd have another one of whatever I'd had the time before – which Brigitte said was "The story of my life, honey," and giggled.

Once Tyrone handed us our drinks, he got right down to business. Beating around the bush is not something Tyrone does. Without any preamble he told Brigitte and Dusty that he had narrowed down the list of suspects to three people, two of whom *they* were. This information did not go down well. However, Tyrone told them, they could very easily remove themselves from that list. All they had to do was tell us what they had really been doing between the hours of approximately ten to twelve and twenty past on New Year's Eve and New Year's Morning.

"I know your stories up to now are untrue," Tyrone added, "Dusty, you were not in Harlow's Bar. Brigitte, you were not dancing with Clifton Chuttle. Since we know you weren't in Harlow's, on the dance floor, in the Gallery or in the lobby it is pretty obvious where you were but I'd rather have you confirm that fact for the benefit of my less perceptive friend here," he nodded towards me.

Brigitte bit his beautifully made-up lower lip (an odd tangerine colour which didn't got at all well with the lavender shirt he was wearing), turned to Dusty, turned back to Tyrone, cocked his head on one side and said, "Can you keep a secret?"

"I can," said Tyrone, "But whether I will is another matter."

Brigitte looked at me. I'm not sure what he expected me to say but whatever it was, I didn't.

"For fuck's sake," Dusty broke in, "I don't know what's the big secret. It was always going to come out one way or another. It might as well be now as later."

Brigitte gritted his teeth but Dusty carried on anyway... "The thing is, Clifton's going to get rid of Dave Buzzard."

For once Tyrone looked gratifyingly confused. This little detail was obviously new to him. "You mean, he's firing him from Mascara Addiction? But didn't he fire him from the other band?"

"Dave's bad news, that's the long and short of it. He's unreliable, he deals."

"Drugs?" I said.

"What else is there to deal in?"

I considered a moment. "Cars?"

"Dave," said Dusty, "is an accident waiting to happen. Beside which, he's not a good singer. I mean, he could just about cut it with The Sexteens. Their style of vocals is pretty much just talking anyway. But he hasn't got a proper singing voice."

"If he was ok with The Sexteens, why did he get given the boot from them?" I asked.

"Pete de Gré," Dusty said, "Clifton likes them young, if you know what I mean."

"I think I can guess..."

"Pete auditioned for Mascara Addiction initially.," Dusty said, "That was last August. He obviously wasn't right for the band. Clifton thought he'd be ok in The Sexteens but there wasn't a vacancy. So he *made* a vacancy. Dave Buzzard got swapped into Mascara Addiction. He's never been right for us but what Clifton wants, Clifton gets. And Clifton wanted Pete."

"How old is Pete exactly?" Tyrone asked.

"He turned sixteen in September."

"But wait a minute," I said, "Interesting as this is, what's it got to do with..."

"Me and Brigitte? Have you met Velma?"

I said I had.

"She's my girlfriend," Dusty says, "She plays Theodora's girlfriend for the cameras. But she was always mine. That's how

Theo met her. Well, she isn't my girlfriend any more. Or anyway, she thinks she is, because I haven't told her yet but..." – he smiled at Brigitte, "Now I've got someone else."

"Someone a whole lot prettier too!" said Brigitte, momentarily overcoming his usual bashfulness. Dusty smiled and kissed Brigitte.

"So the way it is," said Dusty, "is that, first of all, I didn't want Velma to know and, secondly, I didn't want Clifton to know because as far as Mascara Addiction goes, we are all supposed to be straight. He'd blow a gasket if he knew I was dating Brigitte. He's pretty anti-gay, as a matter of fact."

"But I thought you said he was screwing Pete," I said.

"As far as Clifton's concerned, what you do behind closed doors and what gets written about you in the press are two different things. So anyway, one way and another, it's been hard for me and Brigitte, you know. We have to be, what's the word...?"

"Discreet," said Brigitte.

"So that night," Tyrone said, "you needed somewhere discreet to go and... well, do whatever it was that, um, you, well..."

Brigitte helped him out: " 'Fuck' is the word you are looking for."

"Yes, um, exactly. All the store rooms were locked. In the cloakroom, Bad Tommy was showing his Brighton Belle to The Ape. Everywhere else was full of people. The only place where you could get any privacy was the office."

"Well, we could have tried the bogs, I suppose," said Brigitte, "But, dahling, I have not sunk that low!"

"So, yeah," Dusty confirmed, "About ten to twelve, we slipped into Theo's office. We locked the door behind us and we saw in the New Year in our own way."

"With a bang!" said Brigitte.

"Which," said Tyrone, fixing his eye on Brigitte, "Just brings us to the little story that you concocted with Clifton Chuttle."

"Oh, that! Well, I never thought anyone would believe us, anyway. I mean, dahling, really! Do you honestly think that Clifton Chuttle is the best I can do! What happened was that we snuck out of the office, me and Dusty. Must have been about ten past twelve, I'd say. Dusty sneaks off, I know not where. And I wait a few seconds more so that we are not seen together. Then I leave. Only as I'm leaving there's Clifton in the upstairs corridor. He sees me. I'm not sure if he saw Dusty too so I just smile and I say, Oh, fancy seeing you here! And he's still smiling so I'm guessing he never saw Dusty and he says, What you doing here? Something you didn't ought to? And he laughs. With someone you didn't ought to? And he laughs again. And I say, Yea, maybe. Don't tell anyone though, will you. So he says, Don't worry, you can trust me. If anyone asks I'll say I was with you. And *I* say, Oh, that's a good idea. And he says, Yeah, I'll say we was having a dance. Give you an alibi, like. If anyone asks. So that's what we said. I was kind of hoping nobody'd find out."

"Fuck them!" said Dusty, "We can't keep this a secret for ever. Truth is, I love Brigitte." and they kissed again. It was a very heart-warming scene, really. True, it would have been more heart-warming if a drag queen hadn't been singing 'Gimme! Gimme! Gimme! (A Man After Midnight)' while doing rude things with balloons the whole time. But even so, as heart-warming scenes in hot and sweaty drag-pubs go, this was one of the most heart-warming.

When they finally released their suction grip on one another, a thought flitted through Brigitte's mind and, having flitted, it made its way to his mouth – "Which means," he said, "That we can't have killed Theodora!"

"Agreed," said Tyrone, "Absolutely."

"So who was it then?"

"Let me buy you another drink," I said.

Chapter 20

There is something curiously bleak about Kentish Town High Road at ten past eleven on a wet Thursday night in January. The road is not busy enough to be bustling and not quiet enough to be tranquil. Cars come and go, people straggle homeward, occasionally a drunk or a beggar hunched in a doorway mumbles something listless as you walk past them.

A thin, depressing drizzle sifted down upon us as we hunched down and pulled up the collars of our jackets. I cursed myself silently for forgetting to bring an umbrella.

"How are the bones?" Tyrone asked.

For a split second I thought he was asking a medical question. Since I couldn't recall breaking any bones and arthritis was not a problem, I tried to think of some other explanation. It came to me in a flash: Scruffy.

"I was unable to get any bones," I said, "But the rump steak went down pretty speedily."

Tyrone harrumphed. "You need bones," he said.

As I think I have mentioned before, Tyrone has the disconcerting habit of picking up on a conversation at the point where it had been left off. The fact that the conversation in question had taken place two nights ago and that we'd had a good many conversations in the intervening period was neither here nor there.

"What I can't figure out," I said, "Is why Clifton would have killed Theodora. There doesn't seem to be any motive."

"No," Tyrone agreed, "There doesn't. But there must be one."

"Yes, but what?"

"That is something you will have to find out."

A young woman who had been walking towards us suddenly stopped. She was neatly dressed in a long black overcoat and a black headscarf tied over short-cropped blonde hair. She smiled at Tyrone. "Excuse me," she said, "I wonder if you might have two 50p pieces?"

Tyrone rummage in his pocket, brought out a handful of change and flipped through it coin by coin until he found two 50p

168

coins. Having done so, he put the remainder of the change back into his pocket, handed the 50p coins to the woman and held out his hand, palm up.

"What d'you want?" she said.

"I was expecting you give me a pound," he said.

"Fat chance!" she hissed and off she walked at a brisk pace.

"Strange person," I said.

"Not really," Tyrone replied, "She asked for two 50p pieces, I gave them to her. A logical transaction."

They say there is a fine line between genius and madness. That line is drawn finer than most in Tyrone. On arriving at my flat, I opened the front door and flipped on the hallway light. To say that Scruffy came bounding out of the living room to greet us would be overstating it. Well, in fact, it would be a bald-faced lie. Scruffy remained stretched out on the settee. He did, however, find the energy to roll over on his back and allow us to stroke his tummy and scratch him behind the ears. That done, I made a couple of cups of coffee, rolled a non-tobacco cigarette and sat chatting to Tyrone for another twenty minutes or so during which the conversation focussed largely upon the mystery of The Trollettes' absence from The Black Cap, after which Tyrone left in search of a cab.

I was still profoundly dissatisfied with Tyrone's supposed 'solution' to the murder and I was not reticent in letting Scruffy have an earful on the subject. Had I been guilty of placing too much faith in Tyrone's brilliant intellect, had I let him bamboozle me with all his talk of equations and spreadsheets? Were we, in short, completely on the wrong track?

On the one hand, the evidence against Chuttle was persuasive. He was in all the wrong places at all the right times. He had every opportunity to do the two dastardly deeds of poisoning the mascara and throttling Theodora.

What he didn't have was any reason for doing so.

The nearest to a motive we'd managed to come up with was some petty dispute about whether he would or would not record a song with Theodora doing the singing. If he'd refused to do so, Theodora might have been a bit miffed but I couldn't see why that would bother Chuttle. He was a hard-headed businessman by all accounts. Miffed would-be artistes must be an everyday occurrence to him. It's not the sort of thing that would make him want to go off and pour cyanide in a chap's mascara and then promptly garrotte the same chap with his own silk scarf in the gentleman's lav.

Part of me had the urge to go running off to the nearest police station or phoning up Scotland Yard and demanding to speak to the to their top bobby. Another part of me thought we'd been on a wild goose chase and ended up catching a perpetrator who was only slightly less improbable than Rod Hull's emu. It had seemed a fine adventure at the outset. Now I was starting to think I'd been making a fool of myself all along.

Clifton Chuttle couldn't have done it.

He had no motive.

He couldn't be the killer.

And that, frankly, was that.

Scruffy gave me an odd look with one eyebrow raised and his tongue hanging from the corner of his mouth.

"Well," I said, "What do you think?"

Immediately, I realised the stupidity of what I'd done. I'd asked a dog for advice on a murder. That was the last straw. Tomorrow, I'd do two important things. One: I'd stop trying to solve murders. Two: the dog definitely had to go.

Chapter 21

Eight o'clock in the morning is not a time with which I am intimately familiar. It is a time when the night still lingers and the day can't make up its mind whether or not it wants to get itself underway. It is a time at which all civilised people should be tucked up under the duvet contemplating another two hours or so of restful snoozing.

A dog's tongue thrust unannounced into the deepest crevices of one's auditory canal is, alas, not at all conducive to the above.

On the contrary it tends to tear one from deep sleep into adrenaline-pumping wakefulness with no intervening period. And thus it was that, on the morning of Friday, January the 4th, 1980, I found myself leaping around my bedroom throwing any objects that came close to hand at a small, smelly, scurrying dog who seemed to be under the impression that this was a wonderful game which his beloved master was enjoying every bit as much as he was.

I really must get a lock for the bedroom door. Shutting the door is not a sufficient barrier. The door handle on the outer side is just as effective when pressed by a canine paw as by a human hand. I must also get a water glass and a digital alarm clock, these being two of the objects that came closer to hand on the morning in question and which did not survive the game which the beloved master was playing with the aforementioned scurrying, smelly dog.

Two minutes later, the dog was locked out into the back yard which I picturesquely refer to as the 'garden' to engage in whatever furtive mayhem took its fancy while the beloved master slumped in the kitchen over a bowl of muesli and several cups of strong black coffee, meditating upon the grisliness of the dawn that was cracking all around him.

At any rate, the one good thing that resulted from my early awakening was that, by nine o'clock I was moderately bright eyed and bushy tailed and by ten o'clock I was in Brixton. Not, I should say, that, given a perfectly free choice, Brixton would have been top of my list of places to be at ten o'clock in the morning. Tucked up in bed would have been choice number one. A villa on the Cote d'Azur with a full set of servants attending to my every whim might have come in at a close second. However, since neither of these were on offer, Brixton called to me like a siren and I responded by popping onto the Morden train, changing at Stockwell and emerging into the cold light of a balmy South London morning on the sultry shores of the London Riviera, otherwise known as the Brixton Road.

From there it was no more than a brisk ten minute saunter to the recording studio. Janis looked aghast when she saw me. In words of few syllables, she let me know that it was her opinion that I had been up all night engaging in nameless pleasures of the flesh (several of which she named) and that she was about to cop the fag-end of my night of debauchery. I put her mind at ease. While it is true that I am not generally at my most alert during the morning hours, I let her know in no uncertain terms that, when the occasion demands, I am ready to answer the call of the bugle and gird my loins at a moment's notice. Metaphors, I should say, have never been my strongest point but if I mixed them a bit, Janis had the good grace not to comment upon the fact.

Other than Janis and myself, the studio was empty. Chums in the music industry keep telling me that studio time is at a premium and that every second counts but the Chuttle studios appear to be the exception to this rule.

"You come to see Pete?" Janis asked.

This was as good an excuse as any. "Is he here?"

She looked at her watch, "You've got to be kidding. Do you know what time it is?"

I assured her that I had a vague idea. "Is he coming in later?"

"Supposed to be here at half past ten. If he's here by eleven, we'll be lucky."

"Recording today?"

Janis shrugged. "Search me. They come, they make a lot of noise, they go. That's pretty much all I know."

Janis was sitting on the settee sorting through a heap of mail on the coffee table in front of her. She was making three piles – one was obviously intended for advertising and circulars; another seemed to be devoted to business correspondence, bills and invoices; a third pile contained just three items. Having nothing better to do, I picked up the small pile of mail and glanced through it. There was a picture postcard from "Jack and the lads" who were on holiday in sunny Barbados and claimed that they were suffering from a surfeit of "sun, sand and sex", there was a letter addressed to "The Manageress" which I assumed to be a mistake and, finally, there was a padded manila envelope.

"Is Clifton coming today?" I said.

"Maybe. Sometimes he does, sometimes he doesn't. Probably he will. But then, you can't have everything, can you?"

"You don't get on with him?"

"Oh we get on all right. It's just the boys. They keep arguing with him. Especially Pete. He's a little swine at times."

Janis had finished sorting the mail and, turning her attention to the second pile, began ripping open the envelopes containing bills. "Shit! Electric bill's overdue again. I wish he'd pay them on time."

"Money's short, maybe?" I said, "That'll all change if The Sexteens get a hit."

"Yeah, if, if. That's a word we hear a lot around here."

"You want me to open some?" I said.

"Not the bills. They're private. Open some of the others if you like."

I opened the one addressed to The Manageress. It contained a folded glossy page showing a huge silver espresso machine. "Your business will take off with real coffee the way the Italians make it!" it promised. I tossed it to one side and opened the manila envelope. There were a couple of photographs inside and a piece of paper. I pulled them out and glanced at them.

"Fuck! Not that!" Janis grabbed the envelope from me, "Stick to the circulars," she said, "I never said open the private stuff."

She went over to the metal filing cabinet in the corner, opened a drawer and took out a big roll of brown sticky tape, tore off a couple of strips, sealed the envelope with it and threw it back into the appropriate heap on the table. She was muttering to herself as she did this – "He'll never notice. That's how they come sometimes anyway, all stuck down like that, he won't know any difference." then she turned to me, "You'd better leave the mail to me. D'you want some coffee?"

"As long as it's the way the Italians make it," I said but she didn't know what I was talking about.

"We got Maxwell House or Blend 37," she said, "Take your pick."

I picked Blend 37.

About ten minutes later, Adam Xeon came in, looking like a paler version of Mrs Addams in The Addams Family. He grunted twice at Janis and she made him a coffee. Then he noticed me, lifted his hand, said "Hey man," and slouched off into the music room, banging the door behind him. Five minutes later, Pete came in, looking unreasonably sprightly for so early in the morning (it still wasn't quite eleven o'clock). Unlike Adam, Pete noticed me straight away. This wasn't really a difficult task since, other than Janis, I was the only person there.

Pete sat next to me on the settee, curling one leg under him and letting the other one dangle on the floor. Refusing an offer of coffee, he turned his full attention on me and, with the sort of manic intensity that only a sixteen year-old has, he told me about all the tracks the band had recorded, all the songs they'd written, the ideas they had, the arguments they'd had, a programme on TV the night before about lemurs, the crap records that Tony Blackburn plays, how Gary Numan was piss poor but Cabaret Voltaire was fucking ace and what did I think of his new haircut?

"Suits you," I said, though his hair looked the same as it always did.

And then Janis said she had to go out to post some letters and would I answer the phone if anyone rang and I said I would and I knew that this was maybe the only chance I'd have that day to talk to Pete alone so if I didn't ask him now, I might never have another opportunity so, once Janis had gone, I said: "You ever done any modelling, Pete?"

And he gave me a knowingly coy look and said, "Depends what sort you mean. Why? You interested?"

"I just wondered if you'd ever worked with a photographer, that's all?"

"Might have."

"Only I saw a photo of you. And I was just wondering...."

"Oh yeah, you did, did you? Where was this then?"

I stood up and walked over to the filing cabinet in the corner. There was a dead plant and two piles of mail on the top. One pile contained bills. The other, smaller pile, contained a post card, a letter addressed to the Manageress and the manila envelope that I had opened and which Janis had sealed again. She had thrown away the third pile which had contained advertising and circulars.

"I'm not sure I was supposed to have seen it," I said.

Pete was still smiling. "If it's what I'm thinking, I'm not sure you are either."

The outer door opened then and in strolled Squirrel. He nodded at me, then he nodded at Pete. "Janis in?" he said.

"Just popped out," I said.

"Clifton in?"

"Not yet," I said, "Adam's in the music room, though."

Squirrel took the hint and went into the music room, leaving me alone with Pete again.

"Did you get paid?" I said.

"You should know me," said Pete, "Never do nothing for nothing. Where'd you see them? Which ones was they? Was it...? I mean, who showed you?"

"Like I said," I said, "I'm not sure I was supposed to have seen. So don't say a word, ok?"

"Wasn't Clifton, was it?"

"What do you think?"

"I don't think it was Clifton."

"No, it wasn't Clifton. Who took them then?"

"The pictures, you mean?"

"That's what I mean."

"Who do you think took them?"

"That's what I'm asking."

"Yeah, but who do you think?"

"Dusty?"

175

He smiled, looked down, sort of wriggled in the settee then looked up again. The expression on his face is what I think is known as 'coquettish'.

"Could be," he said.

"You are not afraid. I mean, if they got out. If anyone was to find out."

"David Cassidy did nude stuff and that was in the '70s. Bert Reynolds did nude stuff. This is the '80s, man, who really gives a fuck? Know what I mean?"

"Yeah," I said, "You're probably right."

"Live on the wild side of life, know what I mean," Pete added, "That's what the fans expect these days."

I thought again about the pictures I'd glimpsed inside the manila envelope. "Yeah," I said, "You're probably right." But I wasn't at all sure that that's what the fans would expect. Not at all.

It was about half past eleven when Lala arrived and by that time I'd had more Blend 37 than I ever wanted to drink in the entire rest of my life. He was wearing a daffodil yellow double-breasted suit today with four buttons at the cuffs. I asked him how he could afford to have all his suits tailored because one thing is for sure, you don't get suits like that off the peg in Marks and Spencer. "My girlfriend works in a theatrical costumiers," was his reply. To be honest, I was so surprised to discover that he had a girlfriend that, by comparison with that fact, the daffodil-yellow suit suddenly seemed unremarkable.

At about twenty to twelve, the band started playing. It was one of those Thump-thump-thump, bipplety-bipplety-bee synthesiser things that are so big among the Futurists. And at ten past twelve, Clifton Chuttle walked in.

He didn't look pleased to see me.

We exchanged a few pleasantries as the cups on the coffee table rattled with the pounding of the bass notes from the next room. He asked me how the magazine was going and I said "Which one?" and he said the one I was writing which was a special tribute to Theodora and I said, oh, that's done. And he said had I come to see Lala? And I said, yes and no. And he said oh, and I said, "Actually I was wondering if I could have a few words with you?"

He didn't seem surprised. In fact, I think he'd been expecting it.

He asked Janis if there'd been any post and she pointed to the two heaps on top of the filing cabinet. I noticed he picked up the one with the manila envelope first and he put the pile of bills on top of it. Then he slipped the whole bundle into a pocket of his jacket so that the manila envelope wasn't visible.

"Better come into the mixing room," he said, "So we can have a chat in private."

I realised now that there was something quite spooky about the mixing room. When he shut the door behind us and the sounds of the outer studio were reduced to no more than a low murmur, I experienced a distinct sense of claustrophobia. The room was small, not much bigger than a moderately spacious elevator. And it was cramped. Most of the room was taken up by that vast mixing console with its bewildering array of sliders and knobs. What's more, far from increasing the sense of space, the window that looked out on the music room only emphasised the smallness of the room in which we were closed. This is probably how fish in an aquarium see the world. In the room beyond I could see Lala, Pete, Adam and Squirrel moving, playing, laughing and shouting at one another silently. But I was cut off from them, locked into a hermetically sealed box like a contestant in a quiz show.

Just in case you have never found yourself locked in a room with a murderer, I should say that it is not an entirely comfortable feeling. It was hot in there but the drops of sweat rolling down my furrowed brow were very much of the cold and clammy variety.

When I had arrived that morning, I was still of the opinion that Tyrone was on the wrong track and that Clifton Chuttle, while he might well be a slippery customer whom you would not, figuratively speaking, wish to trust further than you could throw, was not a killer. Now, I was not so sure.

I had only glimpsed the contents of the manila envelope for a few seconds but it was enough to convince me that something pretty shady was going on. The photographs which the envelope contained were not of the crispest but even so it was pretty easy to tell that one of the two people involved was Pete de Gré. I couldn't be absolutely certain of the identity of the other person but I had a strong idea that a more leisurely inspection might show him to be the very chap who was at that moment sitting at his mixing desk glowering at me.

Blackmail!

It was, of course, entirely possible that the pictures were just innocent holiday snapshots being mailed to Chuttle by the friendly staff of Boots The Chemist. But, frankly, this did not seem probable. The pictures were unposed and grainy. They seemed to have been taken impromptu and in low lighting. The composition, it is true, was artistic but the subject matter did not seem the sort of thing you'd want to have made into prints, put into frames and stick on the mantelpiece. They were, however, precisely the sort of thing a blackmailer might send to his victim.

As far as the Law is concerned, where two men are concerned, consenting adulthood starts at the age of 21. It would be another five years before Pete de Gré arrived at the age. Which meant that, assuming my guess about the identity of the other man was correct and those photographs were to fall into the hands of the police, Clifton Chuttle might be looking forward to an extended period living at Her Majesty's Pleasure.

From Janis's reaction, it was obvious that this wasn't the first such package that Chuttle had received. I still couldn't see what this might have to do with the killing of Theodora. But, as Tyrone keeps reminding me, the odds against extraordinary coincidences are extraordinarily high. Lala's poisoned mascara was no coincidence and I felt sure that the blackmailing of Clifton Chuttle wasn't a coincidence either. But how was I to find out what the connect was?

I asked myself what Tyrone would do in these circumstances. My inclination was to wheedle out the information in some roundabout way. This is not as easy as it sounds. A friendly chat about the weather and the price of petrol somehow doesn't lead up naturally to "Oh, and by the way, I happened to notice some compromising photographs of you and an underage boy in one of your private letters which I accidentally opened just now." Tyrone, I knew, wouldn't bother with diplomacy. He would skip the preliminaries and go straight for the jugular.

I decided to give the more direct approach a try. I opened my mouth with the intention of saying "I know you are being blackmailed," but what came out was "Very cold weather we are having."

Chuttle grunted. "Why don't you just say what you've come to say?"

"I beg your..."

"Don't take me for a fool. You've been snooping around and it's not just to get some snappy quotes for an interview. How much do you know?"

"About what?"

Chuttle clenched his jaw sardonically. This is not a simple manoeuvre. I mean, clenching the jaw is simple enough; it's the sardonic bit that takes practice. If you can do it, however, it produces a dramatic and intimidating effect. Reflexively, I glanced through the window into the music room. Pete, Adam, Lala and Squirrel were still there. I took comfort from the fact that, while they couldn't hear what Clifton and I were saying, they could see us clearly enough. Clifton wouldn't risk doing anything he (or, more to the point, *I*) might regret in front of witnesses.

"Blackmail," I said. I had planned to wrap this up into a full sentence but my nerve failed me. It was as much as I could do to get out a single word so I decided I might as well go for the crucial one.

"What do you know about that?" said Clifton, as he absently pushed one of the sliders on the mixing console.

"You and Pete de Gré," I said.

He stopped pushing the slider and looked me full in the face. "It's you!"

I gasped. "No! No!" I blubbered, "Not me. I'm not the... I mean, I didn't know anything about... it's not me who's been blackmailing you, for God's sake!"

He didn't know who was sending the photos, then. My experience of blackmail is limited to old episodes of Columbo and Ironside. I regretted having paid them less attention as I couldn't remember whether it was usual for a blackmailer's victim to be in the dark about the identity of the blackmailer. I guessed it probably was. Otherwise the victim might be tempted to go to the blackmailer and do whatever was necessary to stop them.

...whatever was necessary to stop them. That's an interesting thought (I thought). How would you stop a blackmailer. You'd hardly invite him out for a cup of tea and a sandwich and then reason with him man to man. "I say, old chap, this blackmailing malarkey. It's really not the done thing, don't you know. I'd really be most awfully obliged if you could give it a bit of a rest." No, a blackmailer, I suspected, is not the sort of person who's open to friendly persuasion. A blackmailer, I suspected, might need to be dealt with in a very unfriendly manner indeed. Such as, for example, putting poison into his mascara or throttling him with his own silk scarf.

Or then again, as an opening gambit, you might just send a threatening letter. Threaten the person who's threatening you and see whose nerve breaks first.

"You sent the letter to Brigitte," I said.

He smiled. "What letter would that be?"

As luck would have it, Tyrone had given me the purloined letter for safe keeping. The safest keeping I had been able to think of on the spur of the moment had been the inside pocket of my jacket and that is where it still was. I pulled it out with a flourish. I am not entirely sure what blenching looks like but I think that what Clifton did was a close approximation.

"Where did you...?"

"You recognise it, then!"

Clifton hesitated so I pushed on, hoping that if I spoke rapidly and in a loud voice, he would not realise that I was bluffing: "You wrote this, didn't you. And if we compare the typeface with the office typewriter..." (I stumbled over my words at this point as it suddenly occurred to me that I wasn't sure if they had an office typewriter. I supposed there must be one, though, so I went on regardless) "...we shall no doubt find that the typeface matches!"

"It was just a harmless prank," Clifton said, "Brigitte thought he could take up where Theodora left off. I decided to nip that in the bud."

"You think Brigitte was blackmailing you?"

"I never said that. It's you are the one who keeps talking about blackmailing."

"I've seen the photographs," I said.

If he'd blenched before, he did the opposite now. His face took on a reddish colour and I didn't think he was blushing with modesty. The reddish colour was accompanied by a good bit more of the jaw clenching though this time without the sardonic overtones. All in all, his face looked like the sort of face you'd expect to see on a man who was seriously contemplating performing acts of physical violence upon you.

"It was Theodora that started it," he said. He opened a drawer beneath his desk and took out a card. It was the sort of card you send to someone when a close relative has died: all white with big white lilies embossed on the front and 'Deepest Sympathy For Your Sad Loss' written in silver. "That's what he sent me," Clifton said, "He came for an audition and I told him I wasn't interested. So he sent me this card. You think it was meant to be a joke? No way. Two weeks later, the photos started arriving."

"And the photos were taken when?"

"Some time last year. September maybe. I don't know."

"It could have been more than one occasion?" I asked.

"I was set up," he said, "Set up. But it wasn't just Theodora. The two of them were in it together. I can see that now. They both wanted me to make them into stars. Neither of them can sing. Neither of them has any musical talent of any description. What's more, Theodora wasn't even good looking. So when I wouldn't play their game, they found a way to get their own back on me. They set me up. And Pete was in on it too. So that makes three of them. Those photos, they're not what they seem. It wasn't me who was making the running, believe me. It was Pete. He's a fuckin' little tart. What they paid him, I don't know. All I know is that when Theodora got bumped off, I thought that would be the end of it. But it wasn't. Brigitte..." – he paused, rolled his eyes like Long John Silver and muttered sourly, "Fucking Brigitte. First she blackmails me and now the little whore thinks she can seduce Dusty."

"Are you sure it's not the other way around?"

"'Ey?"

"Are you sure it isn't Dusty who's..."

"What! Dusty go chasing after that piece of trash! You have got to be kidding. Dusty's a man's man, know what I mean."

I considered the implications of the phrase and nodded uncertainly.

"Dusty's got a girlfriend, for God's sake."

He meant Velma – who was also, theoretically, Theodora's girlfriend. 'Girlfriend for hire,' I thought. Poor Velma, she had a knack of picking the wrong men.

"But how come you've suddenly got it in for Brigitte? I thought you were planning to make a star of him."

"Is that what she told you?"

"It's what you told me."

"Hmm. Well, let's just say that was a convenient lie. Why would I want anything to do with a fuckin' blackmailer?"

"Brigitte's got nothing to do with that," I said, "Believe me."

"I don't believe you. The two of them were in it together. You've seen them, they are both tarts, more like women than men. You seen what come in the post today, have you? That wasn't Theodora. Theodora's dead, remember. That has to fucking Brigitte. I mean, who else could it be? Only Brigitte or…"

It was as though a light had come on in his head. Someone else who might have continued something that Theodora had started. I don't know why Chuttle hadn't thought of him before; maybe because, unlike Theodora and Brigitte, the man is not a 'tart'. But even though he didn't say his name, I was pretty sure that the thought had crossed his mind: if it's not Theodora and it's not Brigitte, it must be Zipgun!

"The tassel," I said, "In the letter you sent to Brigitte…"

"You think it was off Theodora's scarf? You think I bumped off Theodora? Give me a break. It was just a tassel, ok. Scarfs like that are ten a penny. You can nip into any men's shop and buy one. It was just to put the frighteners on the bitch. Shit! *I'm* the victim, man. It's me who's been getting blackmailed. Anonymous letters, photographs, threats. You know how much money I've had to pay out? Had to pay it in used notes, drop off the package in specific places, at specific times. Under a stone. In a crack in the trunk of a tree. Weird, out of the way places. I hung around looking to see who collected once or twice but I never saw him. I think maybe he came days later to get it. But I didn't kill him. Theodora had loads of enemies."

When I glanced through the window now, I noticed that the music room was empty. No, Lala was still there but the others had gone.

"Yeah well, glad we got that sorted out." I backed towards the door and pulled the handle.

"Don't you dare say a word to anyone," Clifton said.

I smiled, "See you," and I was out of there as fast as I could go.

Chapter 22

I knew there was going to be trouble. But I didn't know how much and what kind.

I knew someone who would know though. I hated to admit it, especially to him, but when there are impenetrable problems to be solved, Tyrone is the man for the job.

I found a phone box on the corner of a side street leading onto Brixton Road. I had Tyrone's work number which he'd written on a scrap of paper when we'd first discussed the case a few days earlier in the Pineapple pub. I'd never called him at work before. I didn't even know where he worked or what he did. All I knew that it was something to do with computers and it was, being Tyrone, bound to be pretty damn' clever stuff. I dialled the number and a woman's voice answered: "Good afternoon. Codeword."

"I beg your..."

"Good afternoon. Codeword," she repeated.

At first I assumed that 'Codeword' must be the name of the company he worked for. Then I remembered what Tyrone had said about phoning him. He'd scribbled a word and a number beneath the phone number. The word was: "Marigold."

"Marigold," I said.

"Extension?"

I read out the number: "623."

"Putting you through."

There were two clicks, a clunk and a burble. Then a man's voice came on the line: "MK20 Desk. How can I help?"

"Is Tyrone there?" I asked.

There was a pause. Then I heard the man's muffled voice calling out: "Anyone seen Tyrone?"

Someone else replied something which I couldn't make out. Then the man's voice came on the line again. "He's on site today."

"On site?"

"All day."

"Where's 'on site'?"

The muffled voice again, asking someone "Anyone know where 'on site' is?"

An even more muffled answer which, once again, I couldn't make out, then the man's voice again: "Sorry, old man, can't say exactly. Privileged information and all that."

"Can you give him a message?"

"Not sure. Depends if anyone can find out where he is. I can jot it down and put it on his desk if you like."

"Ok," I said, "That'll have to do."

"Righty-ho, wait till I get a pencil and... ok, fire away."

"Chuttle knows," I said.

"Chuttle?" said the voice, "Spell that."

"C.H.U.T.T.L.E," I said.

"Chuttle knows. Righty-ho, got that."

"Gone to see Zipgun," I continued.

"Zip...?"

"That's Z.I.P.G.U.N," I said, "At S.P.I.V.Z."

"That it?"

"That's it."

"Jolly good. Now let me read this back. Chuttle knows. Gone to see Zipgun at Spivz. Correct?"

"Correct," I said.

"This urgent, old man?" the voice said.

"Pretty urgent."

"Leave it with me, old man. I'll get this to him if I have to do it by carrier pigeon."

"The telephone might be faster," I said.

"Yes," he said. There was something about the way he said that 'Yes' that made me think he did not have a keen sense of humour.

I caught the tube at Brixton and went straight on to Victoria. There I changed onto the District line going east. Ten stops later, I arrived at Aldgate East. From there it was about a ten minute walk, through streets that had changed depressingly little since the days of Jack The Ripper, until I arrived at the cobbled alley leading down to Spivz.

Mascara Addiction were rehearsing. I knew that as soon as I entered from the way the floorboards were throbbing. As I walked down the lobby, I glanced into Harlow's Bar. Brigitte was sitting in a chair with his stacked heels up on a table and the latest issue of Record Mirror in his beautifully manicured hands. When he heard me enter, he peeked over the top of the paper, said "Fuck all!", scrunched it up and threw it on the floor.

"What's up?" I said.

"Record Fucking Mirror is what's up," he said, "Huge fucking article on Simple Fucking Minds and not so much as a paragraph on the late lamented Theodora. I mean, isn't that just so fucking typical! The doyenne... is that the word 'doyenne'?"

"Could be," I said.

"The doyenne of the Cult With No Name."

"The what?" I said.

"Oh, that's what we are, dearheart, didn't you know? Futurism's a thing of the past. We are a cult, dahling, an absolute cult. Everywhere I go people call out to me, "Ere, sweetheart, you look a right cult!'"

"Oh," I said.

"The music press is full of old hippies and middle-aged punks, that's what's the trouble with this country. Everyone who is anyone is in their thirties. Or even older. But I mean to say, you'd think they'd give Theo the centre spread, declare a national day of mourning and supply free black arm bands with every issue. It is, after all, possibly the greatest tragedy of our generation."

"Martyr Of A Doomed Generation," I said.

"You what?"

"That's what we are calling the special edition of Great Hits. Theodora, Martyr Of A Doomed Generation."

"Coming it a bit strong, ain't it?"

"Maybe."

"Do you like my eye shadow?"

I looked closely. Brigitte's eyelids were shimmering with metallic gold.

"Nice," I said, "Where'd you get it?"

"Selfridges."

"How much did it cost?"

Brigitte looked outraged. "I didn't buy it, dahling. What d'you think I am, made of money? I just slip in with a rolled up copy of Record Mirror, try out a few samples and, oops!, one or two seem to have fallen into my Record Mirror. 'Course I didn't notice until after I'd left, did I?"

"You'll get into trouble one of the days," I said, "They'll see you. They'll get you as you go out the doors."

"Wouldn't that be divine! I'd cause such a scene! I'd say it was sexual discrimination. Horrible hairy security guards pickin' on poor little old me."

"How can it be sexual discrimination when you are the same sex?"

"Horrible hairy *lesbian* security guards then!" Brigitte squealed with delight at the thought. "I wonder if I'd be on the News At Ten? Oh, and there's a message."

"What message?"

"For you. From somebody. Said it was super important, so I wrote it down."

"What is it then?"

"I can't remember. Can't remember where I wrote it. Phone rang behind the bar so I answered it and I wrote down the message on... a beer mat, maybe?"

I picked up a beer mat at random and looked at it. There was nothing on it but beer. I picked up another and another and another. Nothing. Then I picked up one more and this time, the jackpot! There was a phone number written in ballpoint pen. Beneath it were the words: "Miss X, Punishes Naughty Boys." I pass the beer mat across to Brigitte. "This?"

"No, don't be silly. Hmm, do you suppose there's good money to be made out of punishing naughty boys?"

"If they are naughty boys with good jobs and healthy bank accounts, I suppose so," I said.

"What would it involve, do you suppose? Dressing up in latex boots and giving them the odd thrash with a cane or something?"

"Look, Brigitte, maybe we can discuss your career at some other time. We were looking for the message."

"What message?"

"The one you wrote down. Somewhere. The important one that you were going to give me!"

"Oh, I remember where I wrote it. On the bloody music paper."

He bent down and picked up the copy of Record Mirror which he had thrown onto the floor a few minutes before. "Yes, here it is.

Just above that horrible picture of Jim Kerr. Oh, I can't make it out. I've got terrible writing. Can you figure it out, love?"

It was a phone number. Brigitte's 6es and 5s were almost indistinguishable and there was another digit that might have been a 9 or an 8. I went to the telephone behind the bar and made a good guess. It wasn't good enough. The woman who answered started asking me strange questions about my feet. It turned out she was a chiropodist in Finchley. I was pretty sure that chiropodists in Finchley wouldn't be pestering me with urgent messages so I had another guess. This time my guess was better. A dentist's reception- ist in Belsize Park answered. That was closer. Geographically, anyway. But still not quite close enough. My third guess was best of all. I actually recognised the voice that answered. It was Tyrone.

"Where are you?" I said.

"I'm on site," he said.

"Where's on site?"

"Where I am," he said.

If it had been anyone else I'd have assumed he was being deliberately obtuse. With Tyrone, however, this kind of conversation is normal. I ask him a question, he answers it. I've tried to explain that the most literal answer is not necessarily the most useful one but it's no good. "If you want a different answer you should ask a different question," he says.

There was a clicking sound on the line. "Are you still there?" I said.

"Where?" he said.

"There."

"It depends on how you define 'there'."

"Ok, never mind," I said, "I've just been to see Chuttle and I think you were right."

"About what?"

"I think he killed Theodora."

I heard a gasp. It wasn't Tyrone. It was closer at hand. I'd forgotten that Brigitte was still there.

"But I told you he killed Theodora," Tyrone said.

"Yes, well, I'm agreeing with you."

I can't think of the right way to convey the supercilious, arrogant, annoying bloody tone of the "humph" that Tyrone made when I said that. There are times when I could throttle him, with or without the assistance of a silk scarf. He not only has the habit of being right about things he has no right to be right about but he knows he's right and makes no secret of his contempt for anyone who doesn't agree that he's right just because he says he's right.

"He's being..." I glanced across the bar at Brigitte.

"He's being what?" said Tyrone.

"What colour shoes have you got on?" I said.

I was hoping I could get across "blackmail" without spilling the Beans to Brigitte at the same time.

"Brown," said Tyrone.

"Well, what colour would they be if they weren't that colour?"

"They *are* that colour. If they weren't that colour they wouldn't be these shoes."

"Oh! I get it. He's being blackmailed," said Brigitte in the background.

I turned to him and said, "Shhhhhh," then I went back to the phone and told Tyrone, "He's being blackmailed."

The phone was silent for all of two seconds. That meant that this had come as news to Tyrone. Blackmailing had not formed any part of his theory up to this point. I had sprung it on him and he was taking a leisurely two seconds (which is a very long time at the speed his brain works) to revise his ideas.

"Which means," said Tyrone, "That he thought he was being blackmailed by Theodora but he is, in fact, being blackmailed by somebody else."

"How can you possibly know that?" I said.

I had planned to reveal this fact myself and bathe in Tyrone's stunned astonishment so I was more than slightly irritated that he'd figured it out for himself.

"You used the present tense," Tyrone said, "What d'you call it, 'present continuous' or something – 'is being'."

"Present progressive," I said. Grammar is an area of human knowledge in which Tyrone is on shaky ground so I always make a point of correcting him even when he isn't, strictly speaking, wrong. He usually ignores me, however, as he did on this occasion, which is pretty damned bloody annoying, I can tell you.

"So if it's a continuous action," he said without so much as pausing for breath, "Then that means that the blackmailing is still going on which means that Theodora, being presently unavailable for the purpose, can't be the person doing it which means that, since Chuttle killed Theodora he must have assumed that Theodora was the blackmailer but in that assumption he was mistaken. Is there anything I've left out?"

"Yes," I snapped, "Who's really doing the blackmailing?"

"Can't be sure of course..."

"Ha! That's something I don't often hear you say!"

"But I'd say with a moderate degree of certainty that it is highly likely to be Dave Buzzard."

I groaned. "That's stupid. Even for you. There is absolutely no reason... I mean, there is nothing to suggest... what possible... he hasn't even..." I paused to try to regain a some semblance of coherence...

"For God's sake, Tyrone, why....?" I was going to say "Why Dave Buzzard" but I caught sight of Brigitte hovering at my side, straining to hear every word I uttered so I just said, "Why him?"

"Simple. We know he has a history of disagreements with Chuttle. He was thrown out of the first group. We have reason to believe he's quite likely to be thrown out of the new one. So he has plenty of reasons for hating Chuttle. He is not exactly a stable personality and seems to have an advanced drug problem. Given the fact that he has no employment and very little prospect of making a career in the music business, I have to ask what he does to make money to pay for his habit. Blackmail is an obvious solution. Next I have to ask myself what would be the most obvious way to blackmail Clifton Chuttle? We already know that he has a keen interest in young men of a less than legal age and that Pete de Gré fits that description. Moreover, it was Pete who replaced Dave Buzzard in The Sexteens. What better way to get back at Chuttle than through Pete? I presume that mere threats wouldn't be sufficient and that some concrete evidence would be necessary. That suggests photographic evidence. What photographers do we know who'd have easy access to Chuttle and Pete de Gré? The two obvious candidates are Dusty Evsky and Dave Buzzard."

I interrupted Tyrone, "Wait, I know that *one* of them..."

I think Tyrone may by now have suspected the reason for my reluctance to say too much at my end and so he began to fill in the gaps for me.

"Dusty?" he said.

"Is a..."

"Photographer," he said.

"Because we saw him."

"Taking photos at Spivz," he said.

"But as for...

"Dave Buzzard?" he said.

"Exactly."

Tyrone made a tutting sound which had the effect of making my fingertips quiver as they toyed with the concept of throttling him once again. "It was you who told me," Tyrone said, "A couple of days ago when you talked to Dave Buzzard in the pub. He told you he worked as a photographer and took some photographs for Chuttle and that was how Chuttle first met him and ended up recruiting him into The Sexteens."

"Ok, well," I really hate it when Tyrone remembers things that I don't, "So what do we do next?"

"You're at Spivz now?"

I told him I was.

"Who else is in the club?"

"Hang on, I'll ask Brigitte."

Brigitte told me that Mascara Addiction were in the hall rehearsing and Zipgun was upstairs in the office. That was it. I passed this information onto Tyrone.

"I'm coming over. Make sure nobody leaves," he said.

"And how do I do that?"

But even before I'd finished asking the question, he'd put the phone down.

I put the phone back on the hook and turned around expecting to see Brigitte. He was there but that wasn't what caught my eye first. What caught my eye was a dazzle of yellow. Daffodil yellow. Lala was standing in the doorway to the bar. The double-breasted daffodil yellow suit was just as dazzling in the afternoon as it had been that morning when I'd first set eyes on it at the studio.

"I thought you were rehearsing or recording or something," I said.

"Clifton's in one of his sulks," Lala replied, "I don't know what you and he were talking about this morning but whatever it was, it hasn't increased the sunniness of his disposition."

"Clifton killed Theodora," Brigitte said.

Lala laughed. "Who says?"

"He does," she pointed an elegant fingernail in my direction. I couldn't help noticing that the crack was no longer there. I presume there must be some special nail-restoring lacquer he'd used to fix it.

"Clifton killed Theodora," Brigitte said, "And now someone's blackmailing him. But it all has to be kept secret. Except it's not a secret any more because we all know about it. Which probably means that..." Brigitte let out a theatrical squeak, "Which probably means that our lives are in danger because Clifton is a cold, calculating killer who will stop at nothing to silence us!"

"What's she talking about?" Lala said, "Is there even a grain of truth in all that?"

I cleared my throat, "Maybe," I admitted, "A grain. Or two. Look, I um, I just want to go and have a listen to the band a minute. Come with me if you like. You stay here, Brigitte."

"On my own!" he said, "What if Clifton comes here, seeking bloody revenge. And finds me here, on my own. No way, honey, I'm sticking with you."

"Brigitte," I begged, "We need someone to answer the phone. In case there are any urgent messages. You know."

He mulled this over.

"In which case," I said, "When the journalists arrive, and the photographers, they'll want to talk to, and photograph, whoever it was who took the urgent messages."

"Which would be me!" Brigitte gushed.

"Exactly!"

"No way," he said, "Do you think I'm totally stupid?"

I presume the question to be rhetorical and said nothing.

"If I was left out here on my own and Clifton Chuttle showed up, armed with a sawn-off shotgun, he'd probably just pump me full of holes. So I wouldn't be in any state to take your urgent messages, would I?"

"How long will you be?" Lala asked.

I shrugged, "Five minutes. Ten maybe."

"I'll stay with Brigitte."

Brigitte didn't look impressed. "Then we'll both be pumped full of holes. Don't see why you think it's any better to be pumped full of holes on my own than in company!"

"Then come with us," I said, "I really don't care one way or the other."

"Where are you going?"

I nodded in the direction of the dance floor. "In there."

"No thanks."

There are times when I think I don't understand people. I don't understand Brigitte, I don't understand Tyrone, I don't understand the people who had written their phone number on a piece of paper, stuffed it into a capsule attached to Scruffy's collar, booted the poor mutt out on the streets and then, when I phoned them, claimed it wasn't their dog. There are times when I wonder if I really understand *me*. Maybe I'm the one who's unhinged and the rest of the world is sane?

"Well, if anyone phones, come and let me know, ok?"

Brigitte was back with his feet up on the table and his nose buried in the scrunched-up copy of Record Mirror. "Mm-hm," he said.

"But if any crazed murderers with sawn-off shotguns come looking for me," I added, "Tell them I'm in a meeting."

I didn't catch what Brigitte said next but it had the word "twat" in it.

Chapter 23

I went the lobby and pushed open the double-doors to the dance floor. There was a noise like an industrial cement-mixer falling onto a flock of sheep. This was the result of something Anvil Evans was doing on his drums while Dave Buzzard seemed to be having orgasms with his guitar against a large stack of speakers. The doors swung shut behind us. A hundred sheep bleated their last, Anvil gave the drums half a dozen thumps for good measure and then there was what should have been silence but was actually a loud ringing inside my head. It's the sound your brain makes to tell you that the band has stopped playing.

Dave Buzzard was the first to spot us. He was dripping with sweat, his hair was plastered to his forehead and his black-and-white Joy Division tee-shirt was so wet it looked as though it had been painted on. He was smiling maniacally, looking at me, shaking his head from side to side and shouting "Wow, man! Fucking wow!"

"Good session?" Lala asked.

Anvil, who was leaning forward with his head almost hanging between his knees, looked up and said, "Killer Instinct. It's the new song. Should be the single."

"Really came together that time," Joe said, thrumming a string on his bass guitar for emphasis.

"It'd be better if I had the synth," Dusty said.

The problem of the Yamaha CS-5 which he shared with Adam Xeon had yet to be resolved, I gathered.

"Don't need the synth, man," Dave said, "Leave the synths for the boy fucking wonders. This is rock for grownups, man."

Dave Buzzard might be a self-important, loud-mouthed irritating git with a severely limited musical talent, but was he also a blackmailer as Tyrone thought? And if so, how would I be able to prove it?

Well, I could try asking him, I suppose...

"I saw Clifton this morning," I said.

"Oh yeah?" said Buzzard, "Still the same ray of sunshine as ever, was he?"

I moved closer to him. "You got a minute? Maybe we could have a word."

"What about?"

"In private, I mean."

"What's he been saying?"

"Who?"

"Clifton. He say something? About me?"

"Nope," I said, "Not a thing. As far as I can tell you're the apple of his eye."

Dave Buzzard shook his head, smiling, "Not me. I think I'm a bit too old for that. Know what I mean?"

"Yes, I think I do."

"In ten minutes. We're gonna break in ten minutes anyway. Just got one more song to do."

"Ok," I said, "I'll wait."

I walked to the back of the hall, as far away from the band as I could get. It wasn't far enough. The next song was louder than the previous one. It still sounded like large metal objects being dropped onto sheep. If this was the coming trend, I thought I'd better start dusting down my old Bing Crosby records. Maybe it would have sounded better if Dave hadn't been doing the singing. He kept reaching for high notes that would have been too high even if he'd wearing stilts and Tom Jones's old trousers. That was where the sheep noises were coming from. Dave has an impressively horrible voice.

I looked at my watch. It was twenty past three. The next ten minutes slouched by more slowly than minutes have any right to. I leant against the wall and admired the decor. The balcony projected overhead, supported by those intricately carved barley twist columns. I wondered why the Victorian had been so fond of elaborate decoration. This place reminded me of Zipgun Dandy's place. The entire building was built to the same design as Zipgun's hideously ornate sideboard. Maybe that's why Spivz had appealed to Zipgun and Theodora. Their tastes clearly didn't run to the subtle and understated. Who knows, maybe the Victorian Mausoleum style of architecture is an acquired taste. It is a taste that I am about as likely to acquire as dog shit. Which reminded me, I was going to have to get a pooper scooper. Scruffy wasn't too fussy about where

195

he did his business and the neighbours were starting to give me funny looks.

"eeeeeeeeee....."

I became vaguely aware of an irritating whining noise. I look around me but couldn't quite place where it was coming from.

"eeeeeeeeeeeeeeeee....." – it was still going.

I noticed that the floorboards had stopped throbbing. Then I noticed that the band had stopped playing. The whining noise was inside my head. It made a change from the ringing noise that had been there before. Dave Buzzard was looking at me. His mouth was moving but I couldn't figure out what he was saying. It sounded like "eeeeeeeeeeeeeeeee....." I concentrated harder. "Readyeeee," that was one word, "Are you readyeeeee?" He looked at his watch. I looked at mine. It was twenty to three. He said they be ten minutes but they'd been twenty. I hadn't noticed. Doesn't time fly when your head is being battered to a pulp by low frequency notes at a health-threatening volume!

"Ok," I mouthed back.

Brigitte was standing in front of the stage, sidling up against Dusty, I noticed. I hadn't heard him come in for obvious reasons.

Dave Buzzard unstrapped his guitar and propped it up against the side of the stage. "Back in five," he said to Dusty and Joe.

On the way out I asked Brigitte if anyone had called. He said that no one had.

Dave and I made our way to Harlow's Bar. Dave went over to the bar and got a bottle of Pilsner Urquell from the refrigerated cabinet. "Want one?" he said, and I said, "Yeah, good idea." I was about to get some money from my wallet but he said, "It's ok."

I wasn't sure it was Ok really but when you're trying to pin down a murderer's blackmailer, I guess your morals tend to slip a bit so I let him pour me a beer and said "Cheers".

The poster over the bar showed Jean Harlow on the cover of 'Hollywood' Magazine. Next to her picture there were two quotes: "I'd fight to hold my man." (Mae West) and "No man is worth fighting for." (Jean Harlow)

Dave saw where I was looking. "I'd go with Harlow," he said, "Every man for himself. So what's Chuttle been saying?"

I drank my beer. I smiled. "How d'you know he's said anything? You got a guilty conscience or something?"

"I ain't got a conscience so it can't be guilty, can it?"

I drank some more beer, put the glass down on a mat, wiped some foam from the corner of my mouth and tried to look nonchalant. It wasn't working. Mainly because I don't know what nonchalant looks like.

"You used to be a photographer," I said. It seemed like a safe opening gambit – telling the suspect what he'd already told me.

"I still am," he said, "It's just that these days my choice of subject matter is a little, well, different."

"In what way?"

"Like I told you. I used to take pictures of aging rockers. Bowie, Roxy, Mott The Hoople. But you have to keep up with the times, don't you. So these days, I try to keep my subjects a bit, you know, younger."

"Pete de Gré young enough?" I said.

Dave smiled so broadly he was showing his upper teeth. "Clifton didn't tell you that, I bet!"

"Tell me what?"

"That I'd been photographing Pete?"

"No. He didn't."

"Or that *anyone* had been photographing Pete?"

"No, he didn't say that either."

"Well?"

It was no use beating about the bush. If you are going to accuse someone of blackmailing, you might as well just come out and say it. I only hoped that Tyrone was right.

"You are blackmailing Clifton, aren't you?"

He picked up his beer, took a good long drink, put it down again, wiped his mouth with the back of his hand and said, "Who says I am?"

"I've seen the photographs."

"What photographs?"

"Clifton and Pete."

"You got some photographs? Show me what you got."

"I haven't got any photographs."

"Then there ain't no photographs."

"But I've seen them and I know where they are."

"Lots of people take photographs. Dusty. He takes photographs. That friend of yours, the biker with the bad attitude."

"Kev?" I said.

"He takes photographs. I bet you got a camera too. Well, haven't you?"

I agreed that I had.

"There you are, then. You take photographs. Everybody takes photographs. Don't know what you're getting at, mate."

"Not everybody takes photographs like that."

"Like what?"

"Low light. Difficult in low light, with no flash."

"Not difficult. Just need a steady hand, fast film. 400 ASA. 1000 ASA if you can get it. All depending on the lighting. Why no flash?"

"I think you know why," I said, "If you'd used flash he'd have known you were there. But these photos were taken in secret. Where were you? Hiding under a bench?"

"Not me. If it had been me, let me think now, where would I hide? Somewhere out of the way. Somewhere nobody would see – or hear me. For instance, if it'd been in the studio and say I was taking pictures of someone in the music room, I reckon I'd hide myself away in the mixing room. Nice and quiet there. With a nice big window to take the shots through."

I must admit that I'd always known Dave Buzzard was shameless but this was gloating.

"So you," I hesitated, decided to play along with his game, "The photographer, I mean, took pictures of Cliff and Pete de Gré through the window onto the music room. And then sent the pictures to Clifton, telling him to pay up or be exposed to the press."

"As a pederast. Sounds possible, I suppose," Dave said.

"Why do you hate Clifton so much, Dave?"

"Why do I hate the filthy pederast so much?" he said, "You mean the pederast who chucked me out of one group and replaced me with his little fuckpig? The one who puts me in another band and, behind my back, plots to get rid of me again. Why do I hate him so much? Wow, tough question. Just can't think of any reason, can you?"

"You knew he suspected Theodora. You told me before about the 'Deepest sympathy' card that Theodora sent him. Was it you who gave Theodora that idea in the first place?"

He shook his head, "You don't give up, do you."

"Why did you hate Theodora?"

"I never hated Theodora."

"I saw you arguing. The night he was killed."

"You never argued with someone you don't hate?"

"You handed him something. You were his supplier, weren't you. What did you do, put up the price, threaten him with blackmail if he didn't pay?"

Dave laughed, "You're funny, the way you keep harping on."

"So Theodora goes back to the office and puts it in the drawer of his desk. The drugs he bought from you. Which is why Zipgun cleared out the desk afterwards. He cleaned it out so that, even after he was dead, Theodora would seem as clean as a whistle."

"Don't believe it, mate. Theo's body was stuffed full with chemicals. You could get a high just by standing next to him. You think the, what d'they call him, the coroner or whatever wouldn't spot that?"

"Doesn't matter, does it?" I said, "As long as the trail doesn't lead back here. Which is a shame really. Because if it had, Zipgun would have had to tell them where the stuff came from. And that would have led them right back to you."

"Well, it didn't, did it."

"So, one way and another, Theodora was very convenient for you. He bought the drugs and paid the money to fuel *your* habit."

"Speculation, mate. You ain't got no evidence."

"And he also gave you a sitting target to pin the blackmailing onto. You know he has a grievance against Chuttle so you fan the flames, you spread tittle tattle between the two of them, make them hate one another more and more, you even get Theodora to send that 'Deepest sympathy' card, which Theodora probably thought was just a joke. But Chuttle didn't. And when the photographs started arriving and the demands for money, Chuttle was already primed to suspect Theodora. He wouldn't suspect you, least of all you. Because you were always so damn' nice."

"True," Dave was smiling with his mouth but his eyes told a different story, "Me and Clifton got on like a house on fucking fire. But Theo. That bastard was taunting Clifton, you know. All the fucking time he was taunting him. I thought, 'You poor soft sod, you're pouring oil on fire, mate. He was like one of them guys they have in bull rings, you know, that stick things in the bull to make him mad and then one day the bull turns round and get his revenge. That's what Clifton did. He'd had enough of Theo's bleeding taunts so one day he turns around and he sticks the fuckin' horns in. It was Clifton what killed Theodora. You finally figured that out."

"Yes, I finally figured that out."

"You're a slow thinker," he said, "But you get there in the end."

"It might have been Clifton who put the scarf around Theodora's neck, but it was you who got him killed."

Dave laughed then. He laughed so long and so hard that tears ran down his cheeks. When he'd finished laughing, he wiped his eyes and he drank off the last of his beer.

"Well, great to talk to you again, man," he said, and he stood up, "But we got a rehearsal to do, you know, so if you don't mind I'll just get back in there and get on with it."

"I know where the pictures are," I said, "I know where we can get the evidence."

He smiled, "And that should worry me? You get pictures of Clifton and Pete and you think I'm the one who should be bothered?"

"That's the least of Clifton's worries," I said, "The photos are not just evidence against him. They are also evidence against you."

The smile dropped from his face like a mask. "Get stuffed," he said, "There ain't no proof. Anyone can take a photograph. The only proof is the negatives. And they don't exist no more. Least, that's my guess. Whoever took them pictures will have got rid of them. Gone up in flames, I shouldn't wonder."

There was a sudden banging sound followed by a crashing. I ran out of the bar just in time to see a figure flailing around on the floor shouting obscenities. It was Tyrone. I gave him a hand, he got to his feet and dusted himself down. "Bloody stupid doors!" he said.

"You didn't try to kick it open, did you?"

When I'd brought him to Spivz the day before, having found that the left-hand door was locked, he had be prepared to give it a good kick until I pointed out that the right-hand door was open.

"I couldn't get the door to open," he said.

"Which one did you try?"

"The right-hand one," he said, turning and pointing to the door on the right, "Yesterday, it was the left-hand one that was locked."

"But the right-hand door is the left-hand door if you face it from the street," I pointed out, "It's only the right-hand door if you face it from here, inside the club. So it's the same one that is locked today as was locked yesterday. And the other one is open."

"That's the left-hand one," he said.

"But it's the right-hand one as you face it from the street. It was open today just as it was yesterday."

He gave me a look of intense suspicion. Actually, now I come to think about it, that's another thing I have over Tyrone. It's not just grammar that baffles him, it's also the difference between left and right. Whenever I explain it to him, he's never entirely sure if I am making it all up.

As Tyrone dusted himself down, Dave Buzzard strolled past us towards the main hall. "Be there if you need me," he said. He was obviously a lot better at nonchalance than I am.

I quickly told Tyrone about my discussion with Clifton that morning and my recent talk with Dave Buzzard. He affected to be unsurprised. I knew he was lying. He was surprised about the about blackmailing. That was something I'd discovered without Tyrone's help. But there is no point arguing with Tyrone so I didn't.

"Where is Zipgun?" he said.

"He's around somewhere. I think Brigitte said he was in the office upstairs. Why?"

"I think you've managed to convince Chuttle that Zipgun is the blackmailer. Which means that it would be altogether safer for him if he is somewhere where Chuttle can't find him."

We took the stairs to the Gallery two at a time, turned right and pushed open the door to the office without knocking. It was empty. It had looked pretty much as it had done on the previous day: dismal and scruffy apart from the impressive oval-shaped mahogany desk on which sat a calendar, an electric typewriter and a phone.

"How many phone lines are there?" said Tyrone.

"What d'you mean?"

"I mean, is this on a separate line from the telephone in the bar downstairs or do they share the same line?"

"Shit! There was a clicking sound," I said, "Do you remember?"

"When you phoned me," Tyrone said, "Yes. There was a clicking noise and you asked me if I was still there."

"So the clicking sounds might have been..."

"Somebody in this office picking up the phone and listening in on our conversation."

"In which case they'd have heard everything. They'd know all there was to know. They'd know about the photographs. They'd know about the blackmailing."

"They'd know who killed Theodora," Tyrone said.

If we'd run up the stairs two at a time we must have run down them three at a time. When I arrived at the bottom, I nearly knocked Lala off his feet. He was standing there staring. "What's going on? You're running around like headless chickens."

"Brigitte," I said, "Where is he?"

"In there listening to..."

I pushed open the double doors to the dance floor. The band were going full throttle. Brigitte was lounging picturesquely against a pillar. I signalled to him to come to us. He sashayed across the dance floor and out into the lobby. The doors closed behind us, muffling the sound of sheep being murdered by cement mixers.

"Have you seen Zipgun?" I said.

"Yeah," Brigitte said.

"When?"

"When he left."

"He *left*? Why didn't you tell me?"

"You didn't ask."

"When did he leave?"

"Ages ago. Just after you made that phone call. When you came into the dance hall and you left me in Harlow's Bar. He seemed in a rush to leave, actually."

"But didn't you tell him I was here?"

"Wasn't time."

"The phone in the bar," I said, "Is that line shared with any other phones?"

"Only the office," Brigitte said, "If someone rings you can answer it down here or up there."

"Shit!" I said.

Tyrone and I theorized frantically on the destination to which Zipgun might be heading in such a hurry. Home? The pub? A holiday in the Bahamas?

Chuttle's studio! It had to be. I grabbed Lala by a daffodil-yellow sleeve and the three of us ran from the building, turned right along the cobbled street and out onto the road where, a couple of minutes later, we hailed a cab, told the driver where we wanted to go (it was a black cab so we didn't need to give directions or worry that we might end up a route that goes via Brighton) and told him to step on it.

On the way, I gave Lala the lowdown on recent events. I asked him who would be at the studio. "Nobody," he said, "Except for Clifton. He sent everyone home, Janis, the band, everyone. Said he wanted to work on the mix for the single: 'Synthetic Sex' and 'Death Of A Clown'. Double A side. You think Zipgun is in danger?"

"Don't know," I said, "All I know for sure is that Zipgun and Chuttle are not a good combination."

Eventually the cab turned down a side-street off the Brixton Road, which is as close as it could get, we paid, tipped, and legged it across the waste ground to the studio.

The sky was overcast and a thin. A light drizzle had begun to fall. The studio, which had always looked desolate, looked bleaker than ever. It crouched there, a squat, whitewashed building surrounded by cracked concrete and weeds. The windows were dark except for one glimmer of light somewhere deep inside the building.

We walked over the weed-pocked concrete and arrived at the front door. I peered through the pane of reinforced glass. There was nothing to be seen, nothing out of the ordinary. So I pushed open the door and we went into the small hallway. The door to the sitting room was on our right. The door to the music room was immediately in front of us; the door had a glass pane in the upper half. About ten feet to the right of the door to the music room, there was another door – the door to the mixing room. That door was solid and opaque but I knew there was a light on in there because it was shining through the great window that divided the mixing room from the music room.

I pushed at the mixing room door but it wouldn't budge. It had been locked from the inside. So I pushed open the door to the music room. The room itself was in darkness which made the light shining through the mixing room window seem all the brighter. Looking towards it was like looking at a theatre set. But there was just one character: Zipgun. He was crouching over the mixing console with his back towards the window. He must have seen me because after a few moments he stood and he turned. He walked towards the glass window and he leant against it with his arms held straight out in front of him, bracing him against the glass. I walked towards him. There was a wild look in his eyes. He was staring at me but he seemed not to see me. And slowly, his hands slid down the window. And I saw that, as they did so, they left wet red streaks on the glass behind them.

Then I noticed the body. It was slumped over the music desk, face upwards, eyes wide open, staring: all that remained of Clifton Chuttle. There was blood everywhere. All over the mixing desk, dripping onto the floor, smeared over Zipgun's clothes, oozing from a sharp, gaping wound across Clifton's throat.

It was Lala who phoned the police. When Zipgun came out of mixing room, there was no expression on his face and he moved slowly and uncertainly like someone dream walking. He washed his hands and used a tea-towel to wipe blood from his clothes. At Lala's suggestion, I made a pot of Russian Caravan tea and the four of us – myself, Zipgun, Lala and Tyrone – sat in the sitting room drinking it and trying to pretend that we were ordinary people, talking about ordinary things on an ordinary day.

It was Zipgun who had first involved me in this dreadful affair when he'd phoned me on New Year's Day. "You've always been the clever one," he had told me, "If anyone can figure out who killed him, it's you."

I'm not sure I can take the credit, really. It had been Tyrone who'd slotted all the pieces together. But anyway, I said to Zipgun, "Well, we did it, didn't we? We did find the killer." He didn't reply. All he said was: "I did it for Theo. They said I didn't love him. They were wrong."

*

Clifton Chuttle had been garrotted with a wire. The blood on Zipgun's hands had been his own, not Chuttle's. There were guitar strings in coloured paper packages hanging from hooks on the wall of the mixing room. He had hit Chuttle, banged his head against the wall and then, as Chuttle sat, dazed, on the floor, Zipgun had calmly taken one of the paper packets, opened it and removed the looped guitar string. It was an E string. He had undone the loop, wrapped the ends around his hands and pulled it tight, making it a weapon capable of strangling and capable of cutting like a cheese wire. When Chuttle managed to stand up, still dazed, Zipgun moved behind him, pressed his knee into Chuttle's back, looped the wire over his neck and pulled and pulled and pulled and first the wire had choked and then the wire had cut and still he pulled and pulled and pulled. And when the choking noises had stopped and when the blood began pumping through the wound in the throat and the body's weight had slumped full against him, only then did Zipgun let go and let the body fall backwards over the mixing desk where it stayed, insert and dripping blood, its lifeless eyes staring upwards at the ceiling.

"They said I didn't love him," he said; he said it over and over again, "They were wrong."

*

The London Broadsheet, Saturday, January 5, 1980
'Dandy' Murder, Man Arrested
by Helen Royce (staff writer)

In a bizarre turn of events, the manager of one of London's trendiest nightspots was arrested yesterday on suspicion of murder.

Zipgun Dandy (real name, Simon Dudley) was taken into custody late last night after reportedly killing a man in the Brixton area.

Unconfirmed reports have identified the murder victim as Clifton Chuttle, the former lead singer of '70s Glam rockers, Cliff Edge and the Stardust Warriors. We understand that in recent years Chuttle had been working as a record producer. The connection between Dandy and the victim is not yet clear.

This is the second time that Dandy's name has been associated with a brutal slaying, earlier this week, Dandy's business partner, 'Theodora' (real name, Terry Binton) was murdered in Spivz nightclub, which he jointly managed with Dandy.

A close friend of Dandy's, who asked to remain anonymous, told us: "He was a lovely man. He was always lots of fun. But when Theodora died he just went to pieces. I don't think he can be guilty. He wouldn't hurt a fly."

Forensic officers are continuing an examination of a cordoned-off property in Brixton where the murder is believed to have taken place. A police spokesman said yesterday: "We can confirm that we are currently interviewing a 23 year-old man in connection with a suspicious death. We would like to emphasise that, in spite of some speculation in the press, we currently have no reason to believe that this incident is directly connected with any other ongoing investigation."

*

Tyrone and I left the studio before the police arrived. I didn't want to get involved and Tyrone said he couldn't get involved "for professional reasons" which he declined to explain. Lala said he'd deal with the police. He'd been talking to them so much lately he was on first name terms with a few of them. I don't know if Zipgun mentioned me or Tyrone to the cops. If he did they can't have thought it was of any importance.

Chapter 24

The days and weeks following seemed, to me, abnormally quiet. Peaceful even. I settled back into the routine of interviewing pop stars and fending off Sanford's suggestions for ever more ludicrous one-shots. Towards the end of January, I got a phone call from a man who informed me that he was J. P. Cartwright's Personal Assistant and he had a call for me from the Managing Director. J. P. Cartwright turned out to be Janis, the former personal assistant to Clifton Chuttle. I hadn't previously known her surname nor even guessed that she had a middle name (the P, she explained, was short for Phyllida).

She told me The Sexteens would be releasing a single in February, two weeks behind the originally planned release date due to "unforeseen circumstances" and would I like to do an interview with the lead singer, Pete de Gré? I said I would, thinking to myself that it could be a very interesting interview if I were given free rein to ask all the questions I'd like to, but I didn't really think that I'd be able to sell an interview about pederasty, blackmail and murder to 'Jackie' and 'My Guy' so I'd probably just end up asking him the same tired old questions about his first kiss (about which he'd lie) and favourite school meals.

Janis had taken over Chuttle's record business. It turns out that, for obscure legal reasons, Janis had been designated Clifton Chuttle's 'company secretary' and a clause in the memorandum of agreement gave her the option of buying the shares at a favourable price, an option of which she had taken full advantage.

In the event, The Sexteens' single was a minor hit, getting to number 27 in the charts. Of course, it was their big summertime hit, 'Microchip Messiah', later in the year that would really propel them to stardom. The rest, as you no doubt know, is pop music history.

Mascara Addiction were less successful. Janis wasted no time in firing Dave Buzzard (he later joined the Heavy Metal band, Satan's Rabbit, who had a minor hit in the mid '80s with 'Scream In The Asylum'). Dusty was elevated to the lead singer of Mascara Addiction and Clyt Garbage (formerly of the punk band, Trash In Japan) was brought in on guitar. They released two singles in 1980, 'Fallen Angels' and 'I Speak Your Fate', but neither charted and the band broke up in early '81.

*

The City Reporter
Guitar-string Killer gets Life
Jack Smith, Crime Correspondent
April 30th, 1980

The man who killed a top record producer by strangling him with a guitar string has been jailed for life.

Simon Dudley, 23, killed Clifton Chuttle at his recording studio in the Brixton area on the 4th of January. Dudley (also known by the assumed name, 'Zipgun Dandy') of Bayswater, West London, was found guilty of murder by an 11-1 majority at the Old Bailey last week.

During the trial, it had been claimed that Mr Dudley had become convinced that Mr Chuttle had been responsible for the death of Dudley's male lover, Mr Terry 'Theodora' Binton. This assertion was described by Judge David Moreton as "an obsessional fantasy".

Mr Binton was strangled in the toilet of the fashionable East London club, Spivz, last New Year's Eve. Mr Dudley and Mr Binton had jointly managed the club. Mr Binton's killer has still not been found. In spite of speculation that Mr Dudley might been involved in the murder of Mr Binton, Judge David Moreton instructed the jury to concentrate solely on the current case and to disregard comments made about the murder of Mr Binton in the course of the trial.

Michael Dailey, QC, defending, said: "This was clearly not an attack which had been planned in advance. He was suffering from depression following the terrible ordeal of losing a loved one. In an emotionally disturbed state, he allowed an argument to become violent.

The killing of Mr Chuttle is an event that will haunt him for the rest of his life."

The judge told Dudley: "There is no doubt in my mind that what you have done was an act of premeditated violence. You deliberately sought out an unarmed man in an isolated situation at a time when you were certain he would be unable to summon assistance. You then subjected your victim to an assault of unimaginable brutality. At no time then or since have you shown the slightest degree of remorse.

"Your actions do not constitute, as you have claimed, an act of justified retaliation. On the contrary. The jury has found, and I agree with them, that you acted out of blind, callous hatred, which prompted you to carry out a sustained, abhorrent and grotesquely violent assault upon a completely innocent victim."

As he was led away, Dudley called out: "They said I didn't love him. They were wrong. I will always love him."

The judge passed a life sentence and said that Mr Dudley must serve a minimum of 18 years.

Epilogue

It was a couple of weeks after the trial – the 16th of May, a Friday – and the sun was struggling through a fine haze and a layer of thin cloud. The BBC was full of news about inflation going up to 21.8 per cent and Mount Saint Helens in America being about to explode, Dexy's Midnight Runners' 'Geno' was being played to death on the radio and Scruffy had caught a sniff of spring in the air and kept scratching at the front door until I relented and took him out for a walk.

We went up to Hampstead Heath. It took half an hour to get there and half an hour to get back with an hour sandwiched between to give us time to go up the grassy slope of Parliament Hill and stare down upon the sprawling cityscape of London laid out like a toy town in front of us. Hampstead Heath on a clear day gives you an unparalleled view of London. Even on a misty day the sight is spectacular with its jumble of low, ancient buildings clustering around taller modern landmarks such as the oddly incongruous Post Office Tower.

It was as we were walking back down the heath towards the exit onto Gospel Oak that I suddenly heard a penetrating shriek. It was a woman's shriek and it was being shrieked in my general direction. Scruffy's ears pricked up in alarm and, without a moment's hesitation, he slipped his paws into top gear and accelerated towards the exit with me trotting along behind, holding onto his lead for dear life.

"Scruffy!" – that was the word being shrieked and it was followed in quick succession by "Stop thief!" and "That man stole my dog!"

We were on the Gordon House Road and getting ready for a sharp turn in the Kentish Town direction before I finally managed to slam on the brakes and get the mutt under some semblance of control.

I realised then the predicament in which I found myself. Here I was blithely walking a dog to which I had no valid claims of ownership. There was she, the shrieking stranger, pointing the finger of blame and denouncing me to all the world (or, at any rate, that bit of the world within shrieking distance of the Gospel Oak side of Parliament Hill) as a heartless stealer of small and scruffy dogs.

As a law abiding citizen, there was only one course of action open to me. I would retrace my steps, proclaim my guilt and throw myself upon the mercy of my shrieking accuser.

Scruffy sat panting at my feet and turned upon me the full force of his big brown eyes.

"That's not going to work," I said, "Not this time. You are not my dog, you have never been my dog, I've never even wanted a dog. You just turned up one day, stuck your tongue in my ear and worked on the assumption that henceforth I would consider it my solemn duty to provide an endless supply of three-piece suites and choice rump steaks. Well, that's all come to an end. Your grieving owner has finally come to reclaim you."

In the distance the shrieks continued shrieking. They were getting closer by the second. Any moment now, the grieving owner would burst through the entrance gate, run up to the quivering pooch, sweep it up into a set of meaty arms and take it back to its former life of misery and woe, unloved, unwanted and uncared for.

Scruffy's head sank pathetically between his little shoulders as he looked pitifully up at me.

In a moment of madness, I picked up the dog, legged it at full speed across the road and took a swift right turn down the Highgate Road in the Kentish Town direction. In that moment, I knew that I had crossed a boundary. I had changed from being a law abiding citizen with an unblemished reputation to being a vile felon, a callous stealer of scruffy dogs.

The truth of the matter is that I have, contrary to my expectations, rather grown to like Scruffy. I am not persuaded that his original owners ever did. When I'd phoned the number in the capsule on his dog collar they had denied all knowledge. What, I wondered, had suddenly provoked this change of heart? My mind wandered over the ways of the blackmailer. The bloody woman was accusing me of stealing her dog. *Stealing*! *Me*!!! Damn' cheek! When in fact I had taken pity upon the poor animal in its time of most need. No doubt she had caught sight of me with her cast-off pet and an idea for making a bit of easy cash had sprung readily to her mind… She'd accused me of dog-rustling. If she ever got Scruffy back, I decided, it would be over my dead body!

The walk back home went at a brisk pace and I kept glancing behind me to make sure that we weren't being followed by dog-nappers. When we got back, I gave Scruffy a Bonio and a scratch behind the ears. Then I made myself a cup of tea and sat down to enjoy some well-earned relaxation.

It wasn't to last.

When the phone rang, my first thought was that it was Sanford with yet another idea for some half-baked one-shot. But it wasn't.

"I'm told you can help us," the voice said. There was something familiar about that gravelly voice but I couldn't place it until he told me his name. My God! The man was a Glam legend. I'd grown up wearing too-tight flares and platform shoes to the sound of his records.

"Our guitarist has been killed," he said, "They found him this morning – hanged with his own fishnets."

I could tell it was going to be another one of those days.

More 1980s Murder Mysteries

If you enjoyed *Killers In Mascara*, you may also enjoy the other novels in Huw Collingbourne's series of *1980s Murder Mysteries*.

The Glam Assassin

The 1970s meet the 1980s – and the result is murder! When the corpse of a Glam Rock guitarist is found hanged by his own fishnet tights, the rock music scene of 1980s London is thrown into panic. As the murders continue, Glam Rock superstar, Stan Buttershaw, recruits a trash pop music journalist, a freelance physicist and a small scruffy dog to try to find the assassin before the assassin finds Stan...

Death Wears Sequins

On a cold, wet night of November, Brigitte meets a mysterious stranger in a dismal jazz bar. Soon he is on the run for his life. The latest New Romantic adventure has the usual cast of characters plus ruthless spies, crazed killers and a high-speed pursuit across snow-covered Dartmoor. Why does a professional assassin want to kill Brigitte? And will he *succeed*....?

Just One More Thing...

I hope you enjoyed reading *Killers In Mascara*. As you end this novel, I am already writing a new one. And you can help me! The one thing an author really needs is readers. And the most important way to attract new readers is to have reviews. That's where *you* come in.

I would be incredibly grateful if you could take a few moments to leave a short **review** of *Killers In Mascara* on Amazon. It's always hard for an indie author (like me) to compete with the big publishing companies. In order to be able to carry on writing, I really need readers. And in order to get readers, I need reviews. Positive reviews on Amazon are like gold dust.

Thanks in advance to anyone who leaves a review. You have no idea how much that means to me!

Incidentally, if you want to keep in touch, be sure to visit the Dark Neon web site and subscribe to my newsletter:

http://darkneon.com/

Or join the Facebook group:

https://www.facebook.com/darkneonbooks/

Best wishes

Huw

Printed in Great Britain
by Amazon

58791634R00121